瑞蘭國際

瑞蘭國際

# 英語領隊導遊
## 考試總整理

**全新修訂版**

400題必考題型 ✚ 250個必考單字 ✚ 230題歷屆考題與解析

陳若慈 著

# 「英語領隊導遊考試」
# 考來考去都是考這些！

從出了第一本關於「英語領隊導遊考試」的書以來，經常收到許多讀者的疑問以及回饋，像是：

「之前自己準備都不知道怎麼讀，若慈老師把重點先列下來真的很有用！」

「若慈老師説用情境來背，真的比自己依年份做考古題來得有效率多了！」

「若慈老師説得對，真的考來考去都是考這些！」

許多讀者還沒念書之前，都習慣直接「面對」考題！覺得反正英文就是把題目練習熟了就好，應該沒有特別訣竅吧！殊不知大部分的讀者，英文不是年久失修，就是忘得差不多了，一次面對一份80題選擇題的英文考題，第一個反應就是頭很昏，好不容易做完題目、對完答案，也不知道重點在哪裡。比較有毅力的同學，就是硬著頭皮再戰下一回！但這些都不是準備英語領隊導遊考試最有效率的方式。

這本書的做法，一樣是教你直接「面對」考題，但跟市面上其他書籍不同的是，這本除了內容100%完全來自於歷屆考題之外，保證毫無添加其他的內容，也就是將考題重新歸類、整理、標出重點過後，直接端到你的面前，讓你好好地消化吸收！這才是最簡單且有效率「認識」考題的方法。

如果你把英語領隊導遊考試，想成是高中會考、或是大學學測指考英文科，那可就大錯特錯了！相信讀者們從小到大、從國中到高中，求學路上所學的英文，和生活可能都沒有太大的關連，只是為了考試而背，背完就忘，且英文考題中的冷僻單字、硬梆梆的文法，和自己想像中只要讀完就可以開口説一些簡單的會話，似乎

也有落差。然而，身為領隊、導遊，最重要的職責就是溝通，也因此，英語領隊導遊考試，都以實務上常見的單字、議題為主，其中包含了交通、住宿、觀光景點等等，都是實際旅途中真正會用到的英文！

　　正由於和其他一般的學校、公職考試相較之下，英語領隊導遊考試不那麼死板，所以學習方法當然也不必死K硬記。建議除了考題之外，只要平時多瀏覽相關的旅遊英文資訊，或是國外的旅遊網站（詳見附錄），那麼在賞心悅目、吸收新知之餘，一定還能練習到英文，不失為準備英語領隊導遊考試實用又輕鬆的方法。

　　本書除了希望讓大家有效率地準備英語領隊導遊考試外，更重要的是，希望讀者能快速地了解、吸收，縮短考前衝刺的寶貴時間，一舉金榜題名，順利成為一名出色的領隊、導遊！

　　有任何問題，也歡迎上
Facebook（https://www.facebook.com/tourguideEnglish）一同討論。

陳若慈

# 關於專門職業及技術人員普通考試導遊人員、領隊人員考試

　　簡單來說，本項考試就是為了取得導遊、領隊證照的考試。然而領隊、導遊考的科目各有不同，唯一相同的是兩者都會考「外語」這科。而《英語領隊導遊考試總整理》，就是為了這兩種應試類別中的科目——外語（英語）所撰寫的。

## 應考資格：

凡中華民國國民，具有下列資格之一者，即可應考：

一、公立或立案之私立高級中學或高級職業學校以上學校畢業，領有畢業證書或學位證書者。（同等學力者，須附教育部核發之同等學力及格證書）

二、初等考試或相當等級之特種考試及格，並曾任有關職務滿四年，有證明文件者。

三、高等或普通檢定考試及格者。

## 應試科目：

　　導遊人員考試分成「筆試」與「口試」二試，第一試「筆試」錄取者，才可以參加第二試「口試」。領隊人員考試則僅有「筆試」。

| 應試<br>類別 | | 應試科目 | |
|---|---|---|---|
| | | 第一試（筆試） | 第二試（口試） |
| 導遊人員 | 外語導遊人員 | 1、導遊實務（一）：包括導覽解說、旅遊安全與緊急事件處理、觀光心理與行為、航空票務、急救常識、國際禮儀。<br>2、導遊實務（二）：包括觀光行政與法規、台灣地區與大陸地區人民關係條例、兩岸現況認識。<br>3、觀光資源概要：包括台灣歷史、台灣地理、觀光資源維護。<br>4、外國語：分英語、日語、法語、德語、西班牙語、韓語、泰語、阿拉伯語、俄語、義大利語、越南語、印尼語、馬來語等十三種，由應考人任選一種應試。 | 採外語個別口試，就應考人選考之外國語舉行個別口試，並依外語口試規則規定辦理。 |
| 領隊人員 | 外語領隊人員 | 1、領隊實務（一）：包括領隊技巧、航空票務、急救常識、旅遊安全與緊急事件處理、國際禮儀。<br>2、領隊實務（二）：包括觀光法規、入出境相關法規、外匯常識、民法債編旅遊專節與國外定型化旅遊契約、台灣地區與大陸地區人民關係條例、兩岸現況認識。<br>3、觀光資源概要：包括世界歷史、世界地理、觀光資源維護。<br>4、外國語：分英語、日語、法語、德語、西班牙語等五種，由應考人任選一種應試。 | 不需口試。 |

※注意！應試科目均採測驗式試題，因此英語考試也都是四選一的選擇題，共計80題。

## 及格標準與成績計算方式：

一、外語導遊人員考試，筆試＋口試平均加總成績滿60分為及格。

筆試：即為第一試，成績占75%（如上方表格外語導遊人員4科：導遊實務（一）＋導遊實務（二）＋觀光資源概要＋外語）。筆試成績滿60分為及格標準，依以上4科成績平均計算。但若筆試有一科為0分（缺考亦以0分計算），或外國語科目成績未滿50分，都不算及格，也不能參加口試。

口試：即為第二試，成績占25%。首先筆試（第一試）平均成績須達60分，才有資格參加口試。口試成績則須滿60分才及格。

簡單來説，也就是筆試成績須及格（滿60分），才有口試資格，口試也須滿60分，才會錄取。而其中任一科均不得缺考、或是0分，且外語筆試至少須達50分，整體才算及格。

二、外語領隊人員考試，筆試平均加總成績滿60分為及格。

以4科筆試成績平均計算（如上方表格外語領隊人員4科：領隊實務（一）＋領隊實務（二）＋觀光資源概要＋外語）。筆試成績平均滿60分為及格標準，但若筆試有一科為0分（缺考亦以0分計算），或外國語科目成績未滿50分，都不算及格。

※注意！導遊、領隊考試平均考試成績須滿60分才算及格，但單就英語筆試這科，若未滿50分，即便其他科目再高分、平均成績有達60分，也不算及格！

## 資格取得：

一、考試及格人員，由考選部報請考試院發給考試及格證書，並函交通部觀光局查
　　照。但外語導遊人員、外語領隊人員考試及格人員，應註明選試外國語言別。

二、前項考試及格人員，經交通部觀光局訓練合格，得申領執業證。


## 相關考試訊息：

測驗名稱：專門職業及技術人員普通考試導遊人員、領隊人員考試

測驗日期：每年3月（筆試）及5月（口試）

放榜日期：當年4月（筆試）及6月（口試）

等　　級：專技普考

測驗地點：分台北、桃園、新竹、台中、嘉義、台南、高雄、花蓮、台東、澎湖、
　　　　　金門、馬祖十二考區舉行。

報名時間：前一年11月至12月初

實施機構：考選部專技考試司


更多相關資料，請上考選部網站查詢。

http://wwwc.moex.gov.tw

# 如何使用本書

　　本書結合題型、單字、考古題、解析，4者並重，是最穩紮穩打的備考用書。從歷屆試題中統整精選出12大類必考情境，按照情境記憶「必考題型」和「必考單字」，練習「牛刀小試」、實戰「歷屆考題精選」，讓你完全命中領隊導遊英語！

## → Step 1 　記憶「必考題型」

**必考題型**

共400個必考題型，每一句都是必考重點，來不及做考古題沒關係，只要多看幾次必考題型，就能像做完數回考古題一樣的事半功倍。

**粗體強調重點**

每句必考題型都以粗體標示出題時的正確答案或關鍵字，一眼就能看出當句重點所在。

**歷屆試題標示**

每句必考題型後面都標上出自哪一個考試年度，而非作者自擬的考題，對考題更有信心。

**延伸題型**

必考題型中，除了以粗體標示重要內容之外，還會附上粗體字與主要題型相關的延伸題型，舉一反三、觸類旁通。

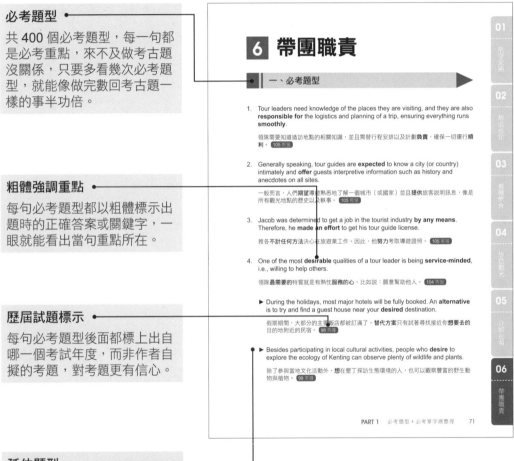

### 6 帶團職責

**一、必考題型**

1. Tour leaders need knowledge of the places they are visiting, and they are also **responsible for** the logistics and planning of a trip, ensuring everything runs **smoothly**.

   領隊需要知道造訪地點的相關知識，並且需替行程安排以及計劃**負責**，確保一切運行順利。 [105 領隊]

2. Generally speaking, tour guides are **expected** to know a city (or country) intimately and **offer** guests interpretive information such as history and anecdotes on all sites.

   一般而言，人們**期望**導遊熟悉地了解一個城市（或國家）並且**提供**旅客說明訊息，像是所有觀光地點的歷史以及軼事。 [105 領隊]

3. Jacob was determined to get a job in the tourist industry **by any means**. Therefore, he **made an effort** to get his tour guide license.

   雅各**不計任何方法**決心在旅遊業工作。因此，他**努力**考取導遊證照。 [105 導遊]

4. One of the most **desirable** qualities of a tour leader is being **service-minded**, i.e., willing to help others.

   領隊**最需要**的特質就是有熱忱**服務**的心。比如說：願意幫助他人。 [104 導遊]

   ▶ During the holidays, most major hotels will be fully booked. An **alternative** is to try and find a guest house near your **desired** destination.

   假期期間，大部分的主要飯店都被訂滿了。**替代方案**只有試著尋找接近你**想要去的**目的地附近的民宿。 [98 領隊]

   ▶ Besides participating in local cultural activities, people who **desire** to explore the ecology of Kenting can observe plenty of wildlife and plants.

   除了參與當地文化活動外，**想**在墾丁探訪生態環境的人，也可以觀察豐富的野生動物與植物。 [99 導遊]

PART 1　必考題型＋必考單字總整理　　71

## → Step 2 記憶「必考單字」

### 二、必考單字　　　　　　　　　MP3-003

| | |
|---|---|
| local flavors n. 當地的美食 | snacks n. 小吃 |
| fragrant adj. 芬芳的 | cuisine n. 料理 |
| culinary adj. 烹飪的 | gastronomy n. 美食 |
| purchase v. 購買 n. 商品 | ingredient n. 食材 |
| spice n. 香料 | exotic adj. 異國的 |

**必考單字**

精選 250 個必考單字，每個情境
都有相關的重要單字，以情境來
記憶，記得快、背得牢。

**詞性＋中譯**

正確的單字詞性、精準的單字中
譯，加深對必考單字的印象。

**標準美語朗讀 MP3**

全書必考單字附有標準美語朗讀
MP3，在準備英語領隊導遊考試
的同時，也能將最道地的發音示
範帶著走。

## → Step 3 練習「牛刀小試」

### 三、牛刀小試

(　　) 1. During their first visit to Taiwan, many foreign tourists _____ the local flavors at the night markets.

(A) recall　　(B) relish　　(C) refill　　(D) reminiscence

(　　) 2. When we have leftover cooked stew or other food with meat, it is suggested that the food should be _____ to room temperature, and then put in the refrigerator.

(A) heated　　(B) cooled　　(C) frozen　　(D) processed

(　　) 3. In order to _____ all the customers with a warm and fragrant atmosphere, the coffee shop owner spent a fortune to redecorate the entire store.

(A) signify　　(B) provide　　(C) launch　　(D) offer

(　　) 4. Once we were seated at the restaurant, it took almost no time before big bamboo steamers full of dumplings arrived, along with _____ on how to eat those xiao long bao.

(A) brunches　　(B) chopsticks　　(C) directions　　(D) functions

(　　) 5. New Orleans has a reputation for having a unique _____ born of many cultures that came together in the old city. Visitors come from all around the world to enjoy the food there.

(A) decor　　(B) license　　(C) tourism　　(D) cuisine

**牛刀小試**

共 300 題牛刀小試，將必考題型
一一還原為題目的形式，透過練
習答題來自我檢測學習成效。

**歷屆考題精選**

精選 230 題歷屆考題，囊括 98 ～ 108 年度歷屆考題，並嚴選常見題目，不放過任何得分關鍵。

**解析**

除了正確答案、中文翻譯之外，有精闢易懂的解析與解題訣竅，更補充相關詞彙與考古題例句，不用死記硬背就能快速找出答案。

## 1 航空交通

● 一、歷屆考題精選

( ) 1. When we get to the airport, we first go to the check-in desk where the airline representatives _____ our luggage. 100 英導

(A) pack　　(B) move　　(C) weigh　　(D) claim

( ) 2. Even though you have _____ your flight with the airline, you must still be present at the check-in desk on time. 99 英導

(A) informed　(B) confirmed　(C) required　(D) given

( ) 3. The flight is scheduled to _____ at eleven o'clock tomorrow. You will have to get to the airport two hours before the takeoff. 99 英導

(A) land　　(B) depart　　(C) cancel　　(D) examine

( ) 4. Though most airlines ask their passengers to check in at the airport counter two hours before the flight, some international flights _____ their passengers to be at the airport three hours before departure. 102 英導

(A) revise　　(B) require　　(C) record　　(D) reveal

( ) 5. You will get a boarding _____ after completing the check-in. 98 英導

(A) pass　　(B) post　　(C) plan　　(D) past

( ) 6. People traveling to a foreign country may need to apply _____ a visa. 98 英導

(A) for　　(B) of　　(C) on　　(D) to

( ) 7. When traveling in a foreign country, we need to carry with us several important documents at all times. One of them is our passport together with the _____ permit if that has been so required. 102 英導

(A) entering　(B) entry　　(C) exit　　(D) ego

( ) 8. Disobeying the airport security rules will _____ a civil penalty. 101 英導

(A) result in　(B) make for　(C) take down　(D) bring on

● 二、試題中譯＋解析

1. When we get to the airport, we first go to the check-in desk where the airline representatives <u>weigh</u> our luggage.

(A) pack 包　　　　　　　(B) move 移動

(C) weigh 秤重　　　　　　(D) claim 認領

**中譯** 當我們到達機場，首先我們到登機櫃台，此處的航空公司工作人員會將我們的行李秤重。

**解析** check-in desk 為登機櫃台，claim baggage 則為認領行李，在 check-in desk 時服務人員會給你行李存根 baggage claim tag，若行李遺失則可到行李領取中心 baggage claim office / counter / center 請求幫忙。

2. Even though you have <u>confirmed</u> your flight with the airline, you must still be present at the check-in desk on time.

(A) informed 告知　　　　　(B) confirmed 確認

(C) required 要求　　　　　(D) given 給予

**中譯** 即便你已經跟航空公司確認班機，你還是必須準時到櫃檯報到。

**解析** confirm 確認；reconfirm 再次確認。confirm flight 確認班機；confirm reservation 確認預約。

3. The flight is scheduled to <u>depart</u> at eleven o'clock tomorrow. You will have to get to the airport two hours before the takeoff.

(A) land 著陸，抵達　　　　(B) depart 起飛

(C) cancell 取消　　　　　 (D) examine 檢驗

**中譯** 班機預定於明天 11 點起飛，你必須在出發前 2 個小時抵達機場。

**解析** depart / take off 起飛；land 著陸、抵達。

01 航空交通

02 旅遊英文

03 氣象與時

04 交通運輸

05 行程規劃

06 學系與主

# 目　次

**PART 1** 必考題型＋必考單字總整理 ................ **13**

PART
1

必考題型
+
必考單字總整理

# 1 航空交通

1. Passengers who do not **comply** with the flight safety rules will be charged a **penalty** fee.

   不**遵守**飛航安全的乘客將會被**罰**款。 `105 英導`

2. We are flying to Hawaii for a vacation tomorrow. We will need to catch the **outbound** flight at 8:00 tomorrow morning.

   我們明天將飛往夏威夷度假。我們明天早上要趕 8 點的**出境**班機。 `105 英導`

3. You need a passport to **board** an international flight and to enter a country.

   你需要護照才能**登機**國際班機並進入一個國家。 `105 英領`

4. **Jet lag** is a temporary sleep problem that can **affect** anyone who quickly travels across multiple time zones.

   **時差**是暫時的睡眠問題，它會**影響**短時間內經過數個時區的人。 `105 英領`

5. In general, your passport must be **valid** for at least six months after the date you enter a foreign country.

   一般來說，你的護照在進入外國國家時，至少須具有**有效**效期 6 個月。 `105 英領`

6. The UK Home Office has **announced** the expansion of its Registered Traveller service to Hong Kong, Singapore, South Korea and Taiwan on 25 January, 2016.

   英國內政部於 2016 年 1 月 25 日**宣布**擴展其登記旅客快速通關計畫（Registered Traveller Service，RTS）至香港、新加坡、南韓以及台灣。 `105 英領`

7. A: Are you **checking** in any bags today?
   B: Just this one. The other's hand luggage.

   A：你今天要**登記（托運）**任何行李嗎？
   B：只有這一個，另一個是手提行李。 `105 英領`

01

航空交通

02

飯店住宿

03

餐廳飲食

04

旅遊觀光

05

介紹台灣

06

帶團職責

8. A: Can you tell me if there are any window seats available?
   B: No. I'm afraid there aren't. The flight's very full. Would you like an **aisle** seat?

   A：請問是否還有任何靠窗的位置？
   B：恐怕沒有。這班飛機很滿。給您靠**走道**的位置好嗎？ `105 英領`

9. Check your bags and clothing to make sure you are not carrying any **banned items** or substances into your destination country.

   進入目的地國家時，檢查並確認一下你們的包包以及隨身衣物是否有攜帶**違禁品**。
   `105 英領`

10. **Air crash** can be caused by either human error or poor weather conditions.

    **空難**可能是人為疏失或是天候不佳的關係。 `104 英領`

11. The plane cannot leave the gate **unless** all passengers are seated and **baggage** is safely stowed.

    **除非**乘客都安全就坐且**行李**被妥善放置，否則飛機不能啟航。 `104 英導`

12. Tourist: Excuse me. Where's the **check-in counter** for American Airlines?
    Worker: It's in Terminal 2. This is Terminal 1.

    旅客：不好意思，請問美國航空的**登機櫃台**在哪？
    工作人員：在第二航廈，這邊是第一航廈。 `103 英領`

13. A **domestic** flight is a form of commercial flight where the departure and the arrival take place in the same country.

    **國內**班機是一種起飛降落都在同一個國家的商業班機。 `103 英導`

14. Worker: If you're on an **international flight**, I believe you have to check in three hours before your flight.

    Tourist: And for **domestic** flights?
    Worker: On those flights you have to check in one and a half hours before.

    工作人員：如果你搭**國際班機**，我想你在起飛前 3 小時就必須辦理報到手續。
    旅客：那**國內**班機呢？
    工作人員：國內班機你只需要 1 個半小時之前報到即可。 `103 英領`

15. Worker: Excuse me, ma'am. One of your bags is **overweight**. I'm going to have to charge you for the **excess weight**.
Tourist: I see. How much **extra** do I have to pay? And can I pay by credit card?
Worker: 30 dollars, ma'am, and yes, we do accept credit cards.

工作人員：不好意思，你其中一個袋子**超重**了，我必須要收你**超重費**。
旅客：了解，我必須**多**付多少錢？我可以用信用卡付費嗎？
工作人員：30 元。可以的，我們接受信用卡。 103 英領

16. The Flight 506 to Amsterdam, scheduled to depart at 11:30 a.m., has been delayed **on account of** a big fog.

**由於**大霧，預計早上 11 點半飛往阿姆斯特丹的 506 號班機被延誤了。 103 英領

17. This tour group got a special promotion **fare**, which requires one stop-over in Japan for about two hours with a **connecting flight**.

這團體拿到了特別的折扣**價**，所以需要於日本暫停約 2 個小時再進行**轉機**。 103 英領

18. The group leader carefully reminds the group that no agricultural products **are allowed** into the USA territory.

領隊小心地提醒團員進入美國領土時不**允許**帶入任何農產品。 103 英領

19. We arrived at the airport two hours before **departure** in order to check in, but we were told that we could not do so as the flight was overbooked.

為了辦理登機手續，我們在飛機**起飛**前 2 個小時到達機場，但卻被告知因為班機超賣而無法登機。 103 英導

20. An airline **inspector** travelling in secret should act normally first and then test the flight attendant with abnormal behaviors such as being drunk, noisy, or difficult to please.

祕密旅行的航空**檢查員**應該一開始表現正常，然後用突發的行為測試空服員，像是喝醉、吵鬧，或是難以被取悅。 103 英導

21. A U.S. flight **bound** for New York last month experienced **turbulence** shortly after take-off from Houston, causing minor injuries to five crew and passengers.

上個月一班美國境內由休士頓飛**往**紐約的班機，在起飛後不久遭受了**亂流**，導致 5 名空服員以及乘客輕微受傷。 103 英導

22. The dangerous situation in which pedestrians and vehicles **compete for** space is being improved by the new policy **implemented** last month.

行人與交通工具**爭**道的危險情況將會因上個月新**實施**的政策而改善。 `105 英導`

23. Foreign countries may **require** that persons considered resident obtain a local driver's license if they are going to drive.

在國外可能會**要求**考慮成為居民並打算開車的人能考取當地駕照。 `105 英領`

24. Taiwan's railroads are far more than just a tool of **transportation**; they embody a deep affinity with the development of local culture and society.

台灣的鐵路不只是一種**交通運輸**工具。它體現了當地文化以及社會發展的緊密性。 `105 英領`

25. As the largest metro subway system in Taiwan, the Taipei MRT **serves** about 1.3 million riders daily. It is fast, convenient, and, most importantly, CLEAN.

台北捷運是台灣最大的捷運系統,每天**運載** 130 萬人次。它快速、方便,最重要的是,乾淨。 `105 英領`

26. Taiwan's railways offer an endless variety of experience, and the scenery lining their **routes** provides an infinite range of fascinating scenery.

台灣的鐵路提供了非常多元的體驗,沿**途**上的風景亦提供了無窮盡的美景。 `105 英領`

27. The train was two hours behind **schedule** because of an accident.

火車因為事故,所以比**表定**時間延遲了 2 小時。 `105 英領`

28. Guests can make use of bicycles for a **leisurely** tour of the surroundings.

遊客可以利用自行車在附近來趟**悠閒的**旅行。 `105 英領`

29. At the start of the bridge is the stairway **leading** down to the trail.

橋的一開始是一段通**往**下方步道的階梯。 `105 英領`

30. The Taipei Metro is both cheap and easy to use. Transfers between lines are **relatively** close to each other, and the stations **serve** most areas of Taipei.

台北捷運既便宜又方便,轉搭的路線**相對**近,且車站**服務**範圍涵括了台北大部分的區域。 `105 英領`

01 航空交通

02 飯店住宿

03 餐廳飲食

04 旅遊觀光

05 介紹台灣

06 帶團職責

31. The subway system in Taipei is very easy to navigate, and is both **bilingual** in Chinese and English.

台北捷運非常容易瀏覽使用，且有中英**雙語**服務。 105 英領

32. The bus doesn't go to the National Museum of Natural Science. You need to **switch** to bus number 100.

這班公車並沒有到國立自然科學博物館，你必須**轉搭** 100 號公車。 105 英領

33. With a new YouBike pricing policy which has led to a **reduction** in turnover rate, it is easier to rent a bicycle in Taipei now.

自從新的 YouBike 定價策略讓周轉率**降低**後，現在更容易在台北租腳踏車了。 105 英領

34. Ultra-high speed tube trains are one of the most **cutting-edge** technologies in the 21st century.

超迴路列車是 21 世紀中最**先進的**科技之一。 104 英領

35. Drinking and eating on the Taipei MRT are strictly **prohibited**.

台北捷運中嚴格**禁止**飲食。 104 英領

36. Tour tickets, once booked, are **subject to** a 10% cancellation **fee** if returned prior to the deadline.

行程的預訂票，**規定**在最後期限前退回的話將會有 10% 的取消**費**。 104 英導

37. Commuters can help **reduce** pollution by occasionally leaving **their** cars at home and using public transportation.

通勤者可以藉由偶爾把**他們的**車留在家、搭乘大眾交通工具來**減少**汙染。 104 英導

38. The baseball game had to be **postponed** for an hour because of a thunderstorm.

棒球比賽因為暴風雨而必須**延期** 1 小時。 104 英導

39. Today, ships are equipped with a large array of electronic devices that help the **navigators** to reach their destinations.

今日，船隻都備有一系列的電子儀器來幫助**領航員**到達目的地。 104 英導

40. Deck chairs operate on a first-come, first-served basis and cannot be reserved. Please take your **belongings** with you when leaving a deck chair for a period of time, or they may be removed.

躺椅採用先到先使用的方式，且不能預訂。當你要離開躺椅一段時間前，請攜帶你的**個人物品**，否則可能會被移走。 104 英導

41. Provision for people with disabilities on public transport is only average in this city, although some new buses are now wheelchair-**accessible**.

雖然有些新的公車**可供**輪椅上下車，但這城市裡提供給身障人士的大眾交通工具仍不夠普及。 103 英導

42. **Budget airlines** boosted their **share** of passenger traffic to nearly 40% last year; at the same time major traditional airlines saw lower volumes.

**廉價航空**去年的載客量提升至 40% 市場**占有率**，而同時間主要的傳統航空的載客量則降低。 103 英導

43. Youbike is a bicycle rental service that **works** with the MRT Easycard, and is widely thought of as the "last mile" in public transportation after you have ridden the bus, train, or MRT.

Youbike 是一種和捷運悠遊卡共同**合作**的腳踏車租借服務，被廣泛地認為是在搭乘巴士、火車或是捷運之後，公眾運輸上的最後一哩路。 103 英導

44. When the 6.3 magnitude earthquake struck Taiwan, the railway administration immediately suspended train service **while** it checked for any possible damage to tracks.

當規模 6.3 的地震襲擊台灣時，鐵路行政處立即停止火車服務，**並且同時**檢查是否有造成任何鐵軌損壞。 103 英導

45. In general, drivers must be careful about walkers. Under current law, motorists must **yield** to pedestrians in a crosswalk.

一般來說，駕駛要小心走路的人。現行法律之下，摩托車騎士必須**禮讓**在斑馬線的行人。 103 英導

46. Flying in **economy class** can be crowded and hot.

坐**經濟艙**會又擁擠又熱。 108 英導

01 航空交通
02 飯店住宿
03 餐廳飲食
04 旅遊觀光
05 介紹台灣
06 帶團職責

47. Some airlines might give you toothpaste and other **personal amenities** when you took a long flight in the past.

在過去你長途飛行時有些航空公司可能會給你牙膏和其他**私人用品**。 `108 英導`

48. Be sure to turn off your **electronic devices** for takeoff and landing.

起飛和降落時一定要關掉你的**電子設備**。 `108 英導`

49. It's faster and less expensive to take the **shuttle** from the airport to the hotel.

搭**接駁車**從機場到飯店是比較快也比較便宜的方式。 `108 英導`

50. Before you leave the bus, be sure to take all of your **belongings** with you.

在你下公車之前，記得帶上你所有的隨身**物品**。 `108 英導`

51. On the MRT of Taiwan, visitors carrying bicycles can get on and off the train only at **designated** stations.

在台灣的捷運上，帶腳踏車的乘客可以在某些**指定的**捷運站上下車。 `108 英導`

52. Smoking is **prohibited** for the duration of the flight.

航行期間**禁止**吸煙。 `108 英領`

53. Due to the **overbooking**, we will upgrade you to business class.

因為**超賣**，我們會將你升級到商務艙。 `108 英領`

54. If your **baggage allowance** exceeds the free checked piece and weight, excess baggage charges will be applied.

如果你的**行李限額**超過了托運的免費件數與重量，將會收取超重費。 `108 英領`

55. At an airport, a **carousel** is a moving surface from which passengers can collect their luggage.

在機場，**行李轉盤**是種會移動的表面讓乘客可以領取他們的行李。 `108 英領`

| | |
|---|---|
| depart **v.** 出發 | departure **n.** 出發 |
| take off **v.** 起飛 | leave the ground **v.** 起飛 |
| land **v.** 著陸 | landing **n.** 著陸 |
| touch down **v.** 著陸 | arrive **v.** 到達 |
| arrival **n.** 到達 | board **v.** 登機 |
| cabin crew / cabin staff **n.** 機組人員 | flight attendants **n.** 空服員 |
| pilot **n.** 駕駛 | passengers **n.** 乘客 |
| flight safety **n.** 飛航安全 | turbulence **n.** 亂流 |
| outbound flight **n.** 出境班機 | inbound flight **n.** 入境班機 |
| domestic flight **n.** 國內班機 | international flight **n.** 國際班機 |
| connecting flight **n.** 轉機班機 | stopover / layover **n.** 短暫停留 |
| check-in baggage / luggage **n.** 托運行李 | carry-on baggage / luggage **n.** 登機行李 |
| aisle seat **n.** 靠走道的位置 | window seat **n.** 靠窗位置 |
| cockpit **n.** 駕駛艙 | overhead compartment / bin / locker **n.** 頭頂置物箱 |
| get off an airplane / a bus / a train **v.** 下飛機 / 巴士 / 火車 | get on an airplane / a bus / a train **v.** 上飛機 / 巴士 / 火車 |
| abroad **adv.** 在國外；到國外 | aboard **adv.** 上交通工具（飛機、公共汽車、火車）；在交通工具上（飛機、公共汽車、火車） |

01 航空交通

02 飯店住宿

03 餐廳飲食

04 旅遊觀光

05 介紹台灣

06 帶團職責

(       ) 1.   Passengers who do not _____ with the flight safety rules will be charged a penalty fee

     (A) undermine      (B) compromise      (C) comply      (D) complete

(       ) 2.   We are flying to Hawaii for a vacation tomorrow. We will need to catch the _____ flight at 8:00 tomorrow morning

     (A) red-eye      (B) outbound      (C) return      (D) overpass

(       ) 3.   You need a passport to _____ an international flight and to enter a country.

     (A) broad      (B) bound      (C) board      (D) abroad

(       ) 4.   Jet _____ is a temporary sleep problem that can affect anyone who quickly travels across multiple time zones.

     (A) gap      (B) lag      (C) leg      (D) tail

(       ) 5.   As the largest metro subway system in Taiwan, the Taipei MRT _____ about 1.3 million riders daily. It is fast, convenient, and, most importantly, CLEAN.

     (A) serves      (B) provides      (C) deserves      (D) preserve

(       ) 6.   This tour group got a special promotion fare, which requires one stop-over in Japan for about two hours with _____.

     (A) a connecting flight          (B) a non-stop flight

     (C) a direct flight          (D) a daily flight

(       ) 7.   The group leader carefully reminds the group that no agricultural products _____ into the USA territory.

     (A) are required      (B) are claiming      (C) are allowed      (D) are bringing

(       ) 8.   At the start of the bridge is the stairway _____ down to the trail.

     (A) putting      (B) sitting      (C) leading      (D) writing

(       ) 9.   Air _____ can be caused by either human error or poor weather conditions.

     (A) plash      (B) crash      (C) flash      (D) splash

( ) 10. The plane cannot leave the gate _____ all passengers are seated and baggage is safely stowed.

    (A) but         (B) if         (C) unless         (D) when

( ) 11. Guests can make use of bicycles for a(n) _____ tour of the surroundings.

    (A) awful         (B) inconvenient     (C) strenuous     (D) leisurely

( ) 12. A _____ flight is a form of commercial flight where the departure and the arrival take place in the same country.

    (A) foreign         (B) domestic         (C) rural         (D) connecting

( ) 13. Worker: If you're on an international flight, I believe you have to check in three hours before your flight.

    Tourist: And for _____ flights?

    Worker: On those flights you have to check in one and a half hours before.

    (A) domestic         (B) country         (C) neighboring     (D) foreign

( ) 14. Worker: Can I see your ticket and your passport, please?

    Tourist: Sure. Here's my passport, and here's my _____.

    (A) paper                       (B) e-ticket

    (C) boarding pass            (D) online purchase

( ) 15. Worker: Excuse me, sir. One of your bags is overweight. I'm going to have to charge you for the excess weight.

    Tourist: I see. How much _____ do I have to pay? And can I pay by credit card?

    Worker: 30 dollars, sir, and yes, we do accept credit cards.

    (A) cash         (B) over         (C) extra         (D) additional

( ) 16. _____ the Wangs got to the station, the train had already left.

    (A) As long as     (B) Now that     (C) By the time     (D) In the past

( ) 17. The bus doesn't go to the National Museum of Natural Science. You need to _____ to bus number 100.

    (A) spread         (B) retreat         (C) fortify         (D) switch

( ) 18. A: Are you _____ in any bags today?

B: Just this one. The other's hand luggage.

(A) bringing　　(B) packing　　(C) checking　　(D) shopping

( ) 19. With a new YouBike pricing policy which has led to a _____ in turnover rate, it is easier to rent a bicycle in Taipei now.

(A) tuition　　(B) reduction　　(C) pension　　(D) compensation

( ) 20. The Taipei Metro is both cheap and easy to use. Transfers between lines are _____ close to each other, and the stations serve most areas of Taipei.

(A) relatively　　(B) easily　　(C) hardly　　(D) rapidly

( ) 21. The subway system in Taipei is very easy to navigate, and is both _____ in Chinese and English.

(A) mutual　　(B) bilingual　　(C) trilingual　　(D) bicultural

( ) 22. China Airlines said yesterday it will work with U.S. based GE Aviation to improve the carrier's fuel efficiency _____ the volatile nature of fuel prices.

(A) in light of

(B) in spite of

(C) in proportion of

(D) in need of

( ) 23. As one source of human-induced global warming, airplanes _____ large volumes of greenhouse gases.

(A) permit　　(B) shovel　　(C) emit　　(D) vanish

( ) 24. A: Can you tell me if there are any window seats available?

B: No. I'm afraid there aren't. The flight's very full. Would you like an _____ seat?

(A) isle　　(B) aisle　　(C) easel　　(D) aerial

( ) 25. Check your bags and clothing to make sure you are not carrying any _____ items or substances into your destination country.

(A) denied　　(B) banned　　(C) lawless　　(D) limited

( ) 26. We arrived at the airport two hours before _____ in order to check in, but we were told that we could not do so as the flight was overbooked.

(A) demand　　(B) departure　　(C) dismissal　　(D) dispute

01

航空交通

02

飯店住宿

03

餐廳飲食

04

旅遊觀光

05

介紹台灣

06

帶團職責

(　　) 27. A U.S. flight bound for New York last month experienced _____ shortly after take-off from Houston, causing minor injuries to five crew and passengers.

       (A) jet lag        (B) boundaries        (C) turbulence        (D) atmosphere

(　　) 28. In general, your passport must be _____ for at least six months after the date you enter a foreign country.

       (A) valid        (B) ruled        (C) checked        (D) rejected

(　　) 29. The UK Home Office has announced the expansion of its _____ Traveller service to Hong Kong, Singapore, South Korea and Taiwan on 25 January, 2016.

       (A) Coded        (B) Enlisted        (C) Registered        (D) Preserved

(　　) 30. The dangerous situation in which pedestrians and vehicles _____ space is being improved by the new policy implemented last month.

       (A) give way to        (B) compete for        (C) speed up        (D) switch to

(　　) 31. Taiwan's railroads are far more than just a tool of _____; they embody a deep affinity with the development of local culture and society.

       (A) method        (B) traffic        (C) vehicle        (D) transportation

(　　) 32. The bicycle path gives cyclists a close and personal feel with the rural valley full of _____ fields and fruit plantations, which are crisscrossed by a network of irrigation canals.

       (A) boulder        (B) rotten        (C) paddy        (D) fallow

(　　) 33. Tourist: Excuse me. Where's the check-in _____ for American Airlines?

       Worker: It's in Terminal 2. This is Terminal 1.

       (A) carrel        (B) barrier        (C) counter        (D) concord

| | | | | |
|---|---|---|---|---|
| 1.（C） | 2.（B） | 3.（C） | 4.（B） | 5.（A） |
| 6.（A） | 7.（C） | 8.（C） | 9.（B） | 10.（C） |
| 11.（D） | 12.（B） | 13.（A） | 14.（B） | 15.（C） |
| 16.（C） | 17.（D） | 18.（C） | 19.（B） | 20.（A） |
| 21.（B） | 22.（A） | 23.（C） | 24.（B） | 25.（B） |
| 26.（B） | 27.（C） | 28.（A） | 29.（C） | 30.（B） |
| 31.（D） | 32.（C） | 33.（C） | | |

# 2 飯店住宿

## 一、必考題型

1. **Luxury hotels** and upscale restaurants have **sprung up** around the **banks** of Sun Moon Lake in Nantou, Taiwan.

   **精品旅館**以及高檔餐廳，在台灣南投日月潭的**岸**邊**如雨後春筍般冒出來**。 105 英導

2. Legal hotels should have public **liability** insurance.

   合法的飯店應該有公共責任保險。 105 英導

3. Illegal short-term rentals are often tucked away in alleys that might **block** evacuation **routes**.

   非法短租經常藏身於巷弄內，這樣可能會**阻擋**逃生**路線**。 105 英導

4. The operator of an illegal short-term rental unit could **be subject to** a **fine** and ordered to immediately close.

   非法短租的經營者可能會**遭受罰款**以及勒令立即停業。 105 英導

5. As a frugal **budget** traveler, he shunned away from fancy hotels.

   身為一名**預算**有限的旅客，他把許多奢華的飯店從清單中刪除。 105 英導

6. Taipei's **licensed accommodations**, with certified management practices, **guarantee** safety and offer travelers peace of mind.

   台灣**有執照的住宿**，有認證的經營方法，能**保障**安全以及讓旅客安心。 105 英導

7. Front Desk: How may we help you?
   Guest: I didn't make a **reservation** , but I'm wondering if you have any rooms **available** for tonight.

   櫃台：我有什麼可以幫你的嗎？
   客人：我沒有**預約**，但我想知道你們今晚是否還**有**任何空房？ 105 英領

8. Thank you for your **hospitality**. I have had a jolly good time during my stay here.

謝謝你的**熱情招待**。我在這邊住得很愉快！ `105 英領`

9. We're so grateful to the warm **hospitality** the host family showed us.

我們很感恩寄宿家庭的**熱情好客**。 `104 英領`

10. In the United States, about 1.8 million people in the **hospitality** industry work in establishments such as hotels, restaurants, casinos, and **amusement parks**.

在美國，大約有 180 萬人在**餐旅**業工作，像是飯店、餐廳、賭場以及**遊樂園**。 `103 英導`

11. With so many legal hotel **options**, let's give up risking a short-term rental.

有這麼多合法的飯店可供**選擇**，我們就不要冒險入住短期出租套房吧！ `105 英領`

12. The Star Lodge boasts 20 years of 80 percent **occupancy**, a record for the state.

星辰旅店吹噓 20 年來有 8 成的**住房率**，是該州的最高紀錄。 `104 英導`

13. During the hotel renovation, special **attention** was given to the lighting fixtures and decorations.

在飯店裝修期間，需要特別**注意**照明設備以及裝飾。 `104 英導`

14. In an effort to **reduce** the number of plastic tooth brushes customers throw away, many hotels have stopped providing **disposable** brushes.

為了**減少**客人丟棄塑膠牙刷的數量，許多飯店已經停止提供**拋棄式**牙刷。 `104 英導`

15. A: Excuse me, ma'am. We are going to leave early tomorrow morning for our flight schedule. Shall we have an early breakfast arrangement for my group?

   B: **What time do you want to have breakfast?**

   A: 不好意思，我們明天因為班機而必須一早離開，我們團員可以早一點吃早餐嗎？
   B: 你們想要幾點用早餐呢？ `103 英領`

16. One advantage of staying in apartment-style hotels is that you can either eat out or keep costs down by self-**catering**.

   住在公寓式旅館的好處之一，就是你可以外食或是自己**煮**以減少花費。 `103 英導`

17. The McDonald's hamburger company is going into the airline **catering** business.

麥當勞漢堡公司即將進入**外燴**產業。 100 英領

18. Tourists have a wide range of budget and tastes, and a wide variety of resorts and hotels have developed to **cater for** them.

旅客有不同的預算以及品味，而各式各樣的度假中心跟飯店也可**滿足**他們的需求。 101 英導

19. **Adjacent** to the theme park and a ten minutes' **stroll** from it, the hotel offers you the best location for your holiday accommodation.

**鄰近**主題公園、約 10 分鐘的**散步路程**，此飯店提供你假日住宿最棒的地點。 103 英導

▶ I just spent a relaxing afternoon taking a **stroll** along the river-walk.

我剛沿著河邊**散步**並度過了一個悠閒的午後。 101 英導

20. To order room service, you can call the reception and ask for food items listed on the hotel's menu. The food **is then brought to** your room for you to enjoy.

要點客房服務時，你可以打給接待中心，並告知飯店菜單上你要的食物選項。**接著**食物**就會被送到**你房間供你享用。 103 英導

21. Some hotels **require** their guests to leave a **deposit** to cover incidental charges to the room.

有些飯店**要求**房客留下一筆**保證金**，以支付客房的額外費用。 103 英導

22. If you **require** an immediate response to a current incident, please telephone our switchboard on 101.

如果你**要求**對於目前意外有立即的回覆，請撥分機 101。 103 英領

23. The travel agent says that we have to pay a **deposit** of $2,000 in advance in order to **secure the reservation** for our hotel room.

旅行社業務表示，我們必須事先付 2000 元**訂金**，以**確保**我們飯店房間的**預約**。 98 英導

24. After many years of travelling, the couples decided to stay in London forever and have a **permanent** home there.

旅行許多年之後，這對情侶決定留在倫敦，並且在那**永遠**定居。 103 英導

01 航空交通
02 飯店住宿
03 餐廳飲食
04 旅遊觀光
05 介紹台灣
06 帶團職責

25. Prices of hotel rooms are very **sensitive** to demand, so special deals and discounts during weekdays could always **attract** more people.

飯店的房價對於需求是非常**敏銳**的，所以平日的特別優惠跟折扣總是**吸引**更多人。
`103 英導`

▶ Considerate people are **sensitive** to others' wants and feelings.

貼心的人總是對於他人的需求以及欲望非常**敏銳**。 `99 英導`

▶ In many Western cultures, it is rude to ask about a person's age, weight, or salary. However, these topics may not be as **sensitive** in East Asia.

在許多西方文化中，問他人的年齡、體重，或是薪水是很無禮的。然而這些話題在東亞可能就不是如此**敏感**。 `99 英導`

26. Although guests are not allowed to eat durians inside the hotel because of their offensive odor, some people manage to **smuggle** them in.

雖然因為其嗆鼻的氣味，房客不被允許在飯店內吃榴槤，但許多人還是設法**偷渡**進來。
`103 英導`

27. Every year the school prepares a celebratory dinner **banquet** for the graduating class. The event will be held at San Francisco's Ritz-Carlton Hotel this year.

每年學校都會替畢業生準備慶祝性的**晚宴**。今年的活動將會於舊金山的麗思卡爾頓酒店舉行。 `103 英導`

28. Each room of this hotel has large windows that provide **spectacular** views of the sparkling Atlantic Ocean.

這間飯店的每一個房間都有大型的窗戶可以提供大西洋動人的**壯觀**景色。 `103 英導`

29. It is **customary** to leave a tip for your maid.

留小費給你的清潔人員是**約定俗成的**方式。 `108 英導`

30. A **resort hotel** is a venue to where travelers can relax. Accordingly, they emphasize **recreational amenities** such as saunas, swimming pools, etc.

所謂的**渡假飯店**是旅人可以放鬆休息的地方。因此，他們強調**休閒設施**像是三溫暖以及游泳池等等。 `108 英導`

legal **adj.** 合法的

short-term rental **adj.** 短租

be subject to **phr.** 依規定、受限於

hospitality **n.** 熱情招待、人情味

renovation **n.** 裝修

catering business **n.** 外燴產業

require **v.** 要求

temporary **adj.** 暫時的

deposit **n.** 預付、保證金、訂金

double **n.** 雙人房

extra bed **n.** 加床

service charge **n.** 服務費

lodging **n.** 住宿

reserved **adj.** （被）保留的

secure reservation **v.** 確保訂位、房

vacant **adj.** 空的

room rate **n.** 房價

high season / peak season **n.** 旺季

illegal **adj.** 非法的

licensed accommodations **n.** 有執照的住宿

guarantee **v.** 保證

options **n.** 選擇

cater **v.** 迎合、滿足

stroll **v.** **n.** 散步

permanent **adj.** 永久的

banquet **n.** 宴會

single **n.** 單人房

twin **n.** 雙人房（兩張單人床）

suite **n.** 套房

accommodation **n.** 住宿

bed down **v.** 下榻

reservation **n.** 預定

re-confirmation **v.** 再確認

vacancy **n.** 空房、空位

in advance **adv.** 事先

low season **n.** 淡季

01 航空交通
02 飯店住宿
03 餐廳飲食
04 旅遊觀光
05 介紹台灣
06 帶團職責

luxurious adj. 奢華的

luxury n. 奢華

facilities n. 設施

amenities n. 設施

boutique n.
流行女裝商店、精品店

satisfactory adj.
令人滿意的、符合要求的

unsatisfactory adj. 不令人滿意的

reception n. 接待處

front desk n. 櫃台

concierge n. 旅館服務台人員、門房

hotel clerk n. 飯店服務員

guest service n. 客戶服務

valet parking service n. 代客泊車

concierge service n. 管家服務

01 航空交通

02 飯店住宿

03 餐廳飲食

04 旅遊觀光

05 介紹台灣

06 帶團職責

## 三、牛刀小試

(　　) 1. One advantage of staying in apartment-style hotels is that you can either eat out or keep costs down by self-_____.

     (A) branding      (B) catering      (C) flavoring      (D) navigating

(　　) 2. _____ to the theme park and a ten minutes' stroll from it, the hotel offers you the best location for your holiday accommodation.

     (A) Adjacent      (B) Aggressive      (C) Applicable      (D) Approximate

(　　) 3. As a frugal _____ traveler, he shunned away from fancy hotels.

     (A) bargain      (B) bounty      (C) boundary      (D) budget

(　　) 4. Although guests are not allowed to eat durians inside the hotel because of their offensive odor, some people manage to _____ them in.

     (A) calculate      (B) exclude      (C) achieve      (D) smuggle

(　　) 5. Taipei's licensed accommodations, with certified management practices, _____ safety and offer travelers peace of mind.

     (A) intercept      (B) guarantee      (C) intimidate      (D) grumble

(　　) 6. To order room service, you call the reception and ask for food items listed on the hotel's menu. The food _____ your room for you to enjoy.

     (A) is then brought to             (B) may then bring in

     (C) to bring is then at           (D) has then brought to

(　　) 7. Front Desk: How may we help you?

     Guest: I didn't make a(n)_____, but I'm wondering if you have any rooms available for tonight.

     (A) conclusion      (B) expectation      (C) reservation      (D) inclusion

(　　) 8. With so many legal hotel _____, let's give up risking a short-term rental.

     (A) options      (B) regulations      (C) restrictions      (D) profits

(　　) 9. The Star Lodge boasts 20 years of 80 percent _____, a record for the state.

     (A) fluency      (B) hospitality      (C) metropolis      (D) occupancy

(　) 10. In an effort to reduce the number of plastic tooth brushes customers throw away, many hotels have stopped providing _____ brushes.

(A) disposable　　(B) ecological　　(C) measurable　　(D) unusable

(　) 11. Some hotels require their guests to leave a _____ to cover incidental charges to the room.

(A) custom　　(B) discount　　(C) deposit　　(D) currency

(　) 12. The operator of an illegal short-term rental unit could be _____ to a fine and ordered to immediately close.

(A) consigned　　(B) certificated　　(C) subject　　(D) subordinate

(　) 13. Prices of hotel rooms are very _____ to demand, so special deals and discounts during weekdays could always attract more people.

(A) commercial　　(B) frequent　　(C) gradual　　(D) sensitive

(　) 14. We're so grateful to the warm _____ the host family showed us.

(A) aloofness　　(B) hospitality　　(C) hostility　　(D) stinginess

(　) 15. In the United States, about 1.8 million people in the _____ industry work in establishments such as hotels, restaurants, casinos, and amusement parks.

(A) hospitality　　(B) missionary　　(C) renaissance　　(D) sanctuary

(　) 16. Every year the school prepares a celebratory dinner _____ for the graduating class. The event will be held at San Francisco's Ritz-Carlton Hotel this year.

(A) engagement　　(B) complex　　(C) disposal　　(D) banquet

(　) 17. Each room of this hotel has large windows that provide _____ views of the sparkling Atlantic Ocean.

(A) cautious　　(B) spectacular　　(C) experimental　　(D) ambitious

(　) 18. Luxury hotels and upscale restaurants have _____ around the banks of Sun Moon Lake in Nantou, Taiwan.

(A) brought in　　(B) lightened up　　(C) sprung up　　(D) called in

(　) 19. During the hotel renovation, special _____ was given to the lighting fixtures and decorations.

(A) attention　　(B) confidence　　(C) introduction　　(D) performance

(　) 20. Legal hotels should have public _____ insurance.

(A) executive　　(B) exempt　　(C) liability　　(D) immune

## 標 準 答 案

| | | | | |
|---|---|---|---|---|
| 1.（B） | 2.（A） | 3.（D） | 4.（D） | 5.（B） |
| 6.（A） | 7.（C） | 8.（A） | 9.（D） | 10.（A） |
| 11.（C） | 12.（C） | 13.（D） | 14.（B） | 15.（A） |
| 16.（D） | 17.（B） | 18.（C） | 19.（A） | 20.（C） |

01 航空交通

02 飯店住宿

03 餐廳飲食

04 旅遊觀光

05 介紹台灣

06 帶團職責

# 3 餐廳飲食

1. During their first visit to Taiwan, many foreign tourists **relish** the local flavors at the night markets.

   許多外國人第一次造訪台灣的時候，他們在夜市很**享受**當地的美食。 105 英導

2. Traditional Chinese food can be found all over Taiwan, but the island's night markets are the places where **snacks** can be found in abundance.

   在全台灣各地可以找到許多傳統的中國菜，但在這島上的夜市則可以找到許多**小吃**。 105 英領

3. In order to **provide** all the customers with a warm and fragrant atmosphere, the coffee shop owner spent a fortune to redecorate the entire store.

   為了**提供**所有顧客一個溫馨芬芳的環境，咖啡店的老闆花了一大筆錢重新裝潢店面。 105 英導

4. New Orleans has a reputation for having a unique **cuisine** born of many cultures that came together in the old city. Visitors come from all around the world to enjoy the food there.

   紐澳良這座古老城市以多元文化匯集而成的獨特**美食**聞名。世界各地慕名而來的遊客都十分享受當地的佳餚。 105 英導

5. Your afternoon tea experience **includes** a glass of good wine and a selection of **culinary delights** designed to **complement** your beverage choice, and of course, live music for your entertainment.

   你的下午茶體驗**包含**一杯好的紅酒，跟一系列設計來與你選擇的飲料**相得益彰**的**美食**，當然還有娛樂你的音樂。 104 英導

6. With special **rates** and **complimentary** breakfasts for two, our Bed & Breakfast **packages** are the perfect way for you to relax and **recharge**.

   有優惠的**房價**跟**免費**的兩人份早餐，B&B **套裝組合**是你放鬆跟**充電**最棒的選擇。 103 英領

▶ With a **complacent** smile, Robert showed how happy he was when he won the swimming contest yesterday.

羅伯**得意的**笑容顯示他有多開心能贏得昨天的游泳比賽。 `99 英導`

▶ Tourists often remark that Taiwan is a beautiful island worthy of visiting; that is a nice **compliment**.

遊客經常評論台灣為一個值得造訪的美麗島嶼，這是很棒的**讚美**。 `103 英領`

7. To be able to work as a chef in the first rate hotel means that you have to have professional **culinary** skills.

能夠在首選的飯店當主廚表示你一定要有專業的**烹飪**技巧。 `104 英領`

8. When we have leftover cooked stew or other food with meat, it is suggested that the food should be **cooled** to room temperature, and then put in the **refrigerator**.

當我們有吃剩的燉菜或是含有肉的食物，建議將食物在室溫中**放涼**，然後再放到**冰箱**。 `104 英導`

9. Naples is rich in historical, artistic and cultural traditions; in addition, it is famous for its **gastronomy** because the city is by tradition the home of pizza.

拿坡里有著豐富的歷史、美學跟文化傳統。此外，它因**美食**聞名，因為傳統上來說，它是披薩的家。 `104 英導`

10. A: Do you like cooking?
    B: No, I'm not **into** it.

A：你喜歡烹飪嗎？
B：不，不怎麼喜歡。 `104 英導`

11. I think you need another knife, Laura. This one you have is so dull that it barely **slices** bread.

我認為你需要另一把刀，羅拉。你現在有的這把很鈍，而且幾乎不能**切**麵包。 `104 英領`

12. The restaurant manager was **replaced** because of her inability to maintain **discipline** among her **employees**.

餐廳經理因為沒有能力維持**員工紀律**，而被**替換**掉了。 `104 英導`

01 航空交通
02 飯店住宿
03 餐廳飲食
04 旅遊觀光
05 介紹台灣
06 帶團職責

13. The fast food restaurant should have been **profitable**, but poor **capital** control forced it into **bankruptcy**.

這間速食餐廳應該要能夠**獲利**，但不當的**資產**管理迫使它**破產**。 104 英導

14. Once we were seated at the restaurant, it took almost no time before big bamboo **steamers** full of dumplings arrived, along with **directions** on how to eat those xiao long bao.

當我們於餐廳就坐後，不消一會兒裝滿餃子的**蒸籠**立刻就送上來，並且同時附上如何吃小籠包的**指示**。 103 英導

15. After you **purchase** good tea, keep it in a dry cool place, **avoiding** direct sunshine. An airtight container is a good choice.

在你**購買**好茶之後，將之放置於涼爽乾燥的地方，**避免**陽光直射。使用密封罐是個好主意。 103 英導

16. The chef uses only the finest **ingredients** to make his special salsa.

主廚只使用最好的**食材**來做他特別的莎莎醬。 103 英導

17. This restaurant is famous for its **exotic** flavors of Indian **cuisine**.

這間餐廳因為其**異國風的**印度**美食**而聞名。 103 英導

▶ Thailand is a pleasure for the senses. Tourists come from around the world to visit the nation's gold-adorned temples and **sample** its delicious **cuisine**.

泰國是個讓人感官感到愉悅的地方。來自世界各地的觀光客會來拜訪此國家以黃金裝飾的廟宇，並品嚐其豐富的美食。 102 導遊

18. Black pepper is perhaps the most commonly used **spice** in the world.

黑胡椒也許是世界上最常用的**香料**。 104 英導

▶ Claire loves to buy **exotic** foods: vegetables and herbs from China, **spices** from India, olives from Greece, and cheeses from France.

克萊兒喜歡買**異國風情的**食物，像是來自中國的蔬菜和草藥、印度來的**香料**、希臘來的橄欖，以及法國來的起司。 99 英導

19. John asked the waitress for a **straw** to drink his iced tea.

約翰向服務生要喝冰茶用的**吸管**。 103 英導

20. The service was terrible at the restaurant, so we didn't leave a **gratuity**.

    餐廳的服務太糟糕，所以我們沒有給**小費**。 `108 英導`

21. Stinky tofu is a distinctive snack in the night market. The tofu is left in **fermented** milk and some ingredients for months, making it pungent and tasty.

    臭豆腐是夜市特有的小吃。豆腐被放在**發酵的**牛奶以及其他材料內數個月，讓它嗆鼻以及可口。 `108 英導`

22. Mary bought her parents a new set of kitchen **utensils** including bowls, knives, and frying pans.

    瑪麗幫他的父母買了一整組的廚房**用具**包含碗、刀以及煎鍋。 `108 英領`

23. Do not undertake hard exercise for a few hours after a meal to allow food to **digest**.

    吃完飯後要讓食物**消化**，幾個小時內不要做太激烈的運動。 `108 英領`

01 航空交通
02 飯店住宿
03 餐廳飲食
04 旅遊觀光
05 介紹台灣
06 帶團職責

## 二、必考單字　MP3-003

local flavors **n.** 當地的美食

fragrant **adj.** 芬芳的

culinary **adj.** 烹飪的

purchase **v.** 購買 **n.** 商品

spice **n.** 香料

snacks **n.** 小吃

cuisine **n.** 料理

gastronomy **n.** 美食

ingredient **n.** 食材

exotic **adj.** 異國的

01 航空交通

02 飯店住宿

03 餐廳飲食

04 旅遊觀光

05 介紹台灣

06 帶團職責

## 三、牛刀小試

( ) 1. During their first visit to Taiwan, many foreign tourists _____ the local flavors at the night markets.

(A) recall      (B) relish      (C) refill      (D) reminiscence

( ) 2. When we have leftover cooked stew or other food with meat, it is suggested that the food should be _____ to room temperature, and then put in the refrigerator.

(A) heated      (B) cooled      (C) frozen      (D) processed

( ) 3. In order to _____ all the customers with a warm and fragrant atmosphere, the coffee shop owner spent a fortune to redecorate the entire store.

(A) signify      (B) provide      (C) launch      (D) offer

( ) 4. Once we were seated at the restaurant, it took almost no time before big bamboo steamers full of dumplings arrived, along with _____ on how to eat those xiao long bao.

(A) brunches      (B) chopsticks      (C) directions      (D) functions

( ) 5. New Orleans has a reputation for having a unique _____ born of many cultures that came together in the old city. Visitors come from all around the world to enjoy the food there.

(A) decor      (B) license      (C) tourism      (D) cuisine

( ) 6. This restaurant is famous for its exotic flavors of Indian _____.

(A) cuisine      (B) ornament      (C) necessities      (D) costumes

( ) 7. Your afternoon tea experience includes a glass of good wine and a selection of culinary delights designed to _____ your beverage choice, and of course, live music for your entertainment.

(A) complement      (B) nurture      (C) propose      (D) relocate

( ) 8. With special rates and _____ breakfasts for two, our Bed & Breakfast packages are the perfect way for you to relax and recharge.

(A) complimentary      (B) compulsory      (C) condescending      (D) commodious

( ) 9. John asked the waitress for a _____ to drink his iced tea.

(A) straw      (B) grinder      (C) fiber      (D) sausage

( ) 10. To be able to work as a chef in the first rate hotel means that you have to have professional _____ skills.

(A) culinary      (B) disciplinary      (C) elocutionary      (D) stationary

( ) 11. I think you need another knife, Laura. This one you have is so dull that it barely _____ bread.

(A) sharpens      (B) slices      (C) spreads      (D) squeezes

( ) 12. The restaurant manager was replaced because of her inability to maintain _____ among her employees.

(A) advocacy      (B) contract      (C) discipline      (D) euphemism

( ) 13. The fast food restaurant should have been profitable, but poor capital control forced it into _____.

(A) bankruptcy      (B) compensation      (C) construction      (D) restoration

( ) 14. _____ you purchase good tea, keep it in a dry cool place, avoiding direct sunshine. An airtight container is a good choice.

(A) After      (B) Though      (C) Before      (D) Whereas

( ) 15. A: Do you like cooking?  B: No, I'm not _____ it.

(A) in      (B) into      (C) onto      (D) toward

( ) 16. Dihua Street is a great place to purchase traditional Chinese foods which _____ great gifts, and many  shops will seal purchases for plane travel.

(A) making      (B) make      (C) makes      (D) made

( ) 17. Traditional Chinese food can be found all over Taiwan, but the island's night markets are the places where _____ can be found in abundance.

(A) sickle      (B) snacks      (C) shacks      (D) sacks

( ) 18. The chef uses only the finest _____ to make his special salsa.

(A) ingredients      (B) properties      (C) vouchers      (D) characteristics

( ) 19. Naples is rich in historical, artistic and cultural traditions; in addition, it is famous for its _____ because the city is by tradition the home of pizza.

(A) astronomy      (B) autonomy      (C) economy      (D) gastronomy

# 標 準 答 案

| 1. ( B ) | 2. ( B ) | 3. ( B ) | 4. ( C ) | 5. ( D ) |
|----------|----------|----------|----------|-----------|
| 6. ( A ) | 7. ( A ) | 8. ( A ) | 9. ( A ) | 10. ( A ) |
| 11. ( B ) | 12. ( C ) | 13. ( A ) | 14. ( A ) | 15. ( B ) |
| 16. ( B ) | 17. ( B ) | 18. ( A ) | 19. ( D ) | |

# 4 旅遊觀光

1. **Tourism** usually brings much-needed money to developing countries. **Furthermore**, it provides **employment** for the local people.

   **觀光業**通常替發展中的國家帶來救命錢。**此外**，也提供了當地人民的**就業機會**。
   [103 英領]

2. The policy of Taiwan tourism is to **reach the goals** of development of international tourism, enhancement of domestic travel quality, and increased foreign-exchange **revenues**.

   台灣觀光政策主要是以**達到**國際觀光發展、加強國內旅遊品質以及增加外匯的**營收**為目標。 [104 英領]

3. We believe travelers can make a positive **contribution** to the countries they visit if they respect their **host** communities and spend their money wisely.

   我們相信如果旅客尊敬**當地**社區以及有智慧地花錢，他們可以替該國家帶來正面的**貢獻**。 [103 英導]

4. The **income** brought in by tourism will **better** the townspeople' life.

   觀光帶來的**收入**將會**改善**小鎮居民的生活。 [105 英導]

5. Climate tourism has become a new **niche** in the **booming ecotourism** due to the global warming in recent years.

   鑑於地球暖化，氣候觀光已經成為**新興的生態觀光**的新**利基**。 [104 英領]

6. Tourism **expenditure** refers to the amount paid for the acquisition of **consumption** goods and services for and during tourism trips.

   觀光業的**花費**是指在觀光旅行中獲取**消費**性商品及服務的支出費用。 [104 英領]

7. We are on **vacation**. This is our first time in Seattle, where do you **recommend** if my husband and I would like to enjoy a romantic evening?

   我們正在**度假**，這是我們第一次到西雅圖，您**推薦**我跟先生去哪裡度過浪漫的夜晚呢？
   [105 英領]

01

航空交通

02

飯店住宿

03

餐廳飲食

04

旅遊觀光

05

介紹台灣

06

帶團職責

8. Father always takes his **annual** vacation in July so the family can **go abroad** together.

父親總是在 7 月休**年**假，這樣全家就可以一起**出國**。 103 英領

9. If your time in Tokyo is limited, you must sketch out your **itinerary** well to make the most of it.

如果你在東京的時間有限，你必須好好利用時間安排你的**行程**。 105 英領

10. This **itinerary features** Spain's major cities including stops at several famous cathedrals.

這**行程路線**是以造訪西班牙主要的城市**以**及當中幾座著名大教堂**為特色**。 103 英導

11. The long-planned musical festival will debut next year, which will **feature** a dozen shows to attract music lovers.

這計畫已久的音樂劇節慶即將於明年登場，將會**以**一系列的表演**為特色**來吸引音樂愛好者。 105 英導

12. This 2.5km-long tree-lined **boulevard** featuring flower shops and **boutiques** is one of the most beautiful places in Paris.

這條長 2.5 公里的樹蔭**大道**以花店跟**精品店**為特色，是巴黎最美的地方之一。 105 英導

13. Pickpocketing often occurs in **crowded** tourist attractions.

偷竊行為經常發生在**擁擠的**觀光勝地。 104 英領

14. Taj Mahal, regarded by many as the finest example of Mughal architecture, is one of the most popular tourist **attractions** in India.

泰姬瑪哈陵，被視為蒙兀兒建築的最佳範例，是印度最受歡迎的觀光**景點**。 103 英導

15. To gain international **publicity**, the city implements several projects of renovations for the coming **exhibition**.

為了贏得國際性的**宣傳**，城市為了接下來的**展覽**，執行許多翻新的計畫。 105 英導

16. Walt Disney World's Magic Kingdom is the most visited **theme park** in the world.

華特迪士尼的魔幻王國是世界上最多人造訪的**主題公園**。 105 英導

17. As all the details about the trip are on the **brochure**, you better read it carefully **in advance**.

   所有關於行程的細節都在**小冊子**上，你最好**事先**仔細閱讀。 `105 英導`

18. The **safari** will **provide** the excitement of direct contact with animals on land.

   這趟**遊獵**將會**提供**人們與陸地上的動物直接接觸的興奮感。 `105 英導`

19. **A safari park** is a large area of land reserved for wild animals, in which they can move freely and be seen by the public who usually drive through the park in cars.

   **野生動物園**是很大的一塊保護野生動物的區域，動物們可以自由移動，並且讓開車進到公園的民眾可以看到他們。 `103 英導`

20. His one ambition in life was to go on **safari** to Kenya to photograph lions and tigers.

   他人生的雄心壯志之一就是去肯亞**獵遊**，拍攝獅子跟老虎。 `100 英導`

21. The final **destination** for today's trip will be The Lincoln Memorial built to honor the 16th President of the United States, Abraham Lincoln.

   今天最後的**目的地**將會是紀念美國第 16 任總統亞伯拉罕・林肯的林肯紀念堂。 `105 英導`

22. The **highlight** of their trip is to watch the gorgeous fireworks of the tallest building on New Year's Eve.

   他們行程的**重點**為欣賞最高建築在跨年夜時的華麗煙火。 `105 英導`

23. When I travelled to Germany last month, I accidently **ran into** one of my high school teachers in the flea market.

   我上個月到德國旅遊時，在當地的跳蚤市場**碰巧遇見**了我的高中老師。 `105 英導`

24. A local travel agency hung several scenic posters in the company window to **attract** pedestrians to come inside and purchase their historical tour.

   當地旅行社在窗戶掛了許多風景海報，以**吸引**路人進來選購他們的歷史之旅。 `105 英導`

25. It is always a great idea to let at least one person know exactly where you will be staying and how to contact you in an **emergency**.

至少讓一個人知道你究竟住在哪裡，以及**緊急**時該如何聯絡你，一直都是個好主意。
`105 英領`

26. The original paintings are now part of an **exhibition** in the national museum.

這幅原作目前是國家博物館**展覽**的一部分。 `105 英領`

27. Don't miss out on the best London art **exhibitions** including sculptures, paintings, and photography.

不要錯過倫敦最棒的藝術**展覽**，包含雕塑、畫作以及攝影。 `103 英導`

28. The museum offers discounted admission for visitors after 4:30 pm to **alleviate** crowding problems during the early part of the day.

博物館提供遊客 4 點半過後的優惠門票，以**減緩**一天中稍早期間的擁擠問題。 `105 英領`

29. The brightly colored paintings **depict** the **indigenous** village where farmers **sowed** the land with wheat seeds.

這幅色彩明亮的畫作**描繪**出**當地**村莊的農夫於土地**播種**小麥種子。 `105 英領`

30. Adjacent old houses and buildings winding along the street **display** the rhythmic beauty.

蜿蜒於街道上相鄰的老房子跟舊建築**呈現**了韻律的美感。 `105 英領`

31. In the water-theme park, kids as well as adults can **frolic** around water fountains or ride swan-shaped paddleboats on the lake.

在主題水樂園，小孩跟大人都可以在噴泉周邊**嬉戲**，或是搭乘湖面上的天鵝造型腳踏船。
`105 英領`

32. Travelling by long-distance bus is generally the cheapest way to reach the destination, but spending 12 hours on the road is very time-**consuming**.

長程巴士旅遊通常是到達目的地最便宜的方法，但是花 12 個小時在路上實在太**耗時**。
`103 英導`

01 航空交通

02 飯店住宿

03 餐廳飲食

04 旅遊觀光

05 介紹台灣

06 帶團職責

33. **Stroll** west from the Maritime Museum along the waterfront and you will soon **reach** the Amsterdam Center for Architecture.

從海事博物館沿著岸邊往西**散步**，你很快就會**到達**阿姆斯特丹的建築中心。 103 英導

34. Shall we **assume** it will not rain tonight, and plan the outdoor party?

我們是否該**假設**今晚不會下雨，然後計畫戶外派對？ 103 英領

35. A metropolitan area consists of a central city and any suburban areas in its **vicinity**.

大都會地區包含一個主要的城市以及**鄰近地區**的郊區。 104 英導

36. Our trips range from cruising **exotic** islands to closer-to-home excursions to baseball games and music events.

我們的行程範圍從遊船到**異國風情的**島嶼、在家附近的郊遊、到棒球比賽以及音樂比賽。 104 英導

37. He got up **early enough** to watch the first ray of the rising sun.

他起得**夠早**去看日出的第一道光。 103 英領

38. Ask for **permission** before you take close-up photographs of people, and if payment is requested, either pay up or put the camera away.

在拍人物近照之前先請求**允許**，如果需要付費，要不付清、要不就把相機移走。 103 英導

39. Under this travel insurance plan, you are **eligible** to make a claim when your journey has to be cancelled for reasons beyond your control.

在這旅行險內，當你的行程由於不可控制的因素而導致取消時，你**有資格**可以申請理賠。 103 英導

40. There is no reason to stay in the city center; after the shops close, the center becomes a **virtual** ghost town.

沒有理由留在市中心。商家關店之後，市中心就成了**實質上的**的鬼城。 103 英導

41. The climate in the city is tropical, with monthly **mean** temperatures in the range of 19 to 29 degrees and **relative** humidity between 70 and 80%.

這座城市的氣候是熱帶天氣，**平均**月溫度在 19 ～ 29 度之間，**相對**溼度則在 70 ～ 80% 之間。 103 英導

42. When you are in public places, be sure not to leave your personal **belongings unattended**.

當你在公眾場合時，確保不要讓你的個人**物品無人看管**。 [103 英導]

43. The English tour group **visited** Taj Mahal last December.

這團英國團去年 12 月**造訪了**泰姬瑪哈陵。 [104 英領]

44. From a traveler's **perspective**, I have to **admit** that the city has superfluous amount of new **statues** and **monuments**.

從旅客的**觀點**來看，我必須**承認**這座城市有難以計數的新**雕像**跟**紀念碑**。 [103 英領]

45. If you arrive in Skopje before 2014, expect to see quite a bit of construction as the city is currently undergoing a massive **transformation**.

如果你在 2014 年前抵達史高比耶，就可看到很多工程，因為這城市正在進行大幅**轉變**。 [103 英領]

46. Most countries have passed laws to protect their national **heritage** such as valuable historical buildings or things that are important to **cultural preservation**.

大部分的國家都已經通過法律來保護國家**遺產**，像是寶貴的歷史建築，或是對於**文化保存**很重要的東西。 [103 英導]

47. Petronas Twin Towers in Kuala Kumpur are the world's tallest twin towers. Visitors can see the views of the city from the Skybridge as well as from the **observatory** at Level 86.

吉隆坡的雙子星塔是世界上最高的雙子塔。遊客可以從天空之橋上跟 86 層樓的**觀景台**欣賞整座城市。 [103 英導]

48. At the end of the train there is an open **observation** car where you can stand and smell the jungle, listen to the birds, and breathe in the sweet Asian air.

在這列火車最尾端是開放式的**觀景**車廂，人們可以站在此聞叢林的味道、聽鳥叫、呼吸亞洲的甜美空氣。 [103 英領]

49. The jazz concert will be held at the high school **auditorium** in town and is going to be one event you do not want to miss out on.

這場即將在鎮上的高中**禮堂**所舉辦的爵士音樂會，是一場你絕不能錯過的活動。 [103 英導]

01 航空交通
02 飯店住宿
03 餐廳飲食
04 旅遊觀光
05 介紹台灣
06 帶團職責

50. Bollywood movies have recently **appealed to** a global market and **drawn** hundreds of millions of viewers all over the world.

寶萊塢電影最近**吸引**了全球市場，亦**吸引**全世界數千萬的觀眾。 `103 英導`

51. Visitors to San Francisco this morning might be quite disappointed because the Golden Gate Bridge was barely **visible** through the **dense fog**.

今天早上到舊金山的遊客可能會有點失望，因為在**濃霧**中幾乎**看**不**到**金門大橋。
`103 英導`

52. Hawaii is a great location for all kinds of water sports. Some like to go windsurfing **whereas** others like to go water-skiing.

夏威夷是一個適合各類水上運動的好地方。有些人喜歡衝浪，**反之**其他人喜歡滑水。
`103 英導`

53. Sunday is the best day to visit the market. There are many fantastic **stalls** selling fresh local fruits and vegetables.

星期天是造訪市場最好的一天。有許多吸引人的**攤販**會販售當地新鮮的水果跟蔬菜。
`103 英導`

54. A: How many countries are you going to visit when you go on vacation to Asia?
B: **Not very many. I don't have a lot of money.**

A：當你到亞洲度假時，你預計要去幾個國家？
B：沒有很多，我沒有很多錢。 `103 英領`

55. A: My husband and I are leaving for Paris. We are taking a second honey moon.
B: **How romantic. Paris is a beautiful city.**

A：我先生跟我即將前往巴黎。我們將二度蜜月。
B：好浪漫！巴黎是座很漂亮的城市。 `103 英領`

56. There are many **attractions** for tourists including a theme park and a museum.

有很多給遊客的**觀光景點**包含一個主題樂園以及一間博物館。 `108 英領`

57. In order to appreciate the **architecture** of the castle, you need to get off the tour bus and get closer to it.

為了欣賞城堡的**建築**，你需要下遊覽車並靠近一點。 `108 英領`

58. Are there any **sightseeing** tours for the memorial hall?

紀念堂有任何**觀光**導覽嗎？ 108 英領

59. The tour operator will arrange transport and plan your **itinerary**.

旅行社人員將會安排交通以及計劃你的**行程**。 108 英領

60. Taking photographs is **banned** in many museums and historic places. The no-photos policy is now a worldwide phenomenon.

在許多博物館以及歷史景點拍照都是**被禁止的**。不能照相的政策已經是一個全球的現象。 108 英領

61. The Burj Khalifa is a **skyscraper** in Dubai and has been the tallest building in the world since 2008.

哈里發塔是杜拜的**摩天大樓**，從 2008 年以來就是世界最高的建築物。 108 英領

62. We found a **secluded** beach a few miles further on. It is very quiet and private as well as perfect for snorkeling.

我們發現一個幾英里外的**僻靜**海灘。非常安靜以及私密，是完美潛水的地方。 108 英領

01 航空交通
02 飯店住宿
03 餐廳飲食
04 旅遊觀光
05 介紹台灣
06 帶團職責

tourism n. 觀光業

destination n. 目的地

tourist attraction n. 觀光景點

recommend v. 推薦

international adj. 國際的

festival n. 節慶

highlight v. 重點

brochure n. 小冊子

undermine v. 破壞

emergency n. 緊急

expenditure n. 花費

excursion n. 郊遊

gastronomy n. 美食

mission n. 使命

attract v. 吸引

provide v. 提供

domestic adj. 國內的

itinerary n. 行程

feature v. 以～為特色 n. 特色

theme park n. 主題公園

safari n. 遊獵

attract v. 吸引

exhibition n. 展覽

exotic adj. 異國風情的

eligible adj. 有資格的

display v. n. 展示、呈現

01 航空交通

02 飯店住宿

03 餐廳飲食

04 旅遊觀光

05 介紹台灣

06 帶團職責

## 三、牛刀小試

( ) 1. The policy of Taiwan tourism is to reach the goals of development of international tourism, _____ of domestic travel quality, and increased foreign-exchange revenues.

    (A) abatement     (B) debasement     (C) diminishment     (D) enhancement

( ) 2. Climate tourism has become a new _____ in the booming ecotourism due to the global warming in recent years.

    (A) closure     (B) compartment     (C) niche     (D) recess

( ) 3. Tourism _____ refers to the amount paid for the acquisition of consumption goods and services for and during tourism trips.

    (A) deficit     (B) expenditure     (C) reimbursement     (D) revenue

( ) 4. Taj Mahal, regarded by many as the finest example of Mughal architecture, is one of the most popular tourist _____ in India.

    (A) attractions     (B) departments     (C) surroundings     (D) promises

( ) 5. The couple hoped that going on a trip together would _____ their relationship.

    (A) cut short                  (B) focus on

    (C) make fun of             (D) breathe life into

( ) 6. We are on _____. This is our first time in Seattle, where do you recommend if my husband and I would like to enjoy a romantic evening?

    (A) vacation     (B) vacancy     (C) vocation     (D) vaccination

( ) 7. The English tour group _____ Taj Mahal last December.

    (A) will visit     (B) visited     (C) visit     (D) had visited

( ) 8. If Jane had won the race, she would have been given a free trip to England; in other words, _____.

    (A) Jane won the race           (B) Jane got a free trip

    (C) Jane gave a free trip         (D) Jane lost the race

(　) 9.  A metropolitan area consists of a central city and any suburban areas in its _____.

(A) construction　　(B) downtown　　(C) shelter　　(D) vicinity

(　) 10. Our trips range from cruising _____ islands to closer-to-home excursions to baseball games and music events.

(A) exile　　(B) exotic　　(C) exquisite　　(D) extensive

(　) 11. He got up _____ to watch the first ray of the rising sun.

(A) as earliest　　(B) enough early　　(C) very earlier　　(D) early enough

(　) 12. Petronas Twin Towers in Kuala Kumpur are the world's tallest twin towers. Visitors can see the views of the city from the Skybridge as well as from the _____ at Level 86.

(A) environment　　(B) observatory　　(C) glacier　　(D) latitude

(　) 13. Bollywood movies have recently _____ to a global market and drawn hundreds of millions of viewers all over the world.

(A) increased　　(B) appealed　　(C) speculated　　(D) enriched

(　) 14. Anything that gives travelers a taste of the local culture or a personal greeting upon arrival _____ the favorable experience of an airport and the city or country where it's located.

(A) is available for　(B) adjusts to　　(C) adds to　　(D) gets over

(　) 15. This 2.5km-long tree-lined _____ featuring flower shops and boutiques is one of the most beautiful places in Paris.

(A) colleague　　(B) delicacy　　(C) ambulance　　(D) boulevard

(　) 16. To gain international _____, the city implements several projects of renovations for the coming exhibition.

(A) boycott　　(B) expedience　　(C) denunciation　　(D) publicity

(　) 17. Walt Disney World's Magic Kingdom is the most visited _____ in the world.

(A) national museum　　　　　　(B) theme park

(C) roller coaster　　　　　　　(D) Ferris wheel

01 航空交通

02 飯店住宿

03 餐廳飲食

04 旅遊觀光

05 介紹台灣

06 帶團職責

(　) 18. A _____ park is a large area of land reserved for wild animals, in which they can move freely and be seen by the public who usually drive through the park in cars.

(A) shrine　　　(B) botanical　　(C) descendent　　(D) safari

(　) 19. When you are in public places, be sure not to leave your personal _____ unattended.

(A) boarding　　(B) amusement　　(C) themes　　(D) belongings

(　) 20. From a traveler's _____, I have to admit that the city has superfluous amount of new statues and monuments.

(A) assumptive　　(B) anticipative　　(C) prescriptive　　(D) perspective

(　) 21. The _____ of their trip is to watch the gorgeous fireworks of the tallest building on New Year's Eve.

(A) expedition　　(B) resolution　　(C) highlight　　(D) demonstration

(　) 22. When I travelled to Germany last month, I accidenty _____ one of my high school teachers in the flea market.

(A) knocked down　(B) bounced back　(C) waited upon　(D) ran into

(　) 23. The original paintings are now part of an _____ in the national museum.

(A) exhibition　　(B) exposition　　(C) prohibition　　(D) equipment

(　) 24. Only on Sundays _____ without paying.

(A) they could visit the museum　　　(B) you will visit the museum

(C) can you visit the museum　　　　(D) we will visit the museum

(　) 25. The brightly colored paintings depict the indigenous village where farmers _____ the land with wheat seeds.

(A) sowed　　　(B) preserved　　(C) explored　　(D) leased

(　) 26. Adjacent old houses and buildings winding along the street _____ the rhythmic beauty.

(A) connect　　(B) display　　(C) conduct　　(D) restore

(　) 27. When traveling in Switzerland, you may see some high mountains _____ covered by ice and snow.

(A) desperately　　(B) imminently　　(C) perpetually　　(D) radically

( ) 28. The _____ zone is a great place to watch crabs and other wildlife as you enjoy the sound of the waves crashing against the shore.

(A) tropical      (B) radiative      (C) intertidal      (D) defensive

( ) 29. In the water-theme park, kids as well as adults can _____ around water fountains or ride swan-shaped paddleboats on the lake.

(A) flex      (B) frolic      (C) stalk      (D) swap

( ) 30. Travelling by long-distance bus is generally the cheapest way to reach the destination, but spending 12 hours on the road is very time-_____.

(A) consuming      (B) misleading      (C) relieving      (D) violating

( ) 31. Shall we _____ it will not rain tonight, and plan the outdoor party?.

(A) resume      (B) assume      (C) consume      (D) subsume

( ) 32. As all the details about the trip are on the _____, you better read it carefully in advance.

(A) curator      (B) tour manager      (C) passport      (D) brochure

( ) 33. We believe travelers can make a positive contribution to the countries they visit if they respect their _____ communities and spend their money wisely.

(A) guest      (B) host      (C) port      (D) source

( ) 34. A: How many countries are you going to visit when you go on vacation to Asia?

B: _____?

(A) Korea is the country I love best.

(B) Unfortunately I don't have much time left.

(C) Sure, many countries in Asia have wonderful cultures.

(D) Not very many. I don't have a lot of money.

( ) 35. Pickpocketing often occurs in _____ tourist attractions.

(A) crowded      (B) distant      (C) asserted      (D) isolated

( ) 36. A local travel agency hung several scenic posters in the company window to _____ pedestrians to come inside and purchase their historical tour.

(A) retract      (B) attract      (C) distract      (D) deprive

01 航空交通

02 飯店住宿

03 餐廳飲食

04 旅遊觀光

05 介紹台灣

06 帶團職責

( ) 37. If your time in Tokyo is limited, you must sketch out your _____ well to make the most of it.

(A) map      (B) goal      (C) itinerary      (D) blue print

( ) 38. This _____ features Spain's major cities including stops at several famous cathedrals.

(A) forecast      (B) itinerary      (C) restriction      (D) allowance

( ) 39. It is always a great idea to let at least one person know exactly where you will be staying and how to contact you in an _____.

(A) evidence      (B) emergency      (C) immigration      (D) organization

( ) 40. Many people, when traveling in Southeast Asia, try to avoid the monsoon season as it is _____ to travel around.

(A) very harder      (B) much harder      (C) too harder      (D) so harder

( ) 41. Ask for _____ before you take close-up photographs of people, and if payment is requested, either pay up or put the camera away.

(A) capital      (B) justice      (C) permission      (D) substance

( ) 42. There is no reason to stay in the city center; after the shops close, the center becomes a _____ ghost town.

(A) customary      (B) feasible      (C) spectacular      (D) virtual

( ) 43. The climate in the city is tropical, with monthly _____ temperatures in the range of 19 to 29 degrees and relative humidity between 70 and 80%.

(A) mean      (B) plain      (C) rare      (D) surface

( ) 44. Most countries have passed laws to protect their national _____ such as valuable historical buildings or things that are important to cultural preservation.

(A) habitat      (B) continent      (C) anthem      (D) heritage

( ) 45. Visitors to San Francisco this morning might be quite disappointed because the Golden Gate Bridge was barely _____ through the dense fog.

(A) durable      (B) visible      (C) amiable      (D) audible

(　　) 46. The _____ statement of Tourism Malaysia is "marketing Malaysia as a destination of excellence to make tourism industry a major contributor to the socio-economic development of the nation.".

    (A) admission     (B) commission     (C) mission     (D) submission

(　　) 47. The income brought in by tourism will _____ the townspeople' life.

    (A) assimilate     (B) better     (C) worsen     (D) deteriorate

(　　) 48. Hawaii is a great location for all kinds of water sports. Some like to go windsurfing _____ others like to go water-skiing.

    (A) despite of     (B) therefore     (C) whenever     (D) whereas

(　　) 49. Many tourists arriving in Japan naturally _____ their sightseeing in large cities such as Tokyo, Osaka, and Kyoto, not far from the international airports where they arrive.

    (A) commence     (B) embrace     (C) navigate     (D) resemble

| | | | | |
|---|---|---|---|---|
| 1. ( D ) | 2. ( C ) | 3. ( B ) | 4. ( A ) | 5. ( D ) |
| 6. ( A ) | 7. ( B ) | 8. ( D ) | 9. ( D ) | 10. ( B ) |
| 11. ( D ) | 12. ( B ) | 13. ( B ) | 14. ( C ) | 15. ( D ) |
| 16. ( D ) | 17. ( B ) | 18. ( D ) | 19. ( D ) | 20. ( D ) |
| 21. ( C ) | 22. ( D ) | 23. ( A ) | 24. ( C ) | 25. ( A ) |
| 26. ( B ) | 27. ( C ) | 28. ( C ) | 29. ( B ) | 30. ( A ) |
| 31. ( B ) | 32. ( D ) | 33. ( B ) | 34. ( D ) | 35. ( A ) |
| 36. ( B ) | 37. ( C ) | 38. ( B ) | 39. ( B ) | 40. ( B ) |
| 41. ( C ) | 42. ( D ) | 43. ( A ) | 44. ( D ) | 45. ( B ) |
| 46. ( C ) | 47. ( B ) | 48. ( D ) | 49. ( A ) | |

01 航空交通

02 飯店住宿

03 餐廳飲食

04 旅遊觀光

05 介紹台灣

06 帶團職責

# memo

# 5 介紹台灣

## 一、必考題型

1. The Fort San Domingo was originally a wooden fort built by the Spanish in 1629 at Tamsui District, New Taipei City, Taiwan. **It is located** near Hobe Fort, which was built during Qing rule.

   紅毛城原本是 1629 年由西班牙在台灣新北市淡水區所建造的一棟木造堡壘。**它的位置** 靠近清朝統治時期的滬尾砲台。 105 英領

2. Founded in 1999, Yunlin International Puppet Arts Festival has supported **a variety of** performing schools to **showcase** the **heritage** of glove puppetry culture.

   雲林國際偶戲藝術節創辦於 1999 年，如今已扶持**各類**表演藝術學校**展示**多樣化的布袋戲文化**遺產**。 105 英領

3. Chiayi City International Band Festival has recently **attracted** many performing teams from all over the world, **transforming** itself from a southern town into a band music city.

   嘉義市國際管樂節近年來**吸引**了許多世界各地的表演團體，將一個南部小鎮**轉型**成一個管樂之都。 105 英領

4. Since 2001, local governments have **competed** to **hold** Taiwan Lantern Festival, which was recommended as one of the best holiday celebration events by the Discovery Channel in 2007.

   從 2001 年開始，地方政府**爭相舉辦**台灣燈會。這在 2007 年被探索頻道推薦為最佳節慶活動之一。 105 英領

5. Formosa coast of Taitung is **recognized** as the latest surfing competition **venue** in Asia by the Asian Surfing Championship (ASC), **demonstrating** its potential for international sports tourism.

   台東的福爾摩沙海岸收到亞洲國際衝浪組織的**認可**，成為亞洲最新的衝浪比賽**場地**，**展現**了它有推動國際運動賽事觀光的潛力。 105 英領

6.  Artists from home and abroad **crafted** and **exhibited** their sand sculptures along the northeast coast in the Fulong International Sand Sculpture Festival.

    來自國內外的藝術家，在東北角海岸的福隆國際沙雕節**精心製作**並**展示**其沙雕作品。
    `105 英領`

7.  The southern branch of the National Palace Museum can **allow** more people to **marvel** at the museum's many ancient treasures which were originally created for the **enjoyment** of the Chinese imperial households.

    國立故宮博物院南院**讓**更多人可以**悠遊**於館內，並欣賞這些原來是被創作於供中國皇室**玩賞**之用的古文物珍藏。　`105 英領`

8.  In recent years, many disused industrial sites around Taiwan have been **renovated** into cultural-creative hubs, where **local residents** and international travelers like to check out shops selling creative-design household goods and decorations.

    近幾年來，許多廢棄的工業用地已經**重新整修**為文創中心，**當地居民**以及國際旅客都喜歡到處看看這些販賣創意居家小物以及飾品的店家。　`105 英領`

9.  In a recent online **poll**, camping enthusiasts voted for Taiwan's best campsites, which are surrounded by **breathtaking scenery** and are close to mountain trails.

    最近一份網路**票選**中，露營愛好者選出了台灣最棒的露營地，它們大都環繞著**風景勝地**，並鄰近山林小徑。　`105 英領`

10. To **promote** a friendly tourism environment, the Taiwan Tourism Bureau sets up the Information Station mobile website, which can be found by searching for "Taiwan ask me".

    為了**推廣**友善的觀光環境，台灣觀光局設立了借問站行動網頁。可以藉由關鍵字「台灣請問我」進行搜尋。　`105 英領`

11. One of the most **exhilarating** outings in the Taipei area is a trip to Jiufen and Jinguashi, twin historic mining settlements **overlooking** the northeast coast, with a vast swath of blue ocean laid out far below.

    台北地區最**令人興奮的**出遊地點之一就是九份跟金瓜石，這 2 座歷史上著名的礦區都能**遠眺**東北角海岸，底下伴隨廣闊的湛藍海洋。　`105 英領`

12. The skywalk **allows** tourists to take in the **breathtaking** mountain view of the narrow deep valley down which the torrents of the waterfall **cascade**.

    天空步道能**讓**遊客欣賞瀑布從峽谷**奔流而下**的**令人屏息的**山景。　`105 英領`

13. The baroque facades in the old street date back to Taiwan's Japanese Occupation Period (1895~1945) and **contrast with** the mainly concrete houses around the environs.

老街裡的巴洛克建築與周圍主要以水泥所蓋的房子**形成對比**，其外觀更可追溯到台灣的日本殖民時期（1895 ～ 1945）。 `105 英領`

14. The guardian general standing on Mazu's right side is Qianli Yan (Thousand-Mile Eye, or called Gold General), who holds a halberd in his left hand and lifts up his right hand to his forehead, looking into the **distance**.

通常站在媽祖右手邊的護衛是千里眼（或稱金精將軍），他左手拿戟，右手舉起放在額頭前，並看著**遠方**。 `105 英領`

15. Despite a kid, Nezha saved his town people from the Sea Dragon King's **disaster** at the price of his life. Because of his bravery and compassion, he was later regarded as the Third Prince Deity **worshipped** in many temples in Taiwan.

即便還是小孩子，哪吒從海龍王的**肆虐**中用生命拯救村民。因為他的勇敢以及同情心，他後來被視為三太子，並**被供奉**於許多台灣的廟宇。 `105 英領`

16. Sun Wukong was the protagonist of the novel Journey to the West. He could perform 72 **transformations** and leaped 108,000 li (54,000 kilometers) in one somersault.

孫悟空是小說西遊記當中的主角。他可以 72 **變**，翻一次筋斗更能翻越 10 萬 8 千里（相當於 5 萬 4 千公里）。 `105 英領`

▶ If you arrive in Skopje before 2014, expect to see quite a bit of construction as the city is currently undergoing a massive **transformation**.

如果你在 2014 之前造訪史高比耶，你會看到很多城市正在進行的巨大**改造**工程。 `103 英領`

17. With a sweet smile and voice to match, Teresa Teng has become a **legendary** figure in Taiwan.

有著甜美的笑容以及相襯的聲音，鄧麗君成為台灣**傳奇性**的人物。 `105 英導`

18. The Alishan area was originally settled by the Tsou tribe of the Taiwanese **aborigines**; the name **derives** from the aboriginal word *Jarissang*.

阿里山區原來是由台灣**原住民**鄒族所居住。所以名字是**從**原住民話 *Jarissang* 所來的。 `105 英領`

01 航空交通

02 飯店住宿

03 餐廳飲食

04 旅遊觀光

05 介紹台灣

06 帶團職責

19. A number of Taiwanese artists **have strived** to convert old sugar **refineries** into exhibition and performance space.

   一些台灣藝術家**努力**將糖**廠**轉變成展覽以及表演空間。 `105 英領`

20. She **told** me that pearl milk tea was one of the most famous drinks in Taiwan.

   她**告訴**我，珍珠奶茶是台灣最有名的飲料之一。 `104 英領`

21. Tourists often **remark** that Taiwan is a beautiful island worthy of visiting; that is a nice **compliment**.

   遊客通常會**評論**台灣為值得造訪的美麗島嶼，那真是很棒的**讚美**。 `103 英領`

22. Taipei, Taiwan's **vibrant** capital city, is one of CNN's top ten New Year's Eve destinations.

   台北，台灣的**活力**首都城市，是 CNN 最棒的前 10 跨年地點之一。 `103 英領`

23. Dihua Street is a great place to purchase traditional Chinese foods which **make** great gifts, and many shops will seal purchases for plane travel.

   迪化街是個購買傳統中國食物的好地方，這些食物**是**很棒的禮物，許多店家會將商品密封以供帶上飛機。 `103 英領`

24. National Taiwan Museum **was built** way back in 1908 during the Japanese occupation of Taiwan.

   國立台灣博物館**建立**於 1902 年日據時期間。 `103 英領`

25. The second floor explores aboriginal culture, **teaching** visitors about the **aboriginal tribes** so important to Taiwanese history.

   2 樓探索原住民文化，**教導**遊客對台灣歷史很重要的**原住民族群**。 `103 英領`

26. Taipei Zoo will accept reservations for up to 300 visitors per day to meet the panda family. Visitors without reservation can **queue** up for the ticket, though numbers will be limited.

   台北動物園每天接受高達 300 名遊客預約來見熊貓家族。沒有預約者則需要**排隊**買票，但數量有限。 `103 英導`

27. The world-class Kruger National Park, known for its **diversity** of wildlife, has an astonishing **variety** and number of animals.

世界知名的克魯格國家公園，因**多元化**的野生動物而知名，其中有令人驚豔的**多樣**動物。
103 英導

28. At the annual food festival, you can sample a wide **variety** of delicacies.

在一年一度的美食節裡，你可以品嚐**各類**佳餚。 101 英領

29. At Juming Museum, you may see many **masterpieces** of Taiwanese sculptor Ju Ming.

在朱銘博物館，你可以看到很多台灣雕塑家朱銘的**藝術作品**。 108 英導

30. Wuling Farm is a must-see **destination** with attractions of spring cherry blossoms and autumn maples.

武陵農場是必訪之觀光**地點**，春天有櫻花，秋天有楓紅。 108 英導

31. In Taiwan, there are many extinct or **dormant** volcanoes, which provide hot water for Taiwan's health-promoting hot springs.

在台灣，有許多死火山或是休火山，提供台灣促進健康的溫泉。 108 英導

32. Confucius was a great **philosopher** and teacher in ancient China. Today, Confucian temples are seen in Taiwan in honor of this great mentor.

孔子是古代中國偉大的**哲學家**與至聖先師。今日，台灣的孔廟被視為紀念這位偉大老師的地方。 108 英導

33. A crazy Lantern Festival takes place in Yanshui. Rockets and fireworks are aimed at the crowds and explode around them. Participants must wear a helmet and protective clothing to **prevent** injury.

鹽水舉辦瘋狂的元宵節活動。爆竹跟煙火用來瞄準人群以及在其周圍爆炸。參加者必須穿戴安全帽跟保護衣物來**預防**受傷。 108 英導

01 航空交通
02 飯店住宿
03 餐廳飲食
04 旅遊觀光
05 介紹台灣
06 帶團職責

National Palace Museum **n.**
故宮博物院

folk culture **n.** 民俗文化

aboriginal **adj.** 原住民的

indigenous **adj.** 土生土長的

it is believed that... /
legend has it that... **phr.**
傳說中

legendary **adj.** 傳奇的

derive from **v.** 衍生出

compliment **n.** 讚美

complement **v.** 相得益彰

complimentary **adj.** 免費的

complacent **adj.** 自滿的

diversity **n.** 多元化

variety **n.** 多樣性

01 航空交通

02 飯店住宿

03 餐廳飲食

04 旅遊觀光

05 介紹台灣

06 帶團職責

### 三、牛刀小試

( ) 1. The guardian general standing on Mazu's right side is Qianli Yan (Thousand-Mile Eye, or called Gold General), who holds a halberd in his left hand and lifts up his right hand to his forehead, looking into the _____.

    (A) discord     (B) demand     (C) detour     (D) distance

( ) 2. The Fort San Domingo was originally a wooden fort built by the Spanish in 1629 at Tamsui District, New Taipei City, Taiwan. It _____ near Hobe Fort, which was built during Qing rule.

    (A) locates     (B) located     (C) is located     (D) was located

( ) 3. Chiayi City International Band Festival has recently _____ many performing teams from all over the world, transforming itself from a southern town into a band music city.

    (A) impacted     (B) coached     (C) guided     (D) attracted

( ) 4. Taipei Zoo will accept reservations for up to 300 visitors per day to meet the panda family. Visitors without reservation can _____ up for the ticket, though numbers will be limited.

    (A) catch     (B) follow     (C) keep     (D) queue

( ) 5. In recent years, many disused industrial sites around Taiwan have been _____ into cultural-creative hubs, where local residents and international travelers like to check out shops selling creative-design household goods and decorations.

    (A) incorporated     (B) renovated     (C) absorbed     (D) recruited

( ) 6. The Alishan area was originally settled by the Tsou tribe of the Taiwanese aborigines; the name _____ from the aboriginal word *Jarissang*.

    (A) divides     (B) drives     (C) devises     (D) derives

( ) 7. A number of Taiwanese artists have strived to convert old sugar _____ into exhibition and performance space.

    (A) refineries     (B) companies     (C) agencies     (D) bureaus

(　　) 8. To _____ a friendly tourism environment, the Taiwan Tourism Bureau sets up the Information Station mobile website, which can be found by searching for "Taiwan ask me.".

(A) promote　　(B) explore　　(C) modify　　(D) adjust

(　　) 9. Dihua Street is a great place to purchase traditional Chinese foods which _____ great gifts, and many shops will seal purchases for plane travel.

(A) making　　(B) make　　(C) makes　　(D) made

(　　) 10. National Taiwan Museum _____ way back in 1908 during the Japanese occupation of Taiwan.

(A) builds　　(B) built　　(C) is built　　(D) was built

(　　) 11. The baroque facades in the old street date back to Taiwan's Japanese Occupation Period (1895~1945) and _____ with the mainly concrete houses around the environs.

(A) conflict　　(B) contrast　　(C) compare　　(D) comply

(　　) 12. Despite a kid, Nezha saved his town people from the Sea Dragon King's _____ at the price of his life. Because of his bravery and compassion, he was later regarded as the Third Prince Deity worshipped in many temples in Taiwan.

(A) auspices　　(B) protection　　(C) disaster　　(D) conservation

(　　) 13. Founded in 1999, Yunlin International Puppet Arts Festival has supported a variety of performing schools to _____ the heritage of glove puppetry culture.

(A) counter　　(B) assess　　(C) showcase　　(D) abandon

(　　) 14. Sun Wukong was the protagonist of the novel Journey to the West. He could perform 72 _____ and leaped 108,000 li (54,000 kilometers) in one somersault.

(A) reforms　　(B) evolutions　　(C) transformations　(D) remedies

(　　) 15. In a recent online _____, camping enthusiasts voted for Taiwan's best campsites, which are surrounded by breathtaking scenery and are close to mountain trails.

(A) experiment　　(B) petition　　(C) poll　　(D) conference

(　　) 16. With a sweet smile and voice to match, Teresa Teng has become a _____ figure in Taiwan.

(A) traditional　　(B) hostile　　(C) legendary　　(D) dictatorial

( ) 17. She _____ me that pearl milk tea was one of the most famous drinks in Taiwan.

    (A) told         (B) said         (C) talked         (D) spoke

( ) 18. Taipei, Taiwan's _____ capital city, is one of CNN's top ten New Year Eve destinations.

    (A) vicious       (B) vibrant       (C) vigilant       (D) vicarious

( ) 19. Since 2001, local governments have competed to _____ Taiwan Lantern Festival, which was recommended as one of the best holiday celebration events by the Discovery Channel in 2007.

    (A) reduce       (B) announce       (C) hold       (D) trigger

( ) 20. The second floor explores aboriginal culture, _____ visitors about the aboriginal tribes so important to Taiwanese history.

    (A) teaches       (B) taught       (C) teaching       (D) is taught

( ) 21. The world-class Kruger National Park, known for its _____ of wildlife, has an astonishing variety and number of animals.

    (A) breakdown     (B) diversity     (C) hospitality     (D) prescription

( ) 22. One of the most exhilarating outings in the Taipei area is a trip to Jiufen and Jinguashi, twin historic mining settlements _____ the northeast coast, with a vast swath of blue ocean laid out far below.

    (A) approaching     (B) overlooking     (C) guarding     (D) linking

( ) 23. Artists from home and abroad _____ and exhibited their sand sculptures along the northeast coast in the Fulong International Sand Sculpture Festival.

    (A) identified     (B) purchased     (C) crafted     (D) redressed

( ) 24. The skywalk allows tourists to take in the breathtaking mountain view of the narrow deep valley down which the torrents of the waterfall _____.

    (A) trickle       (B) tumble       (C) cascade       (D) filter

01 航空交通

02 飯店住宿

03 餐廳飲食

04 旅遊觀光

05 介紹台灣

06 帶團職責

# 標 準 答 案

| | | | | |
|---|---|---|---|---|
| 1. ( D ) | 2. ( C ) | 3. ( D ) | 4. ( D ) | 5. ( B ) |
| 6. ( D ) | 7. ( A ) | 8. ( A ) | 9. ( B ) | 10. ( D ) |
| 11. ( B ) | 12. ( C ) | 13. ( C ) | 14. ( C ) | 15. ( C ) |
| 16. ( C ) | 17. ( A ) | 18. ( B ) | 19. ( C ) | 20. ( C ) |
| 21. ( B ) | 22. ( B ) | 23. ( C ) | 24. ( C ) | |

# 6 帶團職責

## 一、必考題型

1. Tour leaders need knowledge of the places they are visiting, and they are also **responsible for** the logistics and planning of a trip, ensuring everything runs **smoothly**.

   領隊需要知道造訪地點的相關知識，並且需替行程安排以及計劃**負責**，確保一切運行**順利**。 `105 英領`

2. Generally speaking, tour guides are **expected** to know a city (or country) intimately and **offer** guests interpretive information such as history and anecdotes on all sites.

   一般而言，人們**期望**導遊熟悉地了解一個城市（或國家）並且**提供**旅客說明訊息，像是所有觀光地點的歷史以及軼事。 `105 英領`

3. Jacob was determined to get a job in the tourist industry **by any means**. Therefore, he **made an effort** to get his tour guide license.

   雅各**不計任何方法**決心在旅遊業工作。因此，他**努力**考取導遊證照。 `105 英領`

4. One of the most **desirable** qualities of a tour leader is being **service-minded**, i.e., willing to help others.

   領隊**最需要的**特質就是有熱忱**服務的心**。比如說：願意幫助他人。 `104 英領`

   ▶ During the holidays, most major hotels will be fully booked. An **alternative** is to try and find a guest house near your **desired** destination.

   假期期間，大部分的主要飯店都被訂滿了。**替代方案**只有試著尋找接近你**想要去的**目的地附近的民宿。 `98 英導`

   ▶ Besides participating in local cultural activities, people who **desire** to explore the ecology of Kenting can observe plenty of wildlife and plants.

   除了參與當地文化活動外，**想**在墾丁探訪生態環境的人，也可以觀察豐富的野生動物與植物。 `99 英導`

5. The passage read by the tour guide is an **excerpt** from a longer work.

   領隊所念的這段文章，是從比較長的作品所**節錄**出來的。 103 英領

6. Being a tour guide, one needs to be more concerned about the major important matters instead of spending too much time on **frivolous** issues.

   身為一名導遊，需要花更多的心力在比較重要的事務上，而不是花在**瑣碎的**事情上。 103 英領

7. Our tour guide was such a sweet lady that we felt **hesitant** to complain to her about the hotel service.

   我們的導遊是一名如此甜美的小姐，所以我們很**猶豫**是否該向她抱怨飯店的服務。 103 英領

   ▶ When answering questions of the immigration officer, it is advisable to be straight forward and not **hesitating**.

   回答移民官的問題時，建議實話實說，並且不要**猶豫**。 102 英導

8. What **useful information** our tour guide has provided!

   我們導遊提供的**資訊**真是太**實用**了！ 103 英領

9. Our tour leader speaks English and French well, and **so does our tour guide**.

   我們的領隊會說英文跟法文，**我們導遊也是**。 103 英領

10. My friend did not **relinquish** his dream to be a tour leader.

    我的朋友不會**放棄**他成為領隊的夢想。 103 英領

tour guide n. 導遊

travel agent n. 旅行社人員

Tourism Bureau n. 觀光旅遊局

responsible for phr. 對～有責任

desire v. 想望

rely on / depend on / count on v.
依靠、信賴

tour manager n. 領隊

travel agency n. 旅行社

in peak season n. 旺季

challenge n. 挑戰

hesitate v. 猶豫

01 航空交通

02 飯店住宿

03 餐廳飲食

04 旅遊觀光

05 介紹台灣

06 帶團職責

## 三、牛刀小試

(　　) 1. Our tour leader speaks English and French well, and _____.

(A) so does our tour guide　(B) so our tour guide can
(C) neither does our tour guide　(D) nor can our tour guide

(　　) 2. Our tour guide was _____ that we felt hesitant to complain to her about the hotel service.

(A) so a sweet lady　(B) such a sweet lady
(C) so such sweet　(D) such sweet

(　　) 3. One of the most desirable qualities of a tour leader is being _____-minded, i.e., willing to help others.

(A) feeble　(B) peace　(C) service　(D) tolerance

(　　) 4. Being a tour guide, one needs to be more concerned about the major important matters instead of spending too much time on _____ issues.

(A) sensible　(B) voluble　(C) effusive　(D) frivolous

(　　) 5. Tour leaders need knowledge of the places they are visiting, and they are also _____ the logistics and planning of a trip, ensuring everything runs smoothly.

(A) covered with　(B) charged to　(C) on behalf of　(D) responsible for

(　　) 6. Generally speaking, tour guides are _____ to know a city (or country) intimately and offer guests interpretive information such as history and anecdotes on all sites.

(A) prepaid　(B) expected　(C) organized　(D) predicted

(　　) 7. What _____ our tour guide has provided!

(A) a useful information　(B) an useful information
(C) useful information　(D) useful informations

(　　) 8. My friend did not _____ his dream to be a tour leader.

(A) relinquish　(B) distinguish　(C) furnish　(D) astonish

(　　) 9. The passage read by the tour guide is an _____ from a longer work.

(A) excess　(B) excerpt　(C) exception　(D) exemption

01

航空交通

02

飯店住宿

03

餐廳飲食

04

旅遊觀光

05

介紹台灣

06

帶團職責

# 標 準 答 案

| 1. ( A ) | 2. ( B ) | 3. ( C ) | 4. ( D ) | 5. ( D ) |
|----------|----------|----------|----------|----------|
| 6. ( B ) | 7. ( C ) | 8. ( A ) | 9. ( B ) | |

# 7 健康

一、必考題型

1. A direct **link** exists between gaining weight and **inappropriate** diet, according to the medical research.

   根據醫學研究，增重以及**不適當的**飲食之間存有直接的**連結**。 105 英導

2. For the sake of your health, do take proper **vaccination prior to** departure for **epidemic** areas.

   為了你的健康著想，在出發去**傳染**地區**前**，要記得打適當的**疫苗**。 105 英導

3. People should pay attention to their physical condition by having **periodic** health check in order to **prevent diseases**.

   人們應該透過**定期**健康檢查來留意身體的狀況以**預防疾病**。 105 英導

4. Quitting smoking will not only **decrease** the risk of many types of disease, but will also improve a person's **psychological health**.

   戒菸不只**降低**許多疾病的風險，還能改善**心理健康**。 105 英導

5. Even though it controls all of our body movements, the brain itself never **moves**.

   即便大腦掌管身體所有的動作，它本身卻從來不**動**。 104 英領

6. In medicine, an **acute** condition is one that is only a **temporary** problem, such as a sprained ankle. However, a **chronic** one recurs over and over. Migraine headaches are an example of this kind of condition.

   醫學上來說，**急性**情況只是**暫時的**問題，像是扭傷的腳踝。然而**慢性**疾病則是指反覆發作的狀態。偏頭痛就是符合這類情況的例子。 104 英導

7. Some families have children in **chronic** health conditions. At times, the pressure may be overwhelming to every individual in the family and the challenges can **affect** the quality of family life.

有些家庭的孩子有**慢性**疾病的狀況。有時候，每一個家庭份子會碰到排山倒海而來的壓力，而其中的挑戰也會**影響**家庭生活的品質。 `99 英導`

8. Diabetes is a **chronic** disease which is difficult to **cure**. Management concentrates on keeping blood sugar levels as close to normal as possible without presenting undue patient danger.

糖尿病是一種**慢性**且難以**治癒**的疾病。日常管理上，需注意血糖高低是否接近正常值，不要讓病人有過度危險的狀況發生。 `100 英導`

9. Last year, I wanted to go trekking in the Gobi Desert, but my doctor did not **allow** me to because I was not in very good **physical shape**.

去年我想去戈壁沙漠健行，但因為我的**身體狀況**不是很好，我的醫生不**允許**我去。 `103 英領`

10. Hand soaps **provided** in restrooms in public venues have been found to contain **exceedingly** high numbers of viable bacteria.

公共場所廁所**提供**的洗手皂，被檢驗出有**超**高量的細菌。 `103 英領`

▶ Tourism usually brings much-needed money to developing countries. Furthermore, it provides employment for the local people.

觀光業通常替發展中的國家帶來救命錢。此外，也提供了當地人民的就業機會。 `103 英領`

▶ What useful information our tour guide has provided!

我們導遊**提供**的資訊非常有用！ `103 英領`

▶ The mission of The Walt Disney Company is to be one of the world's leading producers and providers of entertainment and information.

華特迪士尼公司的願景就是成為世界娛樂與資訊製造提供的領導指標。 `104 英領`

▶ Each room of this hotel has large windows that **provide spectacular** views of the sparkling Atlantic Ocean.

這間飯店的每一個房間都有大型的窗戶可以**提供**大西洋動人的**壯觀**景色。 `103 英導`

11. Twins aren't always twice as nice; they have much higher risks of being born **premature** and having serious health problems.

雙胞胎不總是 2 倍的好。他們有比較高的**早產**以及嚴重健康問題的風險。　`103 英領`

▶ As children grow and **mature**, they will leave behind childish pursuits, and no longer be so selfish and undisciplined as they used to be.

當小孩長大變**成熟**後，他們將會把幼稚的行為拋下，且不再和以前一樣自私、沒有紀律。　`99 英導`

▶ The decision was not **mature** at all as there was **little** time for discussion before the vote.

這個決定並不**成熟**，因為在投票之前**幾乎沒有**時間可以討論。　`104 英導`

12. When arriving in Thimphu, the capital of Bhutan, some visitors find it difficult to **adjust** to the city's high **altitude** and need to seek medical help.

當到達不丹的首都廷布時，許多遊客發現他們很難**適應**該城市的高**海拔**，並且需要醫療上的協助。　`103 英導`

▶ The airplane is cruising at an **altitude** of 30,000 feet at 700 kilometers per hour.

飛機目前以每小時 700 公里的速度，航行於**海拔** 30,000 英呎上。　`98 英領`

13. Chloe McCardel, an Australian endurance athlete, had to abandon her attempt to swim from Cuba to Florida after she was **stung** by a jellyfish.

克洛伊 ‧ 麥卡德爾，一位澳洲的耐力運動員，因為被水母**螫傷**而必須放棄她試圖從古巴游到佛羅里達的計畫。　`103 英導`

14. Cold symptoms usually **last** for about a week. If the **symptoms persist** or worsen, you will want to see a doctor **immediately**.

感冒症狀通常**延續**約一個禮拜，如果**症狀持續**沒有好轉或惡化，你應該**立刻**看醫生。　`103 英導`

15. If you **require** an immediate response to a current **incident**, please telephone our switchboard on 101.

如果你**要求**得到目前**意外**的立即回覆，請撥分機 101。　`104 英領`

16. Many skin diseases are **contagious** and can be passed from one person to another.

    許多皮膚病都是透過**接觸傳染的**，而且可以從一個人傳到另一個人。 `103 英導`

17. Scarlet fever is a **contagious** disease, which is transferable from one person to another.

    猩紅熱是一種**接觸傳染性**的疾病，是經由人與人接觸傳染。 `99 英導`

18. Most antibiotics are only available with a **prescription** from your doctor.

    大多數的抗生素只能從醫生的**處方籤**獲得。 `108 英領`

19. Body temperatures can **fluctuate** and become unstable when you are ill.

    體溫會**改變**並且在你生病的時候變得不穩定。 `108 英領`

07 健康

08 職場學校

09 人格個性

10 社交禮儀

11 金錢買賣

12 社會時事

| | |
|---|---|
| provide **v.** 提供 | physical shape **n.** 身體狀況 |
| gain weight / put on weight **v.** 增重 | obesity **n.** 肥胖 |
| getting in shape / lose weight **v.** 減重 | disease **n.** 疾病 |
| contagious disease **n.** 接觸傳染疾病 | prevent diseases **v.** 預防疾病 |
| psychological health **n.** 心理健康 | symptom **n.** 症狀 |
| develop a new symptom **v.** 出現新症狀 | chronic health condition **n.** 慢性疾病的情形 |
| vaccination **n.** 疫苗 | exercise **v.** 運動 |
| overweight **adj.** 過胖 | body clock **n.** 生理時鐘 |
| jet lag **n.** 時差 | cure **v.** 治療 |

## 三、牛刀小試

( ) 1. Last year, I wanted to go trekking in the Gobi Desert, but my doctor did not allow me to because I was not in very good _____.

    (A) enjoyable figure              (B) physical shape

    (C) social mind                 (D) careful attention

( ) 2. If you require an _____ response to a current incident, please telephone our switchboard on 10.

    (A) immature    (B) inconvenient    (C) immigrant    (D) immediate

( ) 3. Hand soaps _____ in restrooms in public venues have been found to contain exceedingly high numbers of viable bacteria.

    (A) provide      (B) providing    (C) are provided   (D) provided

( ) 4. A direct _____ exists between gaining weight and inappropriate diet, according to the medical research.

    (A) link         (B) line        (C) circle      (D) button

( ) 5. Twins aren't always twice as nice; they have much higher risks of being born _____ and having serious health problems.

    (A) preliterate    (B) premature    (C) prejudiced    (D) prescribed

( ) 6. For the sake of your health, do take proper _____ prior to departure for epidemic areas.

    (A) vehicle      (B) vegetation    (C) veterinarian   (D) vaccination

( ) 7. People should pay attention to their physical condition by having _____ health check in order to prevent diseases.

    (A) temporary    (B) irregular     (C) periodic    (D) contemporary

( ) 8. Chloe McCardel, an Australian endurance athlete, had to abandon her attempt to swim from Cuba to Florida after she was _____ by a jellyfish.

    (A) stung       (B) drowned     (C) stabbed    (D) dunk

( ) 9. Quitting smoking will not only _____ the risk of many types of disease, but will also improve a person's psychological health.

    (A) decrease     (B) construct    (C) fluctuate    (D) optimize

( ) 10. When arriving in Thimphu, the capital of Bhutan, some visitors find it difficult to adjust to the city's high _____ and need to seek medical help.

    (A) altitude     (B) superstition    (C) significance    (D) economy

## 標準答案

| 1. ( B ) | 2. ( D ) | 3. ( D ) | 4. ( A ) | 5. ( B ) |
|----------|----------|----------|----------|----------|
| 6. ( D ) | 7. ( C ) | 8. ( A ) | 9. ( A ) | 10. ( A ) |

# 8 職場學校

## 一、必考題型

1. Even though I have quit my job, I still need to finish the project because of the contractual **obligation**.

   即便我已辭了工作，因為合約**義務**還是必須完成此專案。 105 英導

2. The purpose of this seminar is to make all the **participants** understand the **crucial** nature of environmental protection.

   這場研討會的目的，就是讓所有**與會者**了解保護自然環境的**重要**本質。 105 英導

3. Because of inexperience, John is not very **confident** in handling such a big team of people.

   因為沒有經驗，約翰對於管理這一大群人不是很有**信心**。 105 英領

4. If you ever need an **emergency** contact number for someone, the **personnel** department keeps a file on each **employee**.

   如果你需要某人的**緊急**連絡電話，**人事**部存有每位**員工**的檔案。 104 英導

5. Beatrix's friend had given her a mock interview before she actually went to meet the **personnel** manager of the company she was applying to.

   貝翠絲的朋友在她和所申請的公司**人事**部經理見面之前，先給她一個模擬面試。 100 英導

6. For five years in a row, the **number** of sick days taken by **employees** has gone down.

   連續 5 年，**員工**請病假的**數目**已經下降。 104 英導

7. At the employee awards banquet, we hope to give all our hardworking employees the **recognition** that they **deserve**.

   在員工表揚宴會上，我們希望給予辛勤工作的員工**應有**的**認可**。 104 英導

8. The restaurant manager was replaced because of her inability to maintain **discipline** among her employees.

   餐廳的經理因為沒有能力維持員工的**紀律**，而被替換掉了。 `104 英導`

9. The manager made it clear that he intended to lay down some new rules to enforce workplace **discipline**.

   經理很明確地表示，他有意制定一些新規定來加強職場**紀律**。 `103 英領`

   ► As children grow and mature, they will leave behind childish pursuits, and no longer be so selfish and **undisciplined** as they used to be.

   當小孩長大變成熟後，他們將會把幼稚的行為拋下，且不再和以前一樣自私、**沒有紀律**。 `99 英導`

10. Starting next quarter, all store managers will be given increased **autonomy**, to make decisions on their own.

    下一季開始，所有的店經理都會擁有能自行做決定的**自主權**。 `104 英導`

11. Event **coordinators** are in charge of organizing all the details required to ensure the success of an event.

    宴會**人員**須負責整理所有的細節來確保宴會的成功。 `104 英領`

12. Let's continue to work with the faith that unearned suffering is **redemptive**.

    讓我們繼續以付出的努力終會有**收穫**的信念工作！ `103 英領`

13. The mission of The Walt Disney Company is to be one of the world's **leading** producers and providers of entertainment and information.

    華特迪士尼公司的願景，就是成為世界娛樂及資訊產業的**領導性**指標。 `104 英領`

14. Doing the housework is one of those things that you can do frequently with **minimal effort**, or infrequently with a whole lot of work.

    做家事就是一種你可以花**最小力氣**經常做，或久久做一次卻得花很多力氣的事情之一。 `103 英領`

    ► **In an effort** to reduce the number of plastic tooth brushes customers throw away, many hotels have stopped providing disposable brushes.

    **為了**減少客人所丟棄的塑膠牙刷數量，許多飯店已經停止提供拋棄式的牙刷。 `103 英導`

▶ A bill to legalize gay marriage in Washington State has won final legislative approval and **taken effect** starting 2012.

華盛頓州同性婚姻合法化的法案已經通過了最後立法同意，並於 2012 年**生效**。
102 英導

▶ Some families have children in **chronic** health conditions. At times, the pressure may be overwhelming to every individual in the family and the challenges can **affect** the quality of family life.

有些家庭的孩子有**慢性**疾病的狀況。有時候，每一個家庭份子會碰到排山倒海而來的壓力，而其中的挑戰也會**影響**家庭生活的品質。 99 英導

▶ Government officials have overlooked the **impact** of inflation on the economy.

政府官員忽略了通貨膨脹對經濟的**影響**。 98 英領

▶ Increasing tourism infrastructure to meet domestic and international demands has raised concerns about the **impact on** Taiwan's natural environment.

為了滿足國內外的需求而增加旅遊業的公共建設，對於台灣的天然環境已經有所**影響**。 102 英導

15. We thought our experimental design was flawless, but it **turns out** that we failed to control an important variable.

我們認為實驗性的設計是完美無瑕的，但**結果**我們卻沒有控制好實驗的變項。 104 英領

16. I have been working on this design problem all day with nothing to show for it. I just seem to be **running around in circles**.

我已經整天都處理這個設計問題但卻徒勞無功。我好像在不斷地**兜圈子**。 104 英領

17. Recently more and more men are **taking on** new roles and entering new careers that previously were nearly all female. For example, we are now seeing more male nurses.

最近越來越多男生**擔負**起新的角色，並進入早先只有女性的行業。舉例來說，我們看到越來越多的男護理師。 104 英領

18. It is said that even today men and women still struggle to **achieve** a balance in their co-existence. In many parts of the world, women are still striving to **occupy** positions previously closed to them.

直到今日男人女人仍要在共存中試著**達到**平衡。世界上很多地方,女人仍須很努力才能**擔任**之前不能做的工作。 `103 英導`

▶ A: Excuse me. Can I take this seat?
 B: Sorry, it is **occupied**.

 A:不好意思。我可以坐這個位子嗎?
 B:抱歉,這座位有人**坐**了。 `101 英導`

▶ The Star Lodge boasts 20 years of 80 percent **occupancy**, a record for the state.

星辰旅社吹噓 20 年來有 8 成**住房率**,是該州的最高紀錄。 `104 英導`

19. Budget airlines boosted their **share** of passenger traffic to nearly 40% last year; at the same time major traditional airlines saw lower volumes.

廉價航空去年提升其**乘客量**至近 40%。而此時段,傳統航空的載量則下降。 `103 英導`

20. When you are interviewed, you had better not volunteer any additional information because that could work **against** you.

當你面試時,你最好不要主動提起任何會對自己**不利**的額外資訊。 `104 英領`

21. Your application materials must be postmarked **no later than** Friday, January 10.

你的申請資料**不得晚於** 1 月 10 號禮拜五前寄出。 `104 英導`

22. Applicants who do not have strong computer skills will not be as **competitive** as those who do.

沒有厲害電腦技能的申請者,將不會比那些有電腦技能的人來得**有競爭力**。 `103 英領`

23. While you are at the conference, take an afternoon to **look around** and check out the **competition**'s booths.

當你在會議上時,請花一下午的時間去**看看競爭者**的攤位。 `104 英導`

24. Living in a highly **competitive** society, some Taiwanese children are forced by their parents to learn many skills at a very young age.

生活在高度**競爭的**社會，有些台灣小孩從小就被逼著學很多技能。 99 英領

25. Most prestigious private schools are highly **competitive** – that is, they have stiffer admissions requirements.

大部分有名氣的私立學校都很**競爭**──也就是說，他們有比較嚴格的入學條件。
100 英導

▶ Paris' Cultural Calendar may be bursting with fairs, salons and auctions, but nothing can quite **compete with** the Biennale des Antiquaires.

巴黎的文化節目可能有展覽、講座和拍賣會，但沒有一個可以和巴黎古董雙年展**相比**。 102 英導

▶ A total of 3,965 athletes from 81 countries will **compete** in the 21st Summer Deaflympics to be hosted by Taipei City from September 5 to September 15 this year.

第 21 屆夏日聽障奧林匹克運動會，此次將由台北市政府於今年 9 月 5 日至 9 月 15 日主辦，來自 81 個國家，總共 3965 位運動員將一同**競技**。 98 英導

26. Professionals who seek career experience outside of their home countries may feel the need to **recharge their batteries** with a new challenge.

在國外尋找職涯機會的專業人士，可能會有用新挑戰重新自我**充電**的需求。
104 英領

27. Everyone attended last week's meeting **except** Mr. Lee, who was out of town on a business trip.

**除了**李先生出差之外，每個人都參加了上週的會議。 104 英導

▶ As for the delivery service of our hotel, FedEx and UPS can make pickups at the front desk Monday through Friday, **excluding** holidays.

我們飯店的寄件服務，是經由聯邦快遞公司以及聯合包裹速遞公司，於週一至週五在櫃台取件，假日**除外**。 101 英領

▶ At the Welcome Center, you will find plenty of resources, **including** maps, brochures, and wireless internet access.

在迎賓中心，你可以發現很多資源，**包含**地圖、小冊子，以及無線網路。 101 英導

28. I missed the meeting this morning. Can someone **fill** me **in** on what happened?

我錯過了今早的會議。誰可以跟我**說**發生了什麼事情嗎？ `103 英導`

29. Sitting through a long presentation can make audience **restless**, so speakers should limit their talks to 30 minutes.

過度冗長的簡報會讓聽眾**不耐煩**，所以講者需要將演講限制在 30 分鐘內。 `104 英導`

30. It is late and I am tired of sitting around waiting for everybody to show up; I wish we could **get going**.

已經很晚了，我受夠了等每個人出現。我希望我們可以**出發**。 `104 英領`

31. She and I **argue** a lot, but if we could just sit down and talk things over, I think we could **work out** our differences.

他跟我有很多**爭執**，但如果我們能夠坐下來好好談，我認為我們可以**解決**我們的想法差異。 `104 英領`

32. A: Bob argues with Bill about almost everything.
B: They just do not see **eye to eye**.

A：包柏幾乎跟比爾爭執每件事情。
B：他們就是互**看不對眼**。 `104 英導`

33. Your **immediate** response will be highly appreciated.

我很感謝你**立即**的反應。 `104 英領`

34. Some publishing companies do not accept **unsolicited** manuscripts. If an author sends them materials that are not invited, they will be immediately rejected.

有些出版社不接受**不請自來的**手稿。如果有作者自行寄給他們資料，會立刻被拒絕。 `104 英導`

35. The decision was not **mature** at all as there was **little** time for discussion before the vote.

這個決定不**成熟**，因為在投票之前**幾乎沒有**時間討論。 `104 英導`

▶ Despite facing an imminent labor shortage as its population ages, Japan has done **little** to open itself up to immigration.

即便隨著人口高齡化，勞工短缺的問題近在眼前，日本在開放移民方面還是做得**很少**。 100 英導

▶ People who earn **little** or no income can receive public assistance, often called welfare.

福利的概念是，賺**很少**或沒賺錢的人可以有大眾救助。 100 英導

▶ Having been unemployed for almost one year, Henry has **little** chance of getting a job.

因為亨利已經失業幾乎 1 年了，他找到工作的機會**很小**。 101 英領

36. Because of threats he received recently, the entrepreneur hired a **bodyguard**.

這名企業家因為最近所收到的威脅而雇了 1 名**保鑣**。 104 英導

37. There was a rumor that there had been a minor accident at the nuclear power plant, but a spokesman for the plant issued a **denial**.

有謠言説核電廠曾有過一個輕微的意外，不過該廠發言人表示**否認**。 104 英導

38. Teamwork plays a vital **role** in fulfilling any mission, particularly at a time when an economic recession is looming on the horizon.

執行任何任務時，團隊合作占了很重要的**角色**，特別是當經濟衰退已開始浮現時。 104 英導

39. The contract is still being discussed as the two parties have not been able to reach an **accord** on several matters.

因為兩方在許多議題上還沒有達到**共識**，所以合約仍在討論中。 104 英導

40. The client requested that the contract be rewritten because several important clauses had been **omitted** from the original.

這名客戶要求重簽合約，因為許多在原本合約中重要的條款都**沒被放入**。 104 英導

41. Having a good logo means people will be able to recognize your **brand** instantly.

擁有一個好的商標，表示人們可以立即地認出你的**品牌**。 104 英導

42. Some retailers, desperate for sales and customer loyalty, have begun training their **employees** in the art of **bargain** with customers.

有些零售商急切地想要業績跟客戶忠誠度，因此已經開始訓練他們的**員工**跟客戶**打交道**的藝術。 `104 英領`

43. Unfortunately, after Epoch Computers merged with that Japanese company, the **value** of its stock **dropped**.

很不幸的，大時代電腦合併日本公司之後，股票的**價值下降**。 `104 英導`

44. Jason always stays **ahead of** other students in Mathematics class.

傑森在數學課的表現總是**領先**其他同學。 `105 英導`

45. At summer camp, Mary **opted out of** rock climbing because, secretly, she was scared of heights.

在夏令營中，瑪莉**決定不**參加攀岩，因為她私底下其實很懼高。 `105 英領`

46. **Despite** Karen starting this project late, her advisor is still full of confidence that she will finish it on time.

**儘管**凱倫很晚才開始她的計畫，指導教授仍深具信心她能如期完成。 `105 英導`

47. Professor Lee thought that the small college town would be a **provincial** place to live, but in fact, he found it quite cosmopolitan.

李教授認為小型的大學城應該是很**偏僻的**居住地，但事實卻是，他發現這裡其實挺大都會的。 `104 英導`

48. The final examination will be a **comprehensive** one that will cover everything we have studied since the beginning of the semester.

期末考會是很**全面的**考試，範圍將會函括所有從學期開始我們學過的所有內容。 `104 英導`

49. After cleaning the hallway, the janitor left a sign saying that the floor was wet and **slippery**.

在清潔走廊後，學校工留下了一個地板仍濕**滑的**標示。 `103 英導`

50. Many parents send their children to some after-school music programs in order to explore their musical interests and **cultivate** their talents.

許多父母送他們的小孩去課後音樂課，是為了探索他們小孩的興趣並**培養**天分。 `103 英導`

51. **Littering** is **forbidden** on campus for sanitary reasons.

因為衛生因素，在校園內**禁止丟垃圾**。 104 英領

► When traveling in a foreign country, we need to carry with us several important documents at all times. One of them is our passport together with the entry **permit** if that has been so required.

當在外國旅遊時，我們需要隨身攜帶幾份重要的文件。如果當被要求時的話，其中可出示的文件之一就是我們的護照和入境**許可證**。 102 英導

► Ask for **permission** before you take close-up photographs of people, and if payment is requested, either pay up or put the camera away.

當拍攝別人近照時，請先請求**許可**，如果需要付費，要不付錢，要不就把相機移走。
103 英導

► Most prestigious private schools are highly competitive – that is, they have stiffer **admissions** requirements.

大部分有名氣的私立學校都很競爭——也就是說，他們有比較嚴格的**入學**條件。
100 英導

► The group leader carefully reminds the group that no agricultural products **are allowed** into the USA territory.

領隊小心地提醒團員，進入美國領土不**允許**帶入任何農產品。 103 英領

► Although guests are not **allowed** to eat durians inside the hotel because of their offensive odor, some people manage to smuggle them in.

雖然客人因為榴槤令人不快的氣味而不被**允許**在飯店內吃榴槤，但仍有些人會設法偷渡進去。 103 英導

► Tourist: What is the baggage **allowance**?
Airline clerk: It is 20 kilograms per person.

旅客：行李的**限額**是多少？
航空公司職員：每個人 20 公斤。 101 英領

► For safety reasons, radios, CD players, and mobile phones are **banned** on board, and they must remain switched off until the aircraft has landed.

由於飛安的因素，收音機、CD 播放器、手機都**禁止**在飛機上使用，且直到飛機降落都必須保持關機的狀態。 101 英領

► **Prohibited items** in carry-on bags will be confiscated at the checkpoints, and no compensation will be given for them

隨身行李中的**違禁品**將會於檢查站被沒收，且沒有任何的補償。 `101 英領`

52. A: What do you think about the plan to build more factories?
    B: Environmentally, I'm afraid it is like opening Pandora's **box**.

    A：你認為增建工廠的計劃如何？
    B：以環境上來說，我覺得這恐怕是打開了潘朵拉的**盒子**。 `104 英導`

53. A: Why are you so busy today?
    B: The boss dropped this big assignment on me **out of the blue**.

    A：你今天為什麼這麼忙？
    B：老闆忽然**沒來由地**丟給我一項大作業。 `104 英導`

54. A: I failed that test--my life is ruined!
    B: **Don't get carried away.** It was only one test.

    A：我考試沒過，我人生毀了。
    B：**別被嚇壞**，這不過是一個考試。 `104 英導`

55. A: It seems I have lost all the work I did on the computer this afternoon.
    B: Oh, no! I am afraid you will have to start from **scratch** again.

    A：看起來我遺失了整個下午在電腦上做的所有工作。
    B：喔不！恐怕你得從**頭**來過了。 `104 英導`

56. A: I see your company has invested in some new machinery.
    B: **Yes, and it's already up and running**.

    A：我看你的公司投資了一些新的機器。
    B：**對，而且已經開始運作了**。 `103 英領`

57. A: I am not **familiar with** this new computer.
    B: It is not that difficult. I am sure you will get the **hang** of it soon.

    A：我不**熟悉**這台新電腦。
    B：這不是那麼難。我相信你很快就會得到**要領**。 `104 英導`

58. Mr. Jones has **got the hang of** being a tour guide. Mr. Jones has learned the skills of being a tour guide.

    瓊斯先生已經**學習到**當一位導遊的**技巧**。 `100 英領`

| | |
|---|---|
| obligation **n.** 義務 | crucial **adj.** 重要的 |
| confident **adj.** 有信心的 | personnel department **n.** 人事部 |
| personnel manager **n.** 人事部經理 | employees **n.** 員工 |
| employment **n.** 就業 | unemployed **adj.** 失業的 |
| unemployment rate **n.** 失業率 | annual **adj.** 年度的 |
| discipline **n.** 紀律 | undisciplined **adj.** 不受規範的 |
| autonomy **n.** 自主權 | in charge of **phr.** 負責 |
| effort **n.** 努力 | effect **n.** 效果 |
| affect **v.** 影響 | impact **n.** 衝擊 |
| market share **n.** 市占率 | apply **v.** 申請 |
| application **n.** 申請 | compete **v.** 競爭 |
| competitive **adj.** 競爭的 | comprehend **v.** 理解 |
| comprehensive **adj.** 全面的 | mature **adj.** 成熟的 |
| premature **adj.** 早熟 | banquet **n.** 宴會 |
| allow / permit (permission / admission) **v.** 允許（ **n.** 許可） | ban / prohibit / forbid **v.** 禁止 |
| get the hang of **phr.** 得到要領 | |

07 健康

08 職場學校

09 人格個性

10 社交禮儀

11 金錢買賣

12 社會時事

( ) 1. There is no sense _____ over such a petty matter.

(A) splitting hair                (B) holding water

(C) carrying the ball            (D) taking into account

( ) 2. Even though I have quit my job, I still need to finish the project because of the contractual _____.

(A) obligation     (B) completion     (C) generation     (D) installation

( ) 3. The purpose of this seminar is to make all the participants understand the _____ nature of environmental protection.

(A) lively          (B) secure         (C) desperate       (D) crucial

( ) 4. The young man _____ to dazzle everyone by scoring 25 points and handing out 7 assists, leading the team to victory.

(A) proceeded     (B) provided      (C) devolved      (D) precancelled

( ) 5. Your application materials must be postmarked _____ Friday, January 10.

(A) no later than    (B) no less than    (C) no more than    (D) no sooner than

( ) 6. Let's continue to work with the faith that unearned suffering is _____.

(A) preemptive     (B) redemptive     (C) emotive       (D) promotive

( ) 7. The final examination will be a(n) _____ one that will cover everything we have studied since the beginning of the semester.

(A) comprehensive           (B) exclusive

(C) preliminary              (D) qualified

( ) 8. I will keep her _____ on the progress of the project.

(A) update       (B) updates      (C) updating      (D) updated

( ) 9. She and I argue a lot, but if we could just sit down and talk things over, I think we could _____ our differences.

(A) put over      (B) hang up      (C) work out      (D) send back

(　) 10. The decision was not mature at all as there was _____ time for discussion before the vote.

(A) few　　　　(B) little　　　　(C) a little　　　　(D) a few

(　) 11. After cleaning the hallway, the janitor left a sign saying that the floor was wet and _____.

(A) slightly　　(B) enormous　　(C) slippery　　(D) enchanted

(　) 12. Many parents send their children to some after-school music programs in order to explore their musical interests and _____ their talents.

(A) cultivate　　(B) disguise　　(C) subside　　(D) moderate

(　) 13. The mission of The Walt Disney Company is to be one of the world's _____ producers and providers of entertainment and information.

(A) deteriorating　(B) leading　　(C) pleading　　(D) overwhelming

(　) 14. We thought our experimental design was flawless, but it turns _____ that we failed to control an important variable.

(A) in　　　　(B) on　　　　(C) out　　　　(D) down

(　) 15. A: Why are you so busy today?
B: The boss dropped this big assignment on me out of the _____.

(A) black　　　(B) blue　　　(C) green　　　(D) red

(　) 16. It is said that even today men and women still struggle to achieve a balance in their co-existence. In many parts of the world, women are still _____ to occupy positions previously closed to them.

(A) striving　　(B) abolishing　　(C) discerning　　(D) inspecting

(　) 17. Applicants who do not have strong computer skills will not be as _____ as those who do.

(A) compensative　(B) comprehensible　(C) comprehensive　(D) competitive

(　) 18. It is late and I am tired of sitting around waiting for everybody to show up; I wish we could _____.

(A) get going　　(B) hang around　　(C) keep alive　　(D) stay young

( ) 19. A: Bob argues with Bill about almost everything.

B: They just do not see _____ to _____.

(A) ear, ear      (B) eye, eye      (C) hand, hand      (D) nose, nose

( ) 20. Event _____ are in charge of organizing all the details required to ensure the success of an event.

(A) administrator      (B) conductor      (C) coordinators      (D) sponsors

( ) 21. Your _____ response will be highly appreciated.

(A) arrogant      (B) belated      (C) immediate      (D) sluggish

( ) 22. Because of threats he received recently, the entrepreneur hired a _____.

(A) bodyguard      (B) cavalry      (C) mariner      (D) meteorologists

( ) 23. Because of inexperience, John is not very _____ in handling such a big team of people.

(A) secure      (B) difficult      (C) confident      (D) considerate

( ) 24. If you ever need an emergency contact number for someone, the _____ department keeps a file on each employee.

(A) parliament      (B) patriotism      (C) personnel      (D) petroleum

( ) 25. Unfortunately, after Epoch Computers merged with that Japanese company, the _____ of its stock dropped.

(A) cost      (B) nature      (C) receipt      (D) value

( ) 26. The building manager has informed us that the west entrance elevators will be out of _____ for the remainder of the week.

(A) courtesy      (B) nowhere      (C) service      (D) work

( ) 27. Recently more and more men are _____ new roles and entering new careers that previously were nearly all female. For example, we are now seeing more male nurses.

(A) taking on      (B) laying off      (C) pointing out      (D) putting down

( ) 28. Father always takes his _____ vacation in July so the family can go abroad together.

(A) ambient      (B) ambivalent      (C) annual      (D) ancillary

( ) 29. The restaurant manager was replaced because of her inability to maintain _____ among her employees.

(A) advocacy      (B) contract      (C) discipline      (D) euphemism

( ) 30. The manager made it clear that he intended to _____ down some new rules to enforce workplace discipline.

(A) lied      (B) laid      (C) lay      (D) lie

( ) 31. The contract is still being discussed as the two parties have not been able to reach an _____ on several matters.

(A) absorption      (B) accord      (C) account      (D) adjudication

( ) 32. Having a good logo means people will be able to recognize your _____ instantly.

(A) age      (B) brand      (C) face      (D) profile

( ) 33. Professor Lee thought that the small college town would be a _____ place to live, but in fact, he found it quite cosmopolitan.

(A) demolished      (B) disrupted      (C) meltdown      (D) provincial

( ) 34. _____ is forbidden on campus for sanitary reasons.

(A) Lecturing      (B) Lingering      (C) Littering      (D) Loitering

( ) 35. A: I failed that test--my life is ruined!

B: Don't get _____ away. It was only one test.

(A) carried      (B) done      (C) excited      (D) moved

( ) 36. Professionals who seek career experience outside of their home countries may feel the need to _____ with a new challenge.

(A) swing back and forth      (B) recharge their batteries

(C) put their heads together      (D) make a mountain out of a molehill

( ) 37. There was a rumor that there had been a minor accident at the nuclear power plant, but a spokesman for the plant issued a _____.

(A) denial      (B) intersection      (C) receipt      (D) spontaneity

( ) 38. Everyone attended last week's meeting _____ Mr. Lee, who was out of town on a business trip.

(A) accept      (B) aspect      (C) except      (D) expect

07 健康

08 職場學校

09 人格個性

10 社交禮儀

11 金錢買賣

12 社會時事

(     ) 39. I missed the meeting this morning. Can someone _____ me in on what happened?

      (A) send       (B) deal       (C) fill       (D) read

(     ) 40. Starting next quarter, all store managers will be given increased _____, to make decisions on their own.

      (A) autonomy       (B) budget       (C) direction       (D) rejection

(     ) 41. Jason always stays _____ other students in Mathematics class.

      (A) in the top       (B) top of       (C) ahead of       (D) ahead

(     ) 42. A: It seems I have lost all the work I did on the computer this afternoon.

      B: Oh, no! I am afraid you will have to start from _____ again.

      (A) scratch       (B) shift       (C) switch       (D) touch

# 標 準 答 案

| | | | | |
|---|---|---|---|---|
| 1. (A) | 2. (A) | 3. (D) | 4. (A) | 5. (A) |
| 6. (B) | 7. (A) | 8. (D) | 9. (C) | 10. (B) |
| 11. (C) | 12. (A) | 13. (B) | 14. (C) | 15. (B) |
| 16. (A) | 17. (D) | 18. (A) | 19. (B) | 20. (C) |
| 21. (C) | 22. (A) | 23. (C) | 24. (C) | 25. (D) |
| 26. (C) | 27. (A) | 28. (C) | 29. (C) | 30. (C) |
| 31. (B) | 32. (B) | 33. (D) | 34. (C) | 35. (A) |
| 36. (B) | 37. (A) | 38. (C) | 39. (C) | 40. (A) |
| 41. (C) | 42. (A) | | | |

# memo

# 9 人格個性

## 一、必考題型

1. He made himself unwelcome by constantly **crashing** a party.

   他讓自己不受歡迎，因為他屢次**擅闖**別人的派對。 `105 英領`

2. Being responsible means that we should learn to take the **consequence** of our own actions.

   負責任表示我們應該要學習對我們所做所為的**後果**。 `104 英領`

3. Generally most of us admire the people whose names **are synonymous with** success, risk-taking, and creative thinking.

   一般來說，我們大部分的人都崇拜那些名字**等同於**成功、冒險以及創意思考的人。 `104 英領`

4. Being creative involves making the best use of your senses: for example, it means looking at the same object from many different **perspectives**.

   創意牽涉到如何善用你所有的感官。比如說，用不同的**眼光**看同一件物品。 `104 英領`

5. My brother is very superstitious. Whenever he sees a black cat, he considers it a bad **omen**.

   我的弟弟非常迷信。不論何時他只要見到黑貓，他覺得就是個壞**徵兆**。 `104 英導`

6. I always thought Dr. Wang was **aloof**. He seldom talked to anyone and seemed cold and distant. But now, I realize that he was just painfully shy!

   我之前總是認為王博士很**冷淡**。他很少跟人交談，看起來似乎很冷淡且有距離感。但現在我才知道他只是極度害羞。 `104 英導`

7. Jane enjoys traveling, and she always travels with great **enthusiasm**.

   珍很喜歡旅行，她總是**熱情十足**地去旅行。 `103 英領`

8. Being **proactive** means that you anticipate problems before they **arise** and come up with solutions ahead of time.

主動出擊表示你在問題**浮現**之前就已經想好了解決之道。　104 英領

aloof adj. 冷淡的

courteous / well-mannered / polite adj. 禮貌的

sunny adj. 陽光性格的

shy adj. 害羞的

down-to-earth adj. 樸實的

childish adj. 幼稚的

considerate adj. 體貼的

sensitive adj. 敏感的

reluctant adj. 不願意的

witty adj. 機智的

eccentric adj. 怪異的

proactive adj. 主動的

discourteous / ill-mannered / impolite adj. 沒禮貌的

outgoing adj. 外向的

humble / modest adj. 謙虛的

mature adj. 成熟的

disciplined adj. 有紀律的

thoughtful adj. 細心的

blunt adj. 遲鈍的

open-minded adj. 開放心胸的

appreciation n. 鑑賞力

(　　) 1.　This girl was very happy to _____ publicity that came with her relationship with the most celebrated soccer player in the world.

　　(A) fall short of　　　　　　　　(B) stay out with

　　(C) go up against　　　　　　　　(D) ride the wave of

(　　) 2.　I always thought Dr. Wang was _____. He seldom talked to anyone and seemed cold and distant. But now, I realize that he was just painfully shy!

　　(A) alert　　　　(B) aloof　　　　(C) dizzy　　　　(D) sober

(　　) 3.　He is not good at talking to strangers. When he tries to make polite conversation, it often _____ uncomfortable silence.

　　(A) fills out　　　(B) takes up　　　(C) lapses into　　　(D) accounts for

(　　) 4.　Being responsible means that we should learn to take the _____ of our own actions.

　　(A) consequence　　(B) fragrance　　(C) eloquence　　(D) subsequence

(　　) 5.　Being creative involves making the best use of your senses: for example, it means looking at the same object from many different _____.

　　(A) invocations　　(B) perspectives　　(C) prosecutions　　(D) incidents

(　　) 6.　My brother is very superstitious. Whenever he sees a black cat, he considers it a bad _____.

　　(A) gist　　　(B) moat　　　(C) omen　　　(D) rumor

(　　) 7.　He made himself unwelcome by constantly _____ a party.

　　(A) joining　　(B) participating　　(C) crashing　　(D) crackling

(　　) 8.　_____ and you will overcome these difficulties.

　　(A) Persecute　　(B) Predominate　　(C) Persevere　　(D) Preserve

(　　) 9.　Jane enjoys traveling, and she always travels with great _____.

　　(A) entertainment　　(B) enormousness　　(C) enthusiasm　　(D) enthronement

(　　) 10. Being _____ means that you anticipate problems before they arise and come up with solutions ahead of time.

　　(A) abstractive　　(B) extractive　　(C) interactive　　(D) proactive

# 標 準 答 案

| | | | | |
|---|---|---|---|---|
| 1. ( D ) | 2. ( B ) | 3. ( C ) | 4. ( A ) | 5. ( B ) |
| 6. ( C ) | 7. ( C ) | 8. ( C ) | 9. ( C ) | 10. ( D ) |

07 健康

08 職場學校

09 人格個性

10 社交禮儀

11 金錢買賣

12 社會時事

# 10 社交禮儀

一、必考題型

1. To **flush** the toilet after use is proper **etiquette**.

   用完馬桶後**沖水**是基本**禮儀**。 105 英導

2. Online dating has become a **trend** for many people looking for potential relationships.

   網路約會已成為尋找潛在關係的一種**潮流**。 104 英領

3. **Netiquette** refers to a set of **social conventions** that facilitate interactions over networks on the world-wide web.

   **網路禮儀**顯示出一系列促進網路上交流的**社會習俗**。 104 英領

4. What the lawyer **advised** the couple was to **confer** with a trained and licensed marriage counselor before the two even contemplated getting a **divorce**.

   律師**建議**這對夫妻在深思**離婚**之前，可以找受過訓練並有執照的婚姻諮商師**討論**。
   104 英領

5. Human beings often like to be part of a group, so it comes as no surprise that they would do something to **look for peer identity**.

   人類通常喜歡成為群體的一部分，因此也不驚訝他們會尋求**同儕認同**。 104 英領

6. George made a terrible social **gaffe**. He asked the hostess at the party when her baby was due, and she said, in an icy voice, "I am NOT pregnant!"

   喬治犯了一個嚴重的社交**錯誤**。他在派對上問了女主人何時寶寶會出生，然後她用尖銳的聲音說：我沒有懷孕！ 104 英導

7. In Australia, about 10% of all divorced people remarry after they **split up** with their first spouses. This figure is about half of what it was in 1970.

   在澳洲，有 10% 的人在第一次**離婚**過後會再婚。這個數字約是 1970 年的一半。
   104 英導

8. Gift **wrapping** refers to the act of enclosing a present in some sort of material. In many cases, it also **adds** much value **to** the gift.

   禮物**包裝**指的是用某種材料將禮物包起來的動作。在許多場合來說，這也可以**增加**禮物的質感。 `103 英導`

9. Although giving gifts is quite popular in Taiwan, it is rude to bring **inappropriate** gifts such as a clock, umbrella, shoes, and so on.

   雖然送禮在台灣很受歡迎，但帶來**不適當的**禮物是很無禮的，像是鐘、雨傘、鞋子等等。 `108 英導`

| | |
|---|---|
| etiquette **n.** 禮儀 | netiquette **n.** 網路禮儀 |
| social conventions **n.** 社會習俗 | social gaffe **n.** 社交錯誤 |
| trend **n.** 潮流 | peer identity **n.** 同儕認同 |
| newlywed **n.** 新婚夫婦 | bachelor **n.** 單身漢 |
| tie the knot **phr.** 結婚 | groom **n.** 新郎 |
| bride **n.** 新娘 | bridal tour / honeymoon **n.** 蜜月旅行 |
| wedding anniversary **n.** 結婚週年 | divorce **n.** 離婚 |
| split up **v.** 離婚 | file for divorce **v.** 提出離婚訴訟 |
| have an affair with **v.** 與～有染 | phenomenon **n.** 現象 |

## 三、牛刀小試

( ) 1. In Australia, about 10% of all divorced people remarry after they _____ with their first spouses. This figure is about half of what it was in 1970.

   (A) pull over      (B) put in      (C) split up      (D) wipe out

( ) 2. What the lawyer advised the couple was to _____ with a trained and licensed marriage counselor before the two even contemplated getting a divorce.

   (A) confer      (B) mingle      (C) revolve      (D) maintain

( ) 3. Online dating has become a _____ for many people looking for potential relationships.

   (A) send      (B) blend      (C) mend      (D) trend

( ) 4. George made a terrible social _____. He asked the hostess at the party when her baby was due, and she said, in an icy voice, "I am NOT pregnant!"

   (A) dainty      (B) gaffe      (C) prefix      (D) screen

( ) 5. To _____ the toilet after use is proper etiquette.

   (A) floss      (B) drain      (C) flush      (D) pump

( ) 6. Human beings often like to be part of a group, so it comes as no surprise that they would do something to _____.

   (A) get an early start      (B) look for peer identity

   (C) come out the winner      (D) make a social statement

( ) 7. _____ refers to a set of social conventions that facilitate interactions over networks on the world-wide web.

   (A) Coquette      (B) Etiquette      (C) Netiquette      (D) Maquette

( ) 8. Gift _____ refers to the act of enclosing a present in some sort of material. In many cases, it also adds much value to the gift.

   (A) editing      (B) spelling      (C) containing      (D) wrapping

## 標準答案

| 1. ( C ) | 2. ( A ) | 3. ( D ) | 4. ( B ) | 5. ( C ) |
|----------|----------|----------|----------|----------|
| 6. ( B ) | 7. ( C ) | 8. ( D ) | | |

07 健康

08 職場學校

09 人格個性

10 社交禮儀

11 金錢買賣

12 社會時事

# 11 金錢買賣

## 一、必考題型

1. Teamwork plays a vital **role** in fulfilling any mission, particularly at a time when an **economic recession** is looming on the horizon.

   實現任何任務時，團體合作扮演很重要的**角色**，特別是當**經濟衰退**即將浮現時。
   104 英導

2. Tourism has helped **boost** the economy for many countries.

   觀光業已經幫忙**振興**了許多國家的經濟。 99 英領

3. Oil price **fluctuation** is always regarded as the barometer of worldwide **economy**.

   油價**浮動**總是被視為世界**經濟**的氣壓計。 103 英導

4. Starting next quarter, all store managers will be given **increased autonomy**, to make decisions on their own.

   從下一季開始，所有商店的經理都會被給予**更多**可以自行做決定的**自主權**。 104 英導

5. The trading company **anticipated** a **rise** in the prices of computer products, but many analysts felt the evidence for this was not supported in the market.

   這件貿易公司**預期**電腦產品價格走**升**，但許多分析師認為市場觀點並不足以證明。
   105 英導

6. The city government must decide **whether** it wants to **increase** taxes or undergo severe **budget cutbacks**.

   市政府必須決定**是否**要**增加**課稅或是遭受嚴重的**預算減縮**。 104 英導

7. After a long period of **economic depression**, the **unemployment rate** has finally **declined**.

   在經過長時間的**經濟蕭條**後，**失業率**終於**下降**了。 104 英領

8. Soon all our natural resources will be **used up** if we do not **reduce** our levels of **consumption**.

如果我們不**減少消耗**的話，我們的自然資源很快就會被**用盡**。 103 英領

9. Even a small **reduction** of salt in the diet can be a big help to the heart.

即便只是在飲食中**減少**些許的鹽分，對於心臟都會有很大的幫助。 99 英領

10. Unfortunately, after Epoch Computers merged with that Japanese company, the **value** of its stock **dropped**.

很不幸的，大紀元電腦合併日本公司之後，股票的**價值**就**下降**了。 104 英導

11. The value of the stocks has **grown by** 1.6 percent in 2013 to ten million US dollars.

股票的價值在 2013 年**漲**了 1.6 個百分點，達到 1000 萬美元。 104 英領

12. A recent **survey** shows that the average American generates twice as much trash as the average European.

最近的**調查**顯示，美國人平均產生的垃圾量是歐洲人的 2 倍。 104 英導

13. In order to save money, she asked to be **transferred** to the branch office near her home town.

為了省錢，他要求**轉調**到離家附近的分公司。 104 英領

14. The fast food restaurant should have been profitable, but poor capital control forced it into **bankruptcy**.

這間速食餐廳應該要能夠獲利，但不好的資產管理迫使這間餐廳**破產**。 104 英導

15. Tourism **expenditure** refers to the amount paid for the acquisition of **consumption** goods and services for and during tourism trips.

旅遊業的**花費**指的是獲取**消耗**品的費用，以及在旅途當中的服務費用。 104 英領

16. Travelling by long-distance bus is generally the cheapest way to reach the destination, but spending 12 hours on the road is very time-**consuming**.

搭乘長程巴士通常是最便宜到達目的地的方式，但花 12 小時在路上真的太**耗**時。
103 英導

17. To take advantage of some good **bargains**, many **consumers** choose to become members of warehouse clubs and start to buy things **in bulk**.

為了好好利用一些**優惠**，許多**消費者**選擇成為倉儲會員且開始**大量**地買東西。 `103 英導`

18. If you are not delighted with your **purchase**, you can take the goods back to your retailer who will **refund** you the **purchase** price.

如果你不喜歡你所買的**物品**，你可以把它帶回你的零售商並**退回**你所**購買**的價錢。
`103 英領`

19. When the show was cancelled, the people who had bought tickets had their money **refunded**.

當表演被取消時，許多買票的人辦理退票**退費**。 `103 英導`

20. The guest is given a **refund** after he makes a complaint to the restaurant.

這名客人跟餐廳抱怨之後就得到**退款**。 `100 英領`

21. Some retailers, desperate for sales and customer loyalty, have begun training their employees in the art of **bargaining** with customers.

有些零售商很急切地想要業績跟客戶忠誠度，已經開始訓練員工與客戶**討價還價**的藝術。 `103 英領`

22. Some hotels require their guests to leave a **deposit** to cover incidental charges to the room.

有些飯店會要求房客留下一筆**保證金**以支付客房的額外費用。 `103 英導`

23. As soon as you **submit** the receipts, the company will **reimburse** you for all costs related to your business trip.

只要你**送出**收據，公司就可以**支付**所有跟出差有關的費用。 `104 英導`

24. Please make sure to keep your receipts so we can **reimburse** you for your travel **expenses**.

請確保將收據妥善保管，這樣我們才可以幫你**支付**你所有的旅行**花費**。 `103 英導`

25. Under this travel insurance plan, you are **eligible** to make a claim when your journey has to be cancelled for reasons beyond your control.

在這旅行險的內容下，當你的行程被不可控制的因素而導致取消時，你**有資格**可以申請理賠。 `103 英導`

26. We have **used up** all of our travel funds for the year; any trips from now on will have to be paid for out of our own pockets.

我們已**用完**今年所有的旅遊基金，現在開始任何旅程的花費都必須從我們的口袋中出。 `104 英領`

27. Many people believe that wealth is like health: **Though** its utter absence can breed misery, having it does not **guarantee** happiness.

許多人相信財富就像健康，**即便**完全沒錢會導致悲慘，但有了錢財也不**保證**幸福。 `104 英領`

28. To keep the bills down, I **got into the habit of** turning off the computer the minute I was finished with it.

為了省錢，我**養成**一旦用完電腦就立刻關機的**習慣**。 `104 英領`

29. Despite ten years of success, the financial stress and burden of the sudden **recession** made the partnership **fail**.

儘管 10 年來都很成功，財務壓力和突如其來的**衰退**跟重擔仍讓合作關係**破裂**。 `104 英導`

30. Terry went into the used-book store just to **browse** through the old books, but he found a **rare** edition of a Hemingway novel that was worth over $1,000.

泰瑞原本走進二手書店只是想**看看**舊書，但他卻從中發現一本價值超過 1000 元的**稀有**版本的海明威小說。 `104 英導`

31. **In addition to** allowing people to buy single shoes, once a season the single shoes bank gives unwanted single shoes to members for free.

**除了**可讓人們買單隻鞋子之外，單鞋銀行每一季都會把沒人要的單鞋免費提供給會員一次。 `103 英領`

32. It is always a good idea to buy **travel insurance**. If you get sick or lose one of your possessions while traveling, the insurance company will pay your medical **expenses** or give you money.

購買**旅遊不便險**是個好主意。當你在旅遊途中生病或遺失個人物品時，保險公司會負擔你的醫療**開銷**並提供賠償。 `103 英領`

33. To save money, Susan always clips **coupons** from the newspaper to use at the grocery store.

為了省錢，蘇珊總是剪下報紙上的**優惠券**去雜貨店使用。 `103 英導`

34. **Bilateral** trade between Taiwan and New Zealand stands at some US$ 1.2 billion annually.

台灣與紐西蘭的**雙邊**貿易每年約可達到美金 12 億。 `105 英導`

35. Can I please have a **receipt** for my purchase?

可以給我買的物品的**收據**嗎？ `108 英導`

36. If you want to find the cheapest airline tickets, **bargains** can usually be found online for best fares.

如果你想要找到最便宜的機票，最好票價的**交易**通常可以在網路上找到。 `108 英導`

37. If you want to **cash** our traveler's checks, you must pay a handling charge. We charge a 2% commission on each traveler's check.

如果你想要**兌現**旅行支票，你必須支付手續費。我們每張旅行支票收 2% 的傭金。 `108 英導`

38. I would like to **claim** a tax refund. Do you know the refund application procedures?

我想要**辦理**退稅。你知道退稅申請的步驟嗎？ `108 英領`

39. Many stores **guarantee** to refund the customers' money if they are not delighted with their purchase.

許多商家**保證**退錢，如果客戶不滿意他們的購買。 `108 英領`

40. Duty free rules and regulations are **subject to** change without notice.

免稅規則與規定**依法**改變不需通知。 `108 英領`

economic **adj.** 經濟上的、經濟學的

economic issues **n.** 經濟問題

economic growth **n.** 經濟成長

economic development **n.** 經濟發展

economic climate **n.** 經濟形勢

economic depression **n.** 經濟蕭條

economic recession **n.** 經濟衰退

economy **n.** 經濟

increase **v.** 增加

rise **v.** 上升

grow **v.** 成長

reduce **v.** 減少

drop **v.** 下降

decline **v.** 下降

cutbacks **n.** 減縮

boost **v.** 振興

fluctuation **n.** 浮動

bankruptcy **n.** 破產

expenditure **n.** 花費

purchase **v.** 購買

refund **n.** 退款

in bulk **adv.** 大量

reimburse **v.** 支付

(     ) 1.   A recent survey shows that the average American generates _____ much trash as the average European.

     (A) twice          (B) twice as        (C) as twice        (D) twice more

(     ) 2.   Please make sure to keep your receipts so we can _____ you for your travel expenses.

     (A) supervise     (B) reimburse     (C) relocate       (D) scatter

(     ) 3.   _____ trade between Taiwan and New Zealand stands at some US1.2billion annually.

     (A) Bilateral      (B) Bipartisan     (C) Unanimous    (D) Unilateral

(     ) 4.   Oil price _____ is always regarded as the barometer of worldwide economy.

     (A) confrontation   (B) fluctuation    (C) prevention    (D) substitution

(     ) 5.   The fast food restaurant should have been profitable, but poor capital control forced it into _____.

     (A) bankruptcy    (B) compensation   (C) construction   (D) restoration

(     ) 6.   Tourism _____ refers to the amount paid for the acquisition of consumption goods and services for and during tourism trips.

     (A) deficit         (B) expenditure    (C) reimbursement   (D) revenue

(     ) 7.   Starting next quarter, all store managers will be given increased _____, to make decisions on their own.

     (A) autonomy    (B) budget       (C) direction       (D) rejection

(     ) 8.   After a long period of economic depression, the unemployment rate has finally _____.

     (A) accelerated    (B) declined      (C) inclined       (D) facilitated

(     ) 9.   Dihua Street is a great place to purchase traditional Chinese foods which _____ great gifts, and many shops will seal purchases for plane travel.

     (A) making      (B) make        (C) makes       (D) made

07 健康
08 職場學校
09 人格個性
10 社交禮儀
11 金錢買賣
12 社會時事

( ) 10. Soon all our natural resources will be used up if we do not _____ our levels of consumption.

(A) calcify        (B) multiply        (C) generate        (D) reduce

( ) 11. Only on Sundays _____ without paying.

(A) they could visit the museum        (B) you will visit the museum

(C) can you visit the museum        (D) we will visit the museum

( ) 12. It is always a good idea to buy _____. If you get sick or lose one of your possessions while traveling, the insurance company will pay your medical expenses or give you money.

(A) medicines        (B) travel guide

(C) duty free goods        (D) travel insurance

( ) 13. To save money, Susan always clips _____ from the newspaper to use at the grocery store.

(A) certificates        (B) warranties        (C) coupons        (D) pouches

( ) 14. Unfortunately, after Epoch Computers merged with that Japanese company, the _____ of its stock dropped.

(A) cost        (B) nature        (C) receipt        (D) value

( ) 15. The value of the stocks has grown _____ 1.6 percent in 2013 to ten million US dollars.

(A) by        (B) into        (C) for        (D) with

( ) 16. In order to save money, she asked to be _____ to the branch office near her home town.

(A) transmitted        (B) transported        (C) transferred        (D) transformed

( ) 17. Travelling by long-distance bus is generally the cheapest way to reach the destination, but spending 12 hours on the road is very time-_____.

(A) consuming        (B) misleading        (C) relieving        (D) violating

( ) 18. Many people believe that wealth is like health: _____ its utter absence can breed misery, having it does not guarantee happiness.

(A) When        (B) Before        (C) Though        (D) Because

( ) 19. We have _____ all of our travel funds for the year; any trips from now on will have to be paid for out of our own pockets.

(A) used up        (B) asked for        (C) carried out        (D) gotten back

( ) 20. _____ you purchase good tea, keep it in a dry cool place, avoiding direct sunshine. An airtight container is a good choice.

(A) After        (B) Though        (C) Before        (D) Whereas

( ) 21. When the show was cancelled, the people who had bought tickets had their money _____.

(A) purchased                    (B) prescribed

(C) replaced                      (D) refunded

( ) 22. Despite ten years of success, the financial stress and burden of the sudden recession made the partnership _____.

(A) fail        (B) failed        (C) to fail        (D) to be failed

( ) 23. To take advantage of some good bargains, many consumers choose to become members of warehouse clubs and start to buy things _____.

(A) at large        (B) in terms        (C) off base        (D) in bulk

( ) 24. Tourism has helped _____ the economy for many countries, and brought in considerable revenues.

(A) boast        (B) boost        (C) receive        (D) recall

( ) 25. If you are not delighted with your purchase, you can take the goods back to your retailer who will _____ you the purchase price.

(A) deliver        (B) refund        (C) exchange        (D) inform

( ) 26. Some retailers, desperate for sales and customer loyalty, have begun training their employees in the art of _____ with customers.

(A) playing        (B) cheating        (C) bargaining        (D) persuading

( ) 27. The trading company _____ a rise in the prices of computer products, but many analysts felt the evidence for this was not supported in the market.

(A) declined        (B) aggregated        (C) anticipated        (D) reduced

( 　　) 28. The city government must decide _____ it wants to increase taxes or undergo severe budget cutbacks.

(A) what　　　　(B) which　　　　(C) whether　　　　(D) while

( 　　) 29. Teamwork plays a vital _____ in fulfilling any mission, particularly at a time when an economic recession is looming on the horizon.

(A) role　　　　(B) task　　　　(C) title　　　　(D) work

( 　　) 30. Under this travel insurance plan, you are _____ to make a claim when your journey has to be cancelled for reasons beyond your control.

(A) dispensable　　(B) eligible　　(C) hospitable　　(D) invaluable

( 　　) 31. Terry went into the used-book store just to _____ through the old books, but he found a rare edition of a Hemingway novel that was worth over $1,000.

(A) browse　　　　(B) haunt　　　　(C) merge　　　　(D) purchase

( 　　) 32. _____ allowing people to buy single shoes, once a season the single shoes bank gives unwanted single shoes to members for free.

(A) Before　　　　　　　　　(B) On the contrary

(C) By taking chance　　　　(D) In addition to

( 　　) 33. Prices of hotel rooms are very _____ to demand, so special deals and discounts during weekdays could always attract more people.

(A) commercial　　(B) frequent　　(C) gradual　　(D) sensitive

( 　　) 34. As soon as you submit the receipts, the company will _____ you for all costs related to your business trip.

(A) charge　　　　(B) reimburse　　　　(C) threaten　　　　(D) warrant

# 標 準 答 案

| 1. ( B ) | 2. ( B ) | 3. ( A ) | 4. ( B ) | 5. ( A ) |
|----------|----------|----------|----------|----------|
| 6. ( B ) | 7. ( A ) | 8. ( B ) | 9. ( B ) | 10. ( D ) |
| 11. ( C ) | 12. ( D ) | 13. ( C ) | 14. ( D ) | 15. ( A ) |
| 16. ( C ) | 17. ( A ) | 18. ( C ) | 19. ( A ) | 20. ( A ) |
| 21. ( D ) | 22. ( A ) | 23. ( D ) | 24. ( B ) | 25. ( B ) |
| 26. ( C ) | 27. ( C ) | 28. ( C ) | 29. ( A ) | 30. ( B ) |
| 31. ( A ) | 32. ( D ) | 33. ( D ) | 34. ( B ) | |

# 12 社會時事

1. Decades of **exploitation** have **resulted in** a severe reduction in the number of the local plants, which are now no longer a common sight.

   數十年的**開採**已經**導致**當地的農作物嚴重縮減，已不復平日景象。　105 英領

2. The **harmful effects** of pesticides and chemical fertilizers made the farm family decide to take a more ecology-friendly approach to farming for the sake of the land, their own health, and the environment **at large**.

   殺蟲劑與化學肥料的**有害作用**，讓農家為了土地、健康以及**整體**環境利益著想，決定採用更為生態友善的方法進行農耕。　105 英領

3. The International Rescue Committee is **providing** relief supplies to **the displaced**.

   國際救援委員會正在**提供**救濟品給**流離失所者**。　105 英導

4. With the street **blocked** by the demonstrators, the cars were unable to move ahead.

   因為示威者已經**擋住**了街道，導致車子無法前進。　105 英導

5. There was a **multitude** of people in Taiwan who **participated** in the **fund-raising** concert after the 921 Earthquake.

   台灣有很大的**一群**人在 921 地震之後**參與募款**音樂會。　105 英導

6. Every September, families of victims **pay tribute to** those who died in the 911 terrorist attacks in the United States.

   每年 9 月，在美國許多受害者家庭會**弔念**因 911 恐怖攻擊而喪生的人。　105 英導

7. There are many refugees from Syria now. If we can help those **in need**, we will make our lives more meaningful.

   現在敘利亞有很多難民。如果我們幫助這些**需要幫忙**的人，我們將會讓我們的生命更有意義。　105 英導

8. Africa has a history of drought and **famine**, which has had the greatest **impact on** undeveloped and poor populations.

   非洲長期以來的乾旱跟**饑荒**，對未開化的貧窮人口有深遠的**影響**。 `105 英導`

9. This non-profit organization was designed to help **underprivileged** families to **apply for** social welfare.

   這個非營利組織是設來幫助**弱勢**家庭**申請**社會福利救濟的。 `105 英導`

10. The police officer's actions in rescuing the dying stray dog from the traffic accident were most **admirable**.

   那名員警救出因交通意外瀕死的流浪狗，其行為值得高度**讚賞**。 `105 英導`

11. The new president expressed his determination to **eliminate corruption** as soon as he took office.

   新任總統剛上任就展現了**消滅貪腐**的決心。 `105 英導`

12. They apply military and economic **sanctions** against terrorism to effectively **deter** its spreading.

   他們對恐怖主義施以軍事以及經濟上的**制裁**以有效**嚇阻**其擴散。 `105 英導`

13. The refugee's **dire** situation **aroused** our sympathy.

   難民的**恐怖**處境**喚醒**了我們的同情心。 `105 英導`

14. Human **trafficking**, which involves controlling people against their will to **exploit** them for forced labor, sexual exploitation, or both, is a crime.

   人口**販賣**，牽涉到強迫勞動、性剝削或是兩者都有，是一種違背意願控制他人的**剝削**行為。 `105 英導`

15. With the fast-growing population plus the **drought**, the **demand** of staple foods **outweighs** the supply.

   人口快速成長再加上**乾旱**，對於主食的**需求**已**超過**供給。 `105 英導`

16. The **operation** of the humanitarian rescue wins much **applause**.

   人道救援的**行動**贏得許多**讚賞**。 `105 英導`

07 健康

08 職場學校

09 人格個性

10 社交禮儀

11 金錢買賣

12 社會時事

17. If the town were **stricter** about drinking and driving, I would not worry so much about driving at night.

如果這城鎮對於酒駕**更嚴格**的話,我就不會這麼擔心在夜晚開車了。 `105 英領`

18. Located in one of the city's poorer neighborhoods, many old houses in this area have been torn down to **make way** for new and better public housing.

位於城市中最貧窮的區域之一,許多這區的老房子都被拆掉,來**讓出空間**給更好的新公眾住宅。 `103 英導`

19. When it comes to catching the bad guys, a **surveillance** camera is a police officer's best friend.

當說到抓壞人,**監視**攝影機是警察最好的朋友。 `103 英領`

20. Taking a photograph in a court is often **prohibited** and sometimes can even be seen as a serious **offense**.

在法院拍照是經常**被禁止的**,而且有時候會被視為很嚴重的**冒犯**。 `103 英導`

21. The man was arrested by the police for producing **fake** LV bags.

這個人因為製造**假的** LV 包包所以被警察逮捕。 `104 英領`

22. The document was finally proved **authentic** and accepted by the court.

這份文件最終被證實為**正本**,並被法院接受。 `103 英領`

23. The police officer wanted to come face to face with the ghostly phenomenon and **expose** it as a hoax.

警方想要跟鬼魅般的現象來個正面對決,卻**發現**是詐騙。 `104 英領`

24. Studies have shown that many people are very concerned about the amount of sex and violence **depicted** in television shows.

研究顯示許多人很關心在電視節目上所**描繪**的性與暴力。 `104 英領`

25. The use of emoticons, punctuation to **depict** a facial expression, is an essential part of the lexicon of the Internet.

用來**描繪**臉部表情的表情符號以及標點符號,是網路上很重要的詞彙。 `103 英導`

26. People everywhere are becoming concerned about the high energy prices. **Rising energy costs** are forcing many offices to **implement** energy-saving measures.

許多地方的人都越來越關心高漲的能源價錢。**節節高升的能源花費**迫使許多辦公室**執行**節省能源的方法。 104 英導

27. The water of this city comes from a **reservoir** located in the mountains nearby.

這座城市的用水是來自於附近山上**水庫**的水。 104 英導

28. **Conservation** of energy has become a very important policy for many countries due to the limited resources.

**節約**能源對許多國家來說都是非常重要的政策，因為資源有限。 104 英領

29. Soon all our natural resources will be used up if we do not **reduce** our levels of consumption.

如果我們不**減少**消耗程度的話，很快的我們的自然資源就會被用盡。 103 英領

30. After the 311 disaster in Japan in 2011, many Japanese began to advocate for the **banning** of the use of nuclear power.

2011 年日本 311 災難之後，許多日本人開始擁護**禁用**核電。 104 英領

31. According to a recent **survey**, more people watch television on Sunday night than on any other night.

根據最近的**調查**，比起其他天的晚上，越來越多人在週日晚上看電視。 104 英導

32. A national bird survey is to be conducted around the New Year's Day holiday to both celebrate the New Year and **raise** public awareness about wildlife protection.

為了慶祝新年並**提高**大眾對於野生動物保護的意識，一份國家的鳥類調查將會在新年假期執行。 103 英領

33. The Agency Against Corruption is forced to **conduct** an investigation into the bribery case of the governor.

反貪腐組織被迫**執行**對於州長貪汙的調查。 104 英領

34. A census analysis published in 2011 showed that almost all of the city's population increase since 2000 can **be accounted for** by an increase in residents between the ages of 20 and 35.

2011 年所出版的人口普查分析顯示，幾乎所有的城市人口都於 2000 年後增加，可**被歸因於** 20 到 35 歲的居民人數增加。 ᴸ103 英領ᴸ

35. Internet technology has nowadays **collapsed** time and space.

網路科技已**瓦解**現今的時間與空間。 ᴸ103 英領ᴸ

36. Since the last half of the twentieth century, our way of life has been **revolutionized** by gadgets of all types: television sets and DVDs, cell phones and computers, just to name a few.

自從 20 世紀後半，我們的生活方式已經被這些各式各樣的小玩意所**革命**了，像是電視機、DVD 撥放器，手機以及電腦。 ᴸ104 英領ᴸ

37. Downloading should **take** about two to four minutes. The time needed will depend on the speed of your internet connection.

下載大約**耗時** 2 至 4 分鐘，需要的時間將會依照你的網路速度。 ᴸ104 英導ᴸ

38. Human knowledge is now in the process of being **converted** into always-available digital formats.

人類的知識現在進入被**轉換**成數位模式的階段。 ᴸ103 英領ᴸ

39. You can carry a cell phone with you **wherever** you go but you can't do this with your PC.

你可以帶著手機**到處**走，但你不能帶著桌機這樣做。 ᴸ103 英領ᴸ

40. Online classes **hold the promise of** enabling teachers and students to communicate, even when they are across the world from each other.

線上課程讓許多師生**抱有許多希望**，即便他們在世界的兩端，還是能夠溝通。 ᴸ103 英領ᴸ

41. More and more public **fueling** stations can be found in places like restaurants, department stores, and airports. Smartphone owners can make use of them when the battery is low.

越來越多餐廳、百貨公司，以及機場這些地方可以找到公共**充電**站。智慧型手機快沒電的時候，可好好利用。 ᴸ103 英導ᴸ

42. Dutch artist Florentijn Hofman was upset about the arrangement for his Rubber Duck installation **on display** in Keelung.

荷蘭藝術家霍夫曼不滿意黃色小鴨於基隆**展出**時的安排。 103 英領

43. Many people agree that America is not only a country of wealth and riches, but also a country of homelessness and **poverty**.

許多人同意美國不只是富裕的國家，同時也是無家可歸以及**貧窮**的國家。 104 英領

44. Should the Prime Minister receive another vote of no confidence, she would be forced to **dissolve** her government.

如果總理收到另一張不信任案的投票，她將會被迫**解散**政府。 104 英領

45. The spy wrote her message in a secret code, but government intelligence agents were able to **decipher** the message.

這名間諜用密碼傳訊給她，但政府特工人員能夠**解碼**這訊息。 104 英導

46. Several new government policies are scheduled to **take effect** today.

許多新政府政策將於今日**生效**。 103 英領

47. More money is needed to improve the **infrastructure** of the nation's rural areas including building roads and establishing clinics.

需要更多的錢來改善國家鄉村地區的**公共建設**，像是鋪路以及蓋診所。 103 英導

48. We must not allow our creative protest to **degenerate** into physical violence.

我們絕不允許將我們的創意的抗爭**降格**為身體上的暴力。 103 英領

49. Human began **cultivating** food about 10,000 years ago; otherwise, they would not have developed a stable food source.

人們約於一萬年前開始**耕種**食物，不然他們無法發展穩定的食物來源。 104 英領

50. Even though the men were the leaders in this tribe, within the family, they were **subordinate** to the women.

即便男人在這部落內是領導者，但在家庭內，他們則是**次於**女人。 104 英領

07 健康

08 職場學校

09 人格個性

10 社交禮儀

11 金錢買賣

12 社會時事

exploitation n. 開採

severe adj. 嚴重的

harmful effects n. 有害作用

participate in v. 參與

pay tribute to v. 致敬

drought n. 乾旱

apply for phr. 申請

eliminate v. 消滅

economic sanctions n. 經濟制裁

humanitarian rescue n.
人道救援的行動

conserve v. 節約

survey n. 調查

result in v. 導致

reduction n. 縮減

at large phr. 整體

fund-raising n. 募款

refugees n. 難民

famine n. 饑荒

admirable adj. 讚賞的

corruption n. 貪腐

human trafficking n. 人口販賣

depict v. 描繪

reduce v. 減少

( ) 1. Studies have shown that many people are very concerned about the amount of sex and violence _____ in television shows.

    (A) polluted     (B) depicted     (C) exported     (D) appointed

( ) 2. People everywhere are becoming concerned about the high energy prices. Rising energy costs are forcing many offices to _____ energy-saving measures.

    (A) complement     (B) compliment     (C) implement     (D) supplement

( ) 3. With the street _____ by the demonstrators, the cars were unable to move ahead.

    (A) tied     (B) blocked     (C) pushed     (D) chained

( ) 4. There was a _____ of people in Taiwan who participated in the fund-raising concert after the 921 Earthquake.

    (A) herd     (B) school     (C) multitude     (D) quantity

( ) 5. Every September, families of victims _____ those who died in the 911 terrorist attacks in the United States.

    (A) contribute to     (B) inspire to     (C) pay tribute to     (D) comply with

( ) 6. This non-profit organization was designed to help _____ families to apply for social welfare.

    (A) undemonstrative         (B) undeniable

    (C) underprivileged         (D) unconscious

( ) 7. The police officer's actions in rescuing the dying stray dog from the traffic accident were most _____.

    (A) credulous     (B) admirable     (C) vulnerable     (D) questionable

( ) 8. After the 311 disaster in Japan in 2011, many Japanese began to advocate for the _____ of the use of nuclear power.

    (A) authorization     (B) banning     (C) enabling     (D) transaction

07 健康

08 職場學校

09 人格個性

10 社交禮儀

11 金錢買賣

12 社會時事

( ) 9. The new president expressed his determination to eliminate _____ as soon as he took office.

    (A) correlation     (B) correspondence     (C) corporation     (D) corruption

( ) 10. That the terrorists should _____ an undefended civilian airliner aroused international indignation.

    (A) fly     (B) launch     (C) hijack     (D) jettison

( ) 11. The refugee's _____ situation aroused our sympathy.

    (A) dear     (B) dire     (C) decorative     (D) descriptive

( ) 12. Decades of _____ have resulted in a severe reduction in the number of the local plants, which are now no longer a common sight.

    (A) civilization     (B) corruption     (C) collaboration     (D) exploitation

( ) 13. The International Rescue Committee is providing relief supplies to _____.

    (A) the displaced     (B) the drowned

    (C) the deceased     (D) the decapitated

( ) 14. Human _____, which involves controlling people against their will to exploit them for forced labor, sexual exploitation, or both, is a crime.

    (A) resources     (B) donation     (C) sacrifice     (D) trafficking

( ) 15. There was a rumor that there had been a minor accident at the nuclear power plant, but a spokesman for the plant issued a _____.

    (A) denial     (B) intersection     (C) receipt     (D) spontaneity

( ) 16. Taking a photograph in a court is often _____ and sometimes can even be seen as a serious offense.

    (A) prohibited     (B) accumulated     (C) celebrated     (D) disordered

( ) 17. With the fast-growing population plus the drought, the demand of staple foods _____ the supply.

    (A) meets     (B) outweighs     (C) satisfies     (D) exploits

( ) 18. The _____ of the humanitarian rescue wins much applause.

    (A) detention     (B) hindrance     (C) upheaval     (D) operation

07 健康

08 職場學校

09 人格個性

10 社交禮儀

11 金錢買賣

12 社會時事

(  ) 19. Although the city is relatively untroubled by crime in comparison with other cities, there is now more street crime than _____.

    (A) it used to      (B) there used to be (C) was there      (D) it has been

(  ) 20. When it comes to catching the bad guys, a _____ camera is a police officer's best friend.

    (A) medium      (B) protection      (C) surveillance      (D) treasure

(  ) 21. Dutch artist Florentijn Hofman was upset about the arrangement for his Rubber Duck installation _____ in Keelung.

    (A) in show      (B) on display      (C) in sail      (D) for touring

(  ) 22. The harmful effects of pesticides and chemical fertilizers made the farm family decide to take a more ecology-friendly approach to farming for the sake of the land, their own health, and the environment _____.

    (A) at best      (B) in general      (C) at large      (D) in advance

(  ) 23. Many people agree that America is not only a country of wealth and riches, but also a country of homelessness and _____.

    (A) relief      (B) venture      (C) poverty      (D) success

(  ) 24. The man was arrested by the police for producing _____ LV bags.

    (A) authentic      (B) fake      (C) genuine      (D) moderate

(  ) 25. The document was finally proved _____ and accepted by the court.

    (A) authentic      (B) confident      (C) dubious      (D) fragile

(  ) 26. The police officer wanted to come face to face with the ghostly phenomenon and _____ it as a hoax.

    (A) float      (B) instill      (C) object      (D) expose

(  ) 27. A census analysis published in 2011 showed that almost all of the city's population increase since 2000 can _____ by an increase in residents between the ages of 20 and 35.

    (A) be responsible for           (B) be accounted for

    (C) be popular with           (D) be important for

( ) 28. Human began _____ food about 10,000 years ago; otherwise, they would not have developed a stable food source.

(A) acquiring　　(B) delivering　　(C) cultivating　　(D) microwaving

( ) 29. Internet technology has nowadays _____ time and space.

(A) coincided　　(B) collapsed　　(C) collaborated　　(D) consisted

( ) 30. Since the last half of the twentieth century, our way of life has been _____ by gadgets of all types: television sets and DVDs, cell phones and computers, just to name a few.

(A) substantiated　(B) compromised　(C) merchandised　(D) revolutionized

( ) 31. The water of this city comes from a _____ located in the mountains nearby.

(A) ford　　(B) hub　　(C) maze　　(D) reservoir

( ) 32. _____ of energy has become a very important policy for many countries due to the limited resources.

(A) Affirmation　(B) Fascination　(C) Conservation　(D) Observation

( ) 33. Online classes _____ enabling teachers and students to communicate, even when they are across the world from each other.

(A) take care of　　　　　　　(B) make up

(C) make an appointment to　　(D) hold the promise of

( ) 34. If the town were _____ about drinking and driving, I would not worry so much about driving at night.

(A) bitter　　(B) stricter　　(C) bleaker　　(D) stronger

( ) 35. Soon all our natural resources will be used up if we do not _____ our levels of consumption.

(A) calcify　　(B) multiply　　(C) generate　　(D) reduce

( ) 36. More money is needed to improve the _____ of the nation's rural areas including building roads and establishing clinics.

(A) infrastructure　(B) obstacle　　(C) commodities　(D) diagnosis

( ) 37. We must not allow our creative protest to _____ into physical violence.

(A) defect　　(B) betray　　(C) resist　　(D) degenerate

07 健康

08 職場學校

09 人格個性

10 社交禮儀

11 金錢買賣

12 社會時事

( ) 38. According to a recent _____, more people watch television on Sunday night than on any other night.

(A) communication          (B) format

(C) medium                 (D) survey

( ) 39. A national bird survey is to be conducted around the New Year's Day holiday to both celebrate the New Year and _____ public awareness about wildlife protection.

(A) raise          (B) switch          (C) divide          (D) arise

( ) 40. Should the Prime Minister receive another vote of no confidence, she would be forced to _____ her government.

(A) approve          (B) condemn          (C) dissolve          (D) evacuate

( ) 41. The Agency Against Corruption is forced to _____ an investigation into the bribery case of the governor.

(A) abduct          (B) conduct          (C) deduct          (D) induct

( ) 42. Downloading should _____ about two to four minutes. The time needed will depend on the speed of your internet connection.

(A) cost          (B) spend          (C) take          (D) waste

( ) 43. Human knowledge is now in the process of being _____ into always-available digital formats.

(A) convicted          (B) condescended   (C) converted          (D) confronted

( ) 44. They apply military and economic _____ against terrorism to effectively deter its spreading.

(A) monopoly          (B) sanctions          (C) bluffing          (D) exploitation

( ) 45. You can carry a cell phone with you _____ you go but you can't do this with your PC.

(A) however          (B) whichever          (C) wherever          (D) whatever

( ) 46. Located in one of the city's poorer neighborhoods, many old houses in this area have been torn down to _____ for new and better public housing.

(A) date back          (B) fall short          (C) get around          (D) make way

(     ) 47. More and more public _____ stations can be found in places like restaurants, department stores, and airports. Smartphone owners can make use of them when the battery is low.

(A) charging      (B) hacking      (C) fueling      (D) boosting

(     ) 48. _____ their military to become weak, their country might be invaded.

(A) If      (B) Were      (C) Should      (D) Suppose

(     ) 49. Africa has a history of drought and _____, which has had the greatest impact on undeveloped and poor populations.

(A) revenue      (B) famine      (C) harvest      (D) possession

(     ) 50. The spy wrote her message in a secret code, but government intelligence agents were able to _____ the message.

(A) accommodate    (B) decipher      (C) monitor      (D) perish

(     ) 51. Several new government policies are scheduled to _____ today.

(A) take effect      (B) avoid contact    (C) go over      (D) work off

## 標 準 答 案

| | | | | |
|---|---|---|---|---|
| 1.（B） | 2.（C） | 3.（B） | 4.（C） | 5.（C） |
| 6.（C） | 7.（B） | 8.（B） | 9.（D） | 10.（C） |
| 11.（B） | 12.（D） | 13.（A） | 14.（D） | 15.（A） |
| 16.（A） | 17.（B） | 18.（D） | 19.（B） | 20.（C） |
| 21.（B） | 22.（C） | 23.（C） | 24.（B） | 25.（A） |
| 26.（D） | 27.（B） | 28.（C） | 29.（B） | 30.（D） |
| 31.（D） | 32.（C） | 33.（D） | 34.（B） | 35.（D） |
| 36.（A） | 37.（D） | 38.（D） | 39.（A） | 40.（C） |
| 41.（B） | 42.（C） | 43.（C） | 44.（B） | 45.（C） |
| 46.（D） | 47.（C） | 48.（B） | 49.（B） | 50.（B） |
| 51.（A） | | | | |

# memo

PART **2**

精選歷屆考題
＋
完全解析

# 1 航空交通

(　　) 1. When we get to the airport, we first go to the check-in desk where the airline representatives _____ our luggage. 100 英導

    (A) pack　　　　(B) move　　　　(C) weigh　　　　(D) claim

(　　) 2. Even though you have _____ your flight with the airline, you must still be present at the check-in desk on time. 99 英導

    (A) informed　　(B) confirmed　　(C) required　　(D) given

(　　) 3. The flight is scheduled to _____ at eleven o'clock tomorrow. You will have to get to the airport two hours before the takeoff. 99 英導

    (A) land　　　　(B) depart　　　　(C) cancel　　　　(D) examine

(　　) 4. Though most airlines ask their passengers to check in at the airport counter two hours before the flight, some international flights _____ their passengers to be at the airport three hours before departure. 102 英導

    (A) revise　　　　(B) require　　　　(C) record　　　　(D) reveal

(　　) 5. You will get a boarding _____ after completing the check-in. 98 英領

    (A) pass　　　　(B) post　　　　(C) plan　　　　(D) past

(　　) 6. People traveling to a foreign country may need to apply _____ a visa. 98 英領

    (A) for　　　　(B) of　　　　(C) on　　　　(D) to

(　　) 7. When traveling in a foreign country, we need to carry with us several important documents at all times. One of them is our passport together with the _____ permit if that has been so required. 102 英導

    (A) entering　　(B) entry　　　　(C) exit　　　　(D) ego

(　　) 8. Disobeying the airport security rules will _____ a civil penalty. 101 英領

    (A) result in　　(B) make for　　(C) take down　　(D) bring on

(　　) 9. Please examine your luggage carefully before leaving. At the security counter, every item in the luggage has to go through thorough _____. 99 英導

     (A) relation　　(B) invention　　(C) inspection　　(D) observation

(　　) 10. For safety reasons, radios, CD players, and mobile phones are banned on board, and they must remain _____ until the aircraft has landed. 101 英領

     (A) switched on　　(B) switch on　　(C) switch off　　(D) switched off

(　　) 11. Prohibited items in carry-on bags will be confiscated at the checkpoints, and no _____ will be given for them. 101 英領

     (A) argument　　(B) recruitment　　(C) compensation　(D) decision

(　　) 12. All passengers shall go through _____ check before boarding. 98 英領

     (A) security　　(B) activity　　(C) insurance　　(D) deficiency

(　　) 13. When answering questions of the immigration officer, it is advisable to be straight forward and not _____. 102 英導

     (A) historic　　(B) hesitating　　(C) hospitable　　(D) heroic

(　　) 14. On my flight to Tokyo, I asked a flight _____ to bring me an extra pillow. 102 英導

     (A) clerk　　(B) employer　　(C) chauffeur　　(D) attendant

(　　) 15. When I take a flight, I always ask for _____ seat, so it is easier for me to get up and walk around. 98 英導

     (A) a window　　(B) a cabinet　　(C) a middle　　(D) an aisle

(　　) 16. The airplane is cruising at an altitude of 30,000 feet at 700 kilometers per hour. 98 英領

     (A) detecting　　(B) moving　　(C) showing　　(D) speeding

(　　) 17. I was very scared when our flight was passing through _____ from the nearby storm. 101 英導

     (A) turbulence　　(B) breeze　　(C) currency　　(D) brilliance

(　　) 18. Please remain _____ while the plane takes off. 99 英領

     (A) seated　　(B) sitting　　(C) sat　　(D) seating

(　) 19. I found myself _____ an airplane. [100 英領]

(A) in broad　　(B) on board　　(C) abroad　　(D) with boarding

(　) 20. After the plane touches down, we have to remain in our seats until we _____ to the gate. [100 英領]

(A) pass by　　(B) stop over　　(C) take off　　(D) taxi in

(　) 21. When you are ready to get off an airplane, you will be told not to forget your personal _____. [99 英導]

(A) utilities　　(B) belongings　　(C) commodities　(D) works

(　) 22. Passengers _____ to other airlines should report to the information desk on the second floor. [101 英領]

(A) have transferred　　　　　(B) transfer
(C) are transferred　　　　　(D) transferring

(　) 23. Due to the delay, we are not able to catch up with our _____ flight. [102 英領]

(A) connecting　　(B) connected　　(C) connect　　(D) connectional

(　) 24. After disembarking the flight, I went directly to the _____ to pick up my bags and trunks. [100 英領]

(A) airport lounge　　　　　(B) cockpit
(C) runway　　　　　　　　(D) baggage claim

(　) 25. A bus used for public transportation runs a set route; however, a _____ bus travels at the direction of the person or organization that hires it. [101 英領]

(A) catering　　(B) chatter　　(C) charter　　(D) cutter

(　) 26. Some cities do not have passenger loading zones. It is advisable to follow the instruction of the tourist guide to get off or get on the tour bus to _____ safety and comfort. [102 英導]

(A) prevent　　(B) guarantee　　(C) keep away　　(D) attend to

(　) 27. Our hotel provides free _____ service to the airport every day. [99 英領]

(A) accommodation　　　　　(B) communication
(C) transmission　　　　　　(D) shuttle

01 航空交通

02 飯店住宿

03 餐廳飲食

04 旅遊觀光

05 介紹台灣

06 帶團職責

(　　) 28. A: "Excuse me. Can I take this seat?"　B: "Sorry, it is _____." 101 英導

(A) empty　　　　(B) closed　　　　(C) occupied　　　(D) complete

## 標 準 答 案

| | | | | |
|---|---|---|---|---|
| 1. ( C ) | 2. ( B ) | 3. ( B ) | 4. ( B ) | 5. ( A ) |
| 6. ( A ) | 7. ( B ) | 8. ( A ) | 9. ( C ) | 10. ( D ) |
| 11. ( C ) | 12. ( A ) | 13. ( B ) | 14. ( D ) | 15. ( D ) |
| 16. ( B ) | 17. ( A ) | 18. ( A ) | 19. ( B ) | 20. ( D ) |
| 21. ( B ) | 22. ( D ) | 23. ( A ) | 24. ( D ) | 25. ( C ) |
| 26. ( B ) | 27. ( D ) | 28. ( C ) | | |

## 二、試題中譯＋解析

1. When we get to the airport, we first go to the check-in desk where the airline representatives <u>weigh</u> our luggage.

(A) pack 包          (B) move 移動

(C) weigh 秤重        (D) claim 認領

**中譯** 當我們到達機場，首先我們到登機櫃台，此處的航空公司工作人員會將我們的行李<u>秤重</u>。

**解析** check-in desk 為登機櫃台，claim baggage 則為認領行李，在 check-in desk 時服務人員會給你行李存根 baggage claim tag，若行李遺失則可到行李領取中心 baggage claim office / counter / center 請求幫忙。

2. Even though you have <u>confirmed</u> your flight with the airline, you must still be present at the check-in desk on time.

(A) informed 告知       (B) confirmed 確認

(C) required 要求        (D) given 給予

**中譯** 即便你已經跟航空公司確認班機，你還是必須準時到報到櫃檯報到。

**解析** confirm 確認；reconfirm 再次確認。confirm flight 確認班機；confirm reservation 確認預約。

3. The flight is scheduled to <u>depart</u> at eleven o'clock tomorrow. You will have to get to the airport two hours before the takeoff.

(A) land 著陸、抵達      (B) depart 起飛

(C) cancell 取消         (D) examine 檢驗

**中譯** 班機預定於明天 11 點起飛，你必須在出發前 2 個小時抵達機場。

**解析** depart / take off 起飛；land 著陸、抵達。

4. Though most airlines ask their passengers to check in at the airport counter two hours before the flight, some international flights <u>require</u> their passengers to be at the airport three hours before departure.

(A) revise 修正

(B) require 需要

(C) record 記錄

(D) reveal 顯示

**中譯** 雖然多數的航空公司要求乘客於班機起飛前 2 個小時到機場的櫃台登記，有些國際線班機還是需要乘客在起飛 3 小時前就到達機場。

**解析** require sb. to do sth. 要求某人做某事。

5. You will get a boarding <u>pass</u> after completing the check-in.

(A) pass 通行證

(B) post 郵件

(C) plan 計畫

(D) past 過去

**中譯** 在完成登機報到手續之後，你將會拿到一張登機證。

**解析** boarding pass 登機證。

6. People traveling to a foreign country may need to apply <u>for</u> a visa.

(A) for

(B) of

(C) on

(D) to

**中譯** 人們到國外旅行可能需要申請簽證。

**解析** visa 簽證，例句：If you're travelling to the United States, you may need a visa. 如果你到美國旅行，你可能需要簽證。（100 英領）

7. When traveling in a foreign country, we need to carry with us several important documents at all times. One of them is our passport together with the <u>entry</u> permit if that has been so required.

(A) entering 進入

(B) entry 進入

(C) exit 出口

(D) ego 自我

中譯 當在外國旅遊時，我們需要隨身攜帶幾份重要的文件。當被要求出示時，其中一項就是我們的護照和<u>入境</u>許可證。

解析 entry 進入（名詞）；enter 進入（動詞）；permit 允許、許可。

8. Disobeying the airport security rules will <u>result in</u> a civil penalty.

(A) result in 導致

(B) make for 走向

(C) take down 寫下、病倒

(D) bring on 引起

中譯 違反機場安全規定會<u>導致</u>民法的刑責。

解析 result in / lead to 皆為導致的意思。

9. Please examine your luggage carefully before leaving. At the security counter, every item in the luggage has to go through <u>inspection</u>.

(A) relation 關係

(B) invention 發明

(C) inspection 檢查

(D) observation 觀察

中譯 在出發前請仔細檢查你的行李。在安檢櫃檯時，行李內的每一項物品都會被<u>檢查</u>。

解析 examine 以及 inspect 都為檢查之意，但 inspect 更有「權力」，因此這裡的 security counter 使用 inspect。

10. For safety reasons, radios, CD players, and mobile phones are banned on board, and they must remain switched off until the aircraft has landed.

(A) switched on 開機
(B) switch on 開機
(C) switch off 關機
(D) switched off 關機

**中譯** 由於飛安的因素，收音機、CD 播放器、手機都禁止在飛機上使用，且必須保持關機的狀態直到飛機降落。

**解析** on board 以及 in flight 都是在飛機上的意思。ban 禁止，例：There is a ban on smoking. 有一個禁菸令。此處選擇 switched off 表關機的「狀態」，故選 switched。

11. Prohibited items in carry-on bags will be confiscated at the checkpoints, and no compensation will be given for them.

(A) argument 爭論
(B) recruitment 招聘
(C) compensation 補償
(D) decision 決定

**中譯** 隨身行李中的違禁品將會於檢查站被沒收，且沒有任何的補償。

**解析** compensate 補償。延伸考題會有：Please examine your luggage carefully before leaving. At the security counter, every item in the luggage has to go through inspection. 在出發前請仔細檢查你的行李。在安檢櫃台時，行李內的每一項物品都會被檢查。（99 英導）

12. All passengers shall go through security check before boarding.

(A) security 安全
(B) activity 活動
(C) insurance 保險
(D) deficiency 缺乏

**中譯** 上機前所有旅客都應該通過安全檢查。

**解析** security 安全。

13. When answering questions of the immigration officer, it is advisable to be straight forward and not <u>hesitating</u>.

(A) historic 有歷史性的

(B) hesitating 猶豫的

(C) hospitable 好客的

(D) heroic 英勇的

中譯 當回答移民官的問題時，建議實話實說，並且不要猶豫。

解析 the immigration officer 移民局；hesitating 猶豫的。

14. On my flight to Tokyo, I asked a flight <u>attendant</u> to bring me an extra pillow.

(A) clerk 店員

(B) employer 雇主

(C) chauffeur 汽車司機

(D) attendant 空服員

中譯 在前往東京的班機上，我要求空服員給我額外的枕頭。

解析 飛機上常見的人員為 flight attendant 空服員；cabin crew 機組人員；captain 機長。另外，stewardess 為空姐，steward 則為空少。此處由 flight to Tokyo 可猜出答案為 attendant 空服員。

15. When I take a flight, I always ask for <u>an aisle</u> seat, so it is easier for me to get up and walk around.

(A) a window 窗戶

(B) a cabinet 機艙

(C) a middle 中間

(D) an aisle 走道

中譯 當我搭飛機時，我總是要求靠走道的座位，這讓我比較容易起身走動。

解析 當於機場櫃檯 check-in 時，通常可要求劃以下的座位 window seat 靠窗的座位、aisle seat 靠走道的座位、middle seat 中間的座位，由題意 easier for me to get up and walk around 可得知為走道的座位。

01 航空交通

02 飯店住宿

03 餐廳飲食

04 旅遊觀光

05 介紹台灣

06 帶團職責

16. The airplane is <u>cruising</u> at an altitude of 30,000 feet at 700 kilometers per hour.

(A) detecting 偵查

(B) moving 移動

(C) showing 顯示

(D) speeding 加速

**中譯** 飛機目前以每小時 700 公里的速度<u>航行</u>於 30,000 英呎的海拔上。

**解析** cruise 飛行，例句：Airliners now cruise the ocean at great speed. 飛機以高速來越洋飛行。

17. I was very scared when our flight was passing through <u>turbulence</u> from the nearby storm.

(A) turbulence 空中亂流

(B) breeze 微風

(C) currency 貨幣

(D) brilliance 光輝

**中譯** 當飛機通過來自附近暴風圈的<u>亂流</u>時，我真是嚇壞了。

**解析** 機上遇到亂流時，經常會廣播以下注意事項：We are now crossing a zone of turbulence. Please return your seats and keep your seat belts fastened. Thank you. 我們正經過亂流區。請回到座位上並保持安全帶繫緊。謝謝。

18. Please remain <u>seated</u> while the plane takes off.

(A) seated 就座的

(B) sitting 就座

(C) sat 坐

(D) seating 座位數

**中譯** 當飛機起飛時，請保持<u>就座</u>。

**解析** remain + 狀態，故選 seated（過去分詞當成形容詞）。

19. I found myself on board an airplane.

(A) in broad

(B) on board 在飛機上

(C) abroad 在國外

(D) with boarding

中譯 我發現我自己在飛機上。

解析 必考片語：on board 在交通工具上。

20. After the plane touches down, we have to remain in our seats until we taxi in to the gate.

(A) pass by 經過

(B) stop over 短暫停留

(C) take off 起飛

(D) taxi in 飛機在跑道上滑行

中譯 飛機降落後，我們必須待在座位上，直到飛機滑入機坪入口。

解析 touch down 著陸；taxi in 飛機在跑道上滑行。

21. When you are ready to get off an airplane, you will be told not to forget your personal belongings.

(A) utilities 日常所需之物

(B) belongings 個人用品

(C) commodities 商品

(D) works 工作

中譯 當你準備下飛機時，你將會被告知別忘了帶走你的隨身物品。

解析 get off an airplane / a bus / a train 下飛機、巴士、火車；get on an airplane / a bus / a train 上飛機、巴士、火車。

01 航空交通

02 飯店住宿

03 餐廳飲食

04 旅遊觀光

05 介紹台灣

06 帶團職責

22. Passengers transferring to other airlines should report to the information desk on the second floor.

(A) have transferred
(B) transfer
(C) are transferred
(D) transferring

中譯 要轉搭其他班機的旅客請到二樓的櫃台報到。

解析 本題考的文法即簡化形容詞子句的步驟：
(1) 去關係代名詞
(2) 將形容詞子句中的動詞改為現在分詞 Ving
(3) 如遇 be 動詞改為 being，則將 being 省略
例句：Passengers transferring to other airlines should report to the information desk on the second floor.
= Passengers who transfer to other airlines should report to the information desk on the second floor.。

23. Due to the delay, we are not able to catch up with our connecting flight.

(A) connecting
(B) connected
(C) connect
(D) connectional

中譯 因為班機延遲，我們無法趕上我們的轉機班機。

解析 catch up 趕上；connecting flight 轉機班機。

24. After disembarking the flight, I went directly to the baggage claim to pick up my bags and trunks.

(A) airport lounge 機場貴賓室
(B) cockpit 駕駛員座艙
(C) runway 逃亡
(D) baggage claim 行李認領處

中譯 下飛機後，我直接走向行李認領處拿我的包包和行李箱。

解析 常考單字：baggage claim 行李認領處。

25.  A bus used for public transportation runs a set route; however, a <u>charter</u> bus
     travels at the direction of the person or organization that hires it.

   (A) catering 餐飲                       (B) chatter 閒聊

   (C) charter 租賃                        (D) cutter 切割機

   **中譯** 用來當大眾運輸工具的巴士有固定的路線，然而，<u>承租的</u>巴士（遊覽車）
   則會依照租車的人或團體來決定行駛路。

   **解析** charter bus 遊覽車；set route 固定的路線。

26.  Some cities do not have passenger loading zones. It is advisable to follow the
     instruction of the tourist guide to get off or get on the tour bus to <u>guarantee</u>
     safety and comfort.

   (A) prevent 防止                        (B) guarantee 保證

   (C) keep away 避開                      (D) attend to 專心於

   **中譯** 有些城市沒有乘客上下車的指定地方，因此建議遵照遊客指南來上下車以
   <u>確保</u>安全及舒適。

   **解析** zone 地帶、地區；instruction 命令、指示；guarantee 保証。

27.  Our hotel provides free <u>shuttle</u> service to the airport every day.

   (A) accommodation 住宿                  (B) communication 溝通

   (C) transmission 傳輸                   (D) shuttle 接駁工具

   **中譯** 我們飯店每天免費提供到機場的接駁巴士服務。

   **解析** THSR Shuttle Bus 台灣高鐵接駁巴士，如從車站至機場兩點固定來回的，
   即稱 shuttle bus。

01 航空交通

02 飯店住宿

03 餐廳飲食

04 旅遊觀光

05 介紹台灣

06 帶團職責

28. A: "Excuse me. Can I take this seat?" B: "Sorry, it is occupied."

(A) empty 空的　　　　　　　　　(B) closed 關閉的

(C) occupied 佔用　　　　　　　(D) complete 完整的

中譯 A：抱歉。我可以坐這個位子嗎？ B：抱歉，這座位有人坐了。

解析 位子有人坐有兩種常見說法：The seat is occupied / taken.，而詢問位子是否有人坐則可以說：Is this seat taken?。

01
航空交通

02
飯店住宿

03
餐廳飲食

04
旅遊觀光

05
介紹台灣

06
帶團職責

# 2 飯店住宿

## 一、歷屆考題精選

( ) 1. If you plan and time it right, some home _____ can let you stay somewhere for free. 101 英導

    (A) abiding    (B) boosting    (C) meditating    (D) swapping

( ) 2. A _____ room or seat is being kept for someone rather than given or sold to someone else. 100 英導

    (A) refrained    (B) restricted    (C) reserved    (D) reversed

( ) 3. You don't have to worry about where to stay tonight. My friend in downtown area will find you a night's _____ . 99 英導

    (A) station    (B) lodging    (C) housekeeper    (D) seat

( ) 4. During the holidays, most major hotels will be fully booked. An _____ is to try and find a guest house near your desired destination. 98 英導

    (A) exchange    (B) alternative    (C) equivalent    (D) applause

( ) 5. Jessica's customers complained because they had to pay twice for their _____. 100 英領

    (A) accommodation        (B) acculturation

    (C) accusation           (D) assimilation

( ) 6. Reservations for hotel accommodation should be made in _____ to make sure rooms are available. 98 英領

    (A) advance    (B) advanced    (C) advances    (D) advancing

( ) 7. The hotels in the resort areas are fully booked in the summer. It would be very difficult to find any _____ then. 102 英領

    (A) vacations    (B) visitors    (C) views    (D) vacancies

(　　) 8. Either the _____ or the cashier's desk of the hotel can help us figure out the exact amount of money and other details we need to join a local tour. `102 英導`

    (A) receiving     (B) reception     (C) resignation     (D) recognition

(　　) 9. Tourists have a wide range of budget and tastes, and a wide variety of resorts and hotels have developed to _____ for them. `101 英導`

    (A) cater     (B) desire     (C) mourn     (D) pray

(　　) 10. Guest: I have made a reservation for a suite overnight.
        Clerk: Yes, we have your reservation right here. Would you please fill out this _____ form and show me your ID? `102 英領`

    (A) reimbursement         (B) registration

    (C) refund         (D) registrar

(　　) 11. A _____ breakfast of coffee and rolls is served in the lobby between 7 and 10 am. `102 英領`

    (A) complete         (B) complimentary

    (C) continuous         (D) complicate

(　　) 12. Working as a hotel _____ means that your focus is to ensure that the needs and requests of hotel guests are met, and that each guest has a memorable stay. `101 英領`

    (A) commander     (B) celebrity     (C) concierge     (D) candidate

(　　) 13. Client: What are this hotel's _____ ?
        Agent: It includes a great restaurant, a fitness center, an outdoor pool, and much more, such as in-room Internet access, 24-hour room service, and trustworthy babysitting, etc. `101 英領`

    (A) installations     (B) utilities     (C) amenities     (D) surroundings

(　　) 14. Is there any problem _____ my reservation? `100 英領`

    (A) in     (B) of     (C) to     (D) with

(     ) 15. Guest: _____.

        Hotel clerk: Our standard room costs NT$3,500 per night. `99 英領`

        (A) Is room service included in your price?

        (B) What is your room rate?

        (C) How much do you charge for a luxury room?

        (D) Do I have to pay for an extra bed?

(     ) 16. It's difficult to find a hotel with a/an _____ room in high season. `99 英領`

        (A) occupied      (B) vacant      (C) lank      (D) unattended

(     ) 17. The _____ at the information desk in a hotel provides traveling information to guests. `99 英領`

        (A) bellhop      (B) concierge      (C) butler      (D) bartender

(     ) 18. When you stay in a hotel, what basic _____ do you think are necessary? `102 英領`

        (A) activities      (B) capabilities      (C) facilities      (D) abilities

01 航空交通
02 飯店住宿
03 餐廳飲食
04 旅遊觀光
05 介紹台灣
06 帶團職責

# 標準答案

| | | | | |
|---|---|---|---|---|
| 1.（D） | 2.（C） | 3.（B） | 4.（B） | 5.（A） |
| 6.（A） | 7.（D） | 8.（B） | 9.（A） | 10.（B） |
| 11.（B） | 12.（C） | 13.（C） | 14.（D） | 15.（B） |
| 16.（B） | 17.（B） | 18.（C） | | |

## 二、試題中譯＋解析

1. If you plan and time it right, some home <u>swapping</u> can let you stay somewhere for free.

(A) abiding 持久的　　　　　　(B) boosting 推動的

(C) meditating 沉思　　　　　　(D) swapping 交換

中譯 如果你計劃的時間恰當，有些交換住家可讓你免費入住。

解析 swap 交換，另一個常見的交換為 exchange，如考題：I really like your scarf. Can I exchange my hat for that? 我真的很喜歡你的圍巾。我可以用我的帽子交換嗎？兩者意思都為交換，但 exchange 比較正式，而 swap 較為口語。

2. A <u>reserved</u> room or seat is being kept for someone rather than given or sold to someone else.

(A) refrained 制止的　　　　　　(B) restricted 受限制的

(C) reserved 保留的　　　　　　(D) reversed 顛倒的

中譯 保留的房間或是座位是代表替某些人而保留，而不能再提供或出售給他人。

解析 reserved （被）保留的；reservations 預定。

3. You don't have to worry about where to stay tonight. My friend in downtown area will find you a night's <u>lodging</u>.

(A) station 車站　　　　　　(B) lodging 住宿

(C) housekeeper 管家　　　　　　(D) seat 座位

中譯 你不需要去擔心今晚在哪過夜。我在市區的朋友會幫你找到住宿一晚的地方。

解析 由 where to stay tonight 可推知答案為 lodging 住宿。

4. During the holidays, most major hotels will be fully booked. An <u>alternative</u> is to try and find a guest house near your desired destination.

(A) exchange 交換

(B) alternative 選擇

(C) equivalent 相當於

(D) applause 鼓掌

中譯 假期期間，大部分的主要飯店都被訂滿了。其他的<u>備案</u>只得試著找看看接近你目的地附近的民宿。

解析 alternative 常見的同義詞有 choice / substitute / replacement。

5. Jessica's customers complained because they had to pay twice for their <u>accommodation</u>.

(A) accommodation 住宿

(B) acculturation 文化適應

(C) accusation 指控

(D) assimilation 吸收

中譯 潔西卡的客人抱怨他們必須支付 2 次<u>住宿</u>費用。

解析 accommodation 住宿，例句：Reservations for hotel accommodation should be made in advance to make sure rooms are available. 旅館的訂房應提早訂，才能確保有房間。（98 英領）

6. Reservations for hotel accommodation should be made in <u>advance</u> to make sure rooms are available.

(A) advance

(B) advanced

(C) advances

(D) advancing

中譯 旅館的訂房應<u>提早</u>預訂，才能確保有房間。

解析 in advance 事先。

01

航空交通

02

飯店住宿

03

餐廳飲食

04

旅遊觀光

05

介紹台灣

06

帶團職責

7. The hotels in the resort areas are fully booked in the summer. It would be very difficult to find any <u>vacancies</u> then.

(A) vacations 假期
(B) visitors 旅客
(C) views 觀點
(D) vacancies 空缺

**中譯** 度假勝地的飯店在夏天時被訂滿了。那時很難找到空房。

**解析** 訂房相關議題經常會考到，如：Reservations for hotel accommodation should be made in advance to make sure rooms are available. 旅館的訂房應提早訂，才能確保有房間。（98 英領）

8. Either the <u>reception</u> or the cashier's desk of the hotel can help us figure out the exact amount of money and other details we need to join a local tour.

(A) receiving 接受
(B) reception 接待處
(C) resignation 辭職
(D) recognition 讚譽

**中譯** 我們可以在飯店的接待處或是收銀台，尋找幫我們釐清正確金額的協助，以及得到其他我們想參加當地旅遊的細節。

**解析** reception 接待處；figure out 理解、明白。

9. Tourists have a wide range of budget and tastes, and a wide variety of resorts and hotels have developed to <u>cater</u> for them.

(A) cater 滿足、投合
(B) desire 期望
(C) mourn 哀悼
(D) pray 祈求

**中譯** 觀光客有不同的預算以及品味，因此也有各式各樣的度假村和飯店來符合他們的需求。

**解析** cater 除了迎合的意思外，亦有承辦伙食之意。cater for the need of the customers 迎合顧客的需求。

10. Guest: I have made a reservation for a suite overnight.

    Clerk: Yes, we have your reservation right here. Would you please fill out this registration form and show me your ID?

    (A) reimbursement 報銷

    (B) registration 註冊

    (C) refund 退款

    (D) registrar 註冊員

    中譯 客人：我已經訂了今晚的套房。

    服務生：是的，我們這邊已經有您的訂位紀錄。麻煩您填上這個登記表格並出示您的身分證件。

    解析 由 fill out form 可知為填寫某個表格，通常住宿時都要填寫 registration form 登記表格。

11. A complimentary breakfast of coffee and rolls is served in the lobby between 7 and 10 am.

    (A) complete 完成

    (B) complimentary 免費

    (C) continuous 連續

    (D) complicate 複雜

    中譯 免費的早餐於早上 7 點到 10 點在大廳供應，提供咖啡和捲餅。

    解析 complimentary 免費，例句：All drinks served on the airplane are complimentary. 所有在飛機上所供應的飲料都是免費的。（98 英領）

12. Working as a hotel concierge means that your focus is to ensure that the needs and requests of hotel guests are met, and that each guest has a memorable stay.

    (A) commander 指揮官

    (B) celebrity 名人

    (C) concierge 門房

    (D) candidate 候選人

    中譯 身為飯店的門房，代表你要確保客戶的需求被滿足，讓每位房客有個難忘的住宿回憶。

    解析 concierge 門房；concierge service 管家服務，其他例句：The concierge at the information desk in a hotel provides traveling information to guests. 旅館服務台人員提供旅遊資訊給客人。（99 英領）

01 航空交通

02 飯店住宿

03 餐廳飲食

04 旅遊觀光

05 介紹台灣

06 帶團職責

13. Client: What are this hotel's <u>amenities</u>?

Agent: It includes a great restaurant, a fitness center, an outdoor pool, and much more, such as in-room Internet access, 24-hour room service, and trustworthy babysitting, etc.

(A) installations 裝置     (B) utilities 實用

(C) amenities 設施     (D) surroundings 環境

中譯 客戶：這間飯店有什麼設施？

代理商：有一間很棒的餐廳、健身房、一座戶外游泳池，其他設施像是室內網路、24 小時客房服務和值得信賴的保母服務。

解析 由 a great restaurant、a fitness center、an outdoor pool 可推知是 amenities 設施。

14. Is there any problem <u>with</u> my reservation?

(A) in       (B) of

(C) to       (D) with

中譯 我的預約有任何問題嗎？

解析 某事有問題，用 with problem。

15. Guest: <u>What is your room rate?</u>

Hotel clerk: Our standard room costs NT$3,500 per night.

(A) Is room service included in your price? 客房服務有包含在價錢裡嗎？

(B) What is your room rate? 你們的房價是多少？

(C) How much do you charge for a luxury room? 對於豪華房間你們收費多少？

(D) Do I have to pay for an extra bed? 我需要替多餘的床付費嗎？

中譯 客人：你們的房價是多少？

飯店人員：我們的標準房每晚要價 3,500 元。

解析 由 NT$3,500 per night 可推知為詢問房價。standard 標準。

16. It's difficult to find a hotel with a/an <u>vacant</u> room in high season.

   (A) occupied 已占滿的　　　　　　(B) vacant 空著的

   (C) lank 細長的　　　　　　　　(D) unattended 沒人照顧的

   中譯 在旺季時很難找到有空房的飯店。

   解析 vacant 形容詞，空的；vacancy 名詞，空房、空位。

17. The <u>concierge</u> at the information desk in a hotel provides traveling information to guests.

   (A) bellhop 旅館侍者　　　　　　(B) concierge 旅館服務台人員

   (C) butler 領班　　　　　　　　(D) bartender 酒保

   中譯 旅館服務台人員提供旅遊資訊給客人。

   解析 concierge 旅館服務台人員。

18. When you stay in a hotel, what basic <u>facilities</u> do you think are necessary?

   (A) activities 活動　　　　　　(B) capabilities 能力

   (C) facilities 設施　　　　　　(D) abilities 能力

   中譯 當你住在飯店時，你認為哪些基本的設備是必須的？

   解析 facilities 設施為重點單字。考題例句如：Guest：What facilities do you have in your hotel? 客人：你們飯店有什麼設施？ Hotel clerk：We have a fitness center, a swimming pool, two restaurants, a beauty parlor, and a boutique. 飯店服務員：我們有一座健身中心、一座游泳池、兩間餐廳、一間美容室和女裝店。（99 英領）

01 航空交通

02 飯店住宿

03 餐廳飲食

04 旅遊觀光

05 介紹台灣

06 帶團職責

# 3 餐廳飲食

## 一、歷屆考題精選

( ) 1. If I had called to reserve a table at Royal House one week earlier, we _____ a gourmet reunion dinner last night. 101 英領

(A) can have

(B) will have had

(C) would have had

(D) would have eating

( ) 2. Waiter: Are you ready to order, sir?

Guest: _____ 99 英導

(A) Your food looks tasty.

(B) OK, I'll have that!

(C) I don't eat meat.

(D) I think so. But what is your specialty?

( ) 3. Our _____ wants to reserve a table for dinner tomorrow. 100 英領

(A) alcoholic   (B) client   (C) gambler   (D) retailer

( ) 4. Would you like to order a/an _____ or refer to the à la carte menu? 100 英領

(A) complex meal

(B) singular meal

(C) set meal

(D) united meal

( ) 5. This restaurant features _____ Northern Italian dishes that reflect the true flavors of Italy. 101 英導

(A) disposable   (B) confident   (C) authentic   (D) dimensional

( ) 6. At the annual food festival, you can _____ a wide variety of delicacies. 101 英領

(A) sample   (B) deliver   (C) cater   (D) reduce

( ) 7. The cake was _____, and tasted bad. 99 英導

(A) stale   (B) nutritious   (C) familiar   (D) indispensable

(　　) 8. Baked goods are not a staple of a traditional Chinese diet, but they have been quickly _____ among China's urban middle classes over the last 10 years. [100 英導]

    (A) dashing on    (B) moving on    (C) catching on    (D) getting on

(　　) 9. People with a low _____ for spicy food should not try the "Hot and Spicy Chicken Soup" served by this restaurant: it brings tears to my eyes. [99 英導]

    (A) prejudice    (B) insistence    (C) tolerance    (D) indulgence

(　　) 10. Many restaurants in Paris offer a _____ of snails for guests to taste. [99 英領]

    (A) plate    (B) group    (C) chunk    (D) loaf

## 標準答案

| | | | | |
|---|---|---|---|---|
| 1.（C） | 2.（D） | 3.（B） | 4.（C） | 5.（C） |
| 6.（A） | 7.（A） | 8.（C） | 9.（C） | 10.（A） |

01
航空交通

02
飯店住宿

03
餐廳飲食

04
旅遊觀光

05
介紹台灣

06
帶團職責

1. If I had called to reserve a table at Royal House one week earlier, we would have had a gourmet reunion dinner last night.

   (A) can have

   (B) will have had

   (C) would have had

   (D) would have eating

   中譯 如果我早一個星期打電話去皇家餐廳預約，我們昨晚可能就能享有美味的團圓飯。

   解析 與過去事實相反，條件子句動詞須用「had + p.p.」，主要子句則是「主詞 + 助動詞 + have + p.p.」。

2. Waiter: Are you ready to order, sir?
   Guest: I think so. But what is your specialty?

   (A) Your food looks tasty. 你的食物看起很好吃。

   (B) OK, I'll have that! 好的，我要這個！

   (C) I don't eat meat. 我不吃肉。

   (D) I think so. But what is your specialty? 應該是。你們的招牌菜是什麼？

   中譯 服務生：你準備好要點了嗎，先生？
       客人：應該是。你們的招牌菜是什麼？

   解析 specialty 招牌菜。

3. Our client wants to reserve a table for dinner tomorrow.

   (A) alcoholic 酗酒

   (B) client 顧客

   (C) gambler 賭徒

   (D) retailer 零售商

   中譯 我們的客人想要為明天晚餐預先訂桌。

   解析 reserve 預約、預訂；reserve a table 訂桌；make reservation 預約。

4. Would you like to order a/an <u>set meal</u> or refer to the à la carte menu?

(A) complex meal

(B) singular meal

(C) set meal 套餐

(D) united meal

中譯 你想要點套餐，還是參考每日菜單？

解析 set meal 套餐。

5. This restaurant features <u>authentic</u> Northern Italian dishes that reflect the true flavors of Italy.

(A) disposable 可丟棄的

(B) confident 有信心的

(C) authentic 道地的

(D) dimensional 尺寸的

中譯 這間餐廳的特色為義大利口味的道地北義大利菜。

解析 由 reflect the true flavors of Italy 可知，是非常 authentic 道地的。reflect 反射、反映，此作反映。

6. At the annual food festival, you can <u>sample</u> a wide variety of delicacies.

(A) sample 品嚐

(B) deliver 傳遞

(C) cater 承辦宴席

(D) reduce 減少

中譯 在一年一度的美食節，你可以品嚐各類佳餚。

解析 由 food festival 與 delicacies 得知，為 sample 品嚐。此處的 sample 也可以用 taste 品嚐來替換。delicacy 美味、佳餚。

7. The cake was <u>stale</u>, and tasted bad.

(A) stale 不新鮮的（腐壞的）

(B) nutritious 營養的

(C) familiar 相似的

(D) indispensable 必要的

中譯 這個蛋糕不新鮮了，且嚐起來不好吃。

解析 stale 不新鮮的；fresh 新鮮的。由 tasted bad 可得知蛋糕已 stale 不新鮮的（腐壞的）。

8. Baked goods are not a staple of a traditional Chinese diet, but they have been quickly catching on among China's urban middle classes over the last 10 years.

(A) dashing on 猛衝

(B) moving on 繼續前進

(C) catching on 流行

(D) getting on 進展

中譯 烘焙食品並非傳統中國菜的主菜，但過去 10 年，已經在中國城市的中產階級之間迅速流行。

解析 staple 主要產品、主食；catch on 有兩種意思：① understand 理解 ② become popular 流行起來。

9. People with a low tolerance for spicy food should not try the "Hot and Spicy Chicken Soup" served by this restaurant: it brings tears to my eyes.

(A) prejudice 偏見

(B) insistence 堅持

(C) tolerance 容忍

(D) indulgence 放縱

中譯 對於辛辣食物容忍度低的人不應該嘗試此餐廳供應的麻辣雞湯，它讓我眼淚直流。

解析 tolerance 容忍度為名詞，tolerable 則為可容忍的（形容詞）。

10. Many restaurants in Paris offer a plate of snails for guests to taste.

(A) plate 盤

(B) group 團體

(C) chunk 大塊

(D) loaf 條

中譯 巴黎的許多餐廳提供一整盤的蝸牛給客戶吃。

解析 plate 盤子；bowl 碗。

01
航空交通

02
飯店住宿

03
餐廳飲食

04
旅遊觀光

05
介紹台灣

06
帶團職責

# 4 旅遊觀光

## 一、歷屆考題精選

( ) 1. The developments of technology and transport infrastructure have made many types of tourism more _____. 101 英導

    (A) affordable     (B) considerable   (C) exclusive     (D) illusive

( ) 2. The prosperity of _____ tourism is related to the policy of our government. 100 英領

    (A) domestic      (B) duplicated     (C) dumb       (D) detour

( ) 3. Increasing tourism infrastructure to meet domestic and international demands has raised concerns about the _____ on Taiwan's natural environment. 102 英導

    (A) impact       (B) input         (C) itinerary     (D) identity

( ) 4. Before you step out for a foreign trip, you should _____ about the accommodations, climate, and culture of the country you are visiting. 101 英領

    (A) insure        (B) require       (C) inquire      (D) adjust

( ) 5. All the _____ on the city rail map are color-coded so that a traveler knows which direction she/he should take. 99 英領

    (A) routes        (B) roads        (C) sights       (D) systems

( ) 6. Don't over pack when you travel because you can always _____ new goods along the way. 101 英導

    (A) watch        (B) acquire       (C) promote     (D) throw

( ) 7. Go to the office at the Tourist Information Center and they will give you a _____ about sightseeing. 99 英領

    (A) destination   (B) deposit      (C) baggage     (D) brochure

( ) 8. In order to _____ the architecture of the building, you really need to get off the bus and get closer to it. 99 英導

    (A) absorb       (B) exhaust      (C) beware      (D) appreciate

(　) 9.　Do not draw attention to yourself by _____ large amounts of cash or expensive jewelry. 100 英領

(A) display　　　(B) displayed　　　(C) displays　　　(D) displaying

(　) 10.　If you take a _____ holiday, all your transport, accommodation, and even meals and excursions will be taken care of. 99 英領

(A) leisure　　　(B) business　　　(C) package　　　(D) luxury

(　) 11.　Your detailed _____ is as follows: leaving Taipei on the 14 of June and arriving at Tokyo on the same day at noon. 102 英領

(A) item　　　(B) identification　(C) itinerary　　　(D) inscription

(　) 12.　Do they have a _____ plan if it rains tomorrow and they can't go hiking? 102 英領

(A) convenience　(B) contingency　(C) continuous　(D) constituent

(　) 13.　I just spent a relaxing afternoon taking a _____ along the river-walk. 101 英導

(A) trot　　　(B) dip　　　(C) stroll　　　(D) look

(　) 14.　I love to go wandering; often I take my bicycle to _____ around the countryside on weekends. 102 英導

(A) tour　　　(B) speed　　　(C) stroll　　　(D) drive

(　) 15.　His one ambition in life was to go on _____ to Kenya to photograph lions and tigers. 100 英導

(A) safari　　　(B) voyage　　　(C) ferry　　　(D) yacht

(　) 16.　They _____ all around the Mediterranean for eight weeks last summer and stopped off at a number of uninhabited islands. 100 英導

(A) campaigned　(B) cruised　　　(C) commuted　(D) circulated

(　) 17.　Even though John has returned from Bali for two weeks, he is still _____ the memories of his holidays. 102 英領

(A) missing　　　(B) forgetting　　　(C) savoring　　　(D) remembering

( ) 18. Thailand is a pleasure for the senses. Tourists come from around the world to visit the nation's gold-adorned temples and sample its delicious _____. `102 英導`

    (A) sky diving                 (B) cuisine

    (C) bungee jumping          (D) horseracing

( ) 19. Paris' Cultural Calendar may be bursting with fairs, salons and auctions, but nothing can quite _____ the Biennale des Antiquaires. `102 英導`

    (A) compete with           (B) comment on

    (C) complain about        (D) compose of

( ) 20. Macau, a small city west of Hong Kong, has turned itself into a casino headquarters in the East. Its economy now depends very much on tourists and visitors whose number is more than double that of the local _____. `102 英導`

    (A) man       (B) shop       (C) worker       (D) population

( ) 21. Strictly speaking, Venice is now more of a _____ city than a maritime business city. `102 英導`

    (A) waterfront     (B) Italian       (C) tourism       (D) modern

( ) 22. I like Rome very much because it has many historic _____ and it is friendly to visitors. `102 英導`

    (A) stories       (B) glory       (C) sites       (D) giants

( ) 23. With its palaces, sculptured parks, concert halls, and museums, Vienna is a _____ city in cultures. `101 英導`

    (A) chronic       (B) elite       (C) provincial       (D) steeped

( ) 24. The oldest of all the main Hawaiian islands, Kauai is _____ for its secluded beaches, scenic waterfalls, and jungle hikes. `101 英導`

    (A) due       (B) known       (C) neutral       (D) ripe

( ) 25. Hong Kong is one of the world's most thrilling Chinese New Year travel destinations. The _____ is the spectacular fireworks display on the second day of the New Year. `100 英導`

    (A) highlight     (B) limelight       (C) insight       (D) twilight

01 航空交通
02 飯店住宿
03 餐廳飲食
04 旅遊觀光
05 介紹台灣
06 帶團職責

( ) 26. This monument _____ the men and women who died during the war. `98 英導`

(A) presides    (B) honors    (C) monitors    (D) memorizes

( ) 27. The _____ of the New Seven Wonders of the World campaign were announced on July 7th, 2007, and the Great Wall of China is one of the winners. `98 英導`

(A) sources    (B) results    (C) revolts    (D) shelters

( ) 28. _____ fireworks shows lit up the sky of cities around the world as people celebrated the start of 2012. `101 英導`

(A) Invisible    (B) Spectacular    (C) Dull    (D) Endangered

( ) 29. The landscape of this natural park is best seen on bike or foot, and there are _____ trails in the area. All paths offer breath-taking sceneries. `101 英導`

(A) sole    (B) simultaneous    (C) numerous    (D) indifferent

( ) 30. The view of _____ waterfalls in the rainforest is spectacular. `101 英導`

(A) ascending    (B) cascading    (C) flourishing    (D) overflowing

( ) 31. Costa Brava is a popular tourist destination in northeastern Spain, thanks to its _____ climate, beautiful beaches, and charming towns. `101 英導`

(A) dreadful    (B) contemporary    (C) moderate    (D) bitter

( ) 32. A good place to end a tour of Rome is the Trevi Fountain. Legend has it that if you toss a single coin into the Trevi, you are _____ a return to Rome. `100 英導`

(A) preserved    (B) obtained    (C) dedicated    (D) guaranteed

( ) 33. Palm Beach is a coastline _____ where thousands of tourists from all over the world spend their summer vacation. `101 英領`

(A) airport    (B) resort    (C) pavement    (D) passage

# 標 準 答 案

| 1. （A） | 2. （A） | 3. （A） | 4. （C） | 5. （A） |
|---------|---------|---------|---------|---------|
| 6. （B） | 7. （D） | 8. （D） | 9. （D） | 10. （C） |
| 11. （C） | 12. （B） | 13. （C） | 14. （A） | 15. （A） |
| 16. （B） | 17. （C） | 18. （B） | 19. （A） | 20. （D） |
| 21. （C） | 22. （C） | 23. （D） | 24. （B） | 25. （A） |
| 26. （B） | 27. （B） | 28. （B） | 29. （C） | 30. （B） |
| 31. （C） | 32. （D） | 33. （B） | | |

01 航空交通

02 飯店住宿

03 餐廳飲食

04 旅遊觀光

05 介紹台灣

06 帶團職責

## 二、試題中譯＋解析

1. The developments of technology and transport infrastructure have made many types of tourism more <u>affordable</u>.

(A) affordable 提供得起的

(B) considerable 值得考慮的

(C) exclusive 排外的

(D) illusive 錯覺的

中譯 科技以及交通建設的發達，使人能夠<u>負擔得起</u>許多不同型態的旅遊。

解析 afford 提供、花費、負擔得起；affordable 提供得起的，如 affordable housing 買得起的房子；affordable risk 承擔得起的風險；development 生長、進化、發展，此作發達。

2. The prosperity of <u>domestic</u> tourism is related to the policy of our government.

(A) domestic 國內的

(B) duplicated 複製的

(C) dumb 啞的

(D) detour 繞道而行

中譯 <u>國內</u>旅遊業的興盛與我們政府政策有關。

解析 domestic 國內的；international 國外的；domestic flight 國內航班；international flight 國際航班；prosperity 興旺、繁榮。可由 our government 推論和 domestic 國內的有關。

3. Increasing tourism infrastructure to meet domestic and international demands has raised concerns about the <u>impact</u> on Taiwan's natural environment.

(A) impact 影響

(B) input 投入

(C) itinerary 旅程

(D) identity 身分

中譯 增加旅遊業的公共建設來滿足國內外的需求，對於台灣的天然環境而言已經有所<u>影響</u>。

解析 infrastructure 公共建設；impact 影響。

01 航空交通

02 飯店住宿

03 餐廳飲食

04 旅遊觀光

05 介紹台灣

06 帶團職責

4. Before you step out for a foreign trip, you should <u>inquire</u> about the accommodations, climate, and culture of the country you are visiting.

(A) insure 保險          (B) require 需要

(C) inquire 詢問        (D) adjust 調整

**中譯** 在你踏出國外旅程之前,你應該先詢問有關那個國家的住宿、天氣和文化。

**解析** step out 踏出;inquire 詢問;accommodations 住宿。

5. All the <u>routes</u> on the city rail map are color-coded so that a traveler knows which direction she/he should take.

(A) routes 路線         (B) roads 道路

(C) sights 景觀         (D) systems 系統

**中譯** 城市鐵路地圖的所有路線用顏色區分,這樣旅人才知道他們要搭哪個方向的列車。

**解析** routes 路線;a train / bus route 火車 / 公車路線。例句:The hiking route of the Shitoushan Trail is not steep and so is suitable for most people, including the elderly and young children. 獅頭山步道的健行路線不太陡峭,所以適合大多數的人,包含老人和小孩。 100 英導

6. Don't over pack when you travel because you can always <u>acquire</u> new goods along the way.

(A) watch 觀看         (B) acquire 得到

(C) promote 晉升       (D) throw 投

**中譯** 旅行時不用帶太多東西,因為你總是可以在旅途中取得新物品。

**解析** acquire 得到、獲取之意。例:We must work hard to acquire a good knowledge of English. 我們必須用功學習才能精通英語。goods 商品、貨物。

7. Go to the office at the Tourist Information Center and they will give you a brochure about sightseeing.

(A) destination 目的地　　　　(B) deposit 存款

(C) baggage 行李　　　　(D) brochure 手冊

中譯 去旅遊中心，他們會給你一本觀光手冊。

解析 Tourist information center 通常會提供 brochure 手冊以及 map 地圖。

8. In order to appreciate the architecture of the building, you really need to get off the bus and get closer to it.

(A) absorb 吸收　　　　(B) exhaust 精疲力盡

(C) beware 當心　　　　(D) appreciate 欣賞

中譯 為了欣賞建築物的結構，你真的需要下車，並靠它近一點。

解析 In order to + V 為了做某事；appreciate 欣賞（動詞）；appreciation of art 藝術鑑賞力。

9. Do not draw attention to yourself by displaying large amounts of cash or expensive jewelry.

(A) display 炫耀　　　　(B) displayed

(C) displays　　　　(D) displaying

中譯 不要藉由展示大量的現金和貴重首飾，引起別人對自己的注意力。

解析 draw attention to 引起對～的注意；by Ving 藉由～的動作。

10. If you take a package holiday, all your transport, accommodation, and even meals and excursions will be taken care of.

(A) leisure 空閒

(B) business 事業

(C) package 包裹

(D) luxury 奢侈

中譯 如果你選擇套裝行程，你所有的交通、住宿和餐食、旅遊都會被打點好。

解析 package holiday 套裝行程；excursion 遠足。

11. Your detailed itinerary is as follows: leaving Taipei on the 14th of June and arriving at Tokyo on the same day at noon.

(A) item 物件

(B) identification 識別

(C) itinerary 行程

(D) inscription 碑文

中譯 你詳細的行程如下：6 月 14 日從台北出發，當天中午抵達東京。

解析 itinerary 行程，例句：The manager gave a copy of his itinerary to his secretary and asked her to arrange some business meetings for him during his stay in Sydney. 經理交給他的祕書一份旅行計畫，並且要求她幫他在雪梨安排一些業務會議。（101 英領）

12. Do they have a contingency plan if it rains tomorrow and they can't go hiking?

(A) convenience 方便

(B) contingency 應變

(C) continuous 連續

(D) constituent 成分

中譯 如果明天下雨他們不能健行的話，他們有緊急備案嗎？

解析 考 contingency plan 備案的用法。

13. I just spent a relaxing afternoon taking a stroll along the river-walk.

(A) trot 小跑

(B) dip 浸泡

(C) stroll 散步

(D) look 看

中譯 我剛剛沿著河邊散步，度過了一個悠閒的下午。

解析 由 spent a relaxing afternoon 可知為 stroll 散步。

14. I love to go wandering; often I take my bicycle to tour around the countryside on weekends.

(A) tour 旅行

(B) speed 速度

(C) stroll 漫步

(D) drive 開車

中譯 我喜歡閒逛，我周末常常騎腳踏車到鄉間旅行。

解析 wander 漫遊、閒逛；take / have / go for a stroll 散步、漫步。

15. His one ambition in life was to go on safari to Kenya to photograph lions and tigers.

(A) safari 狩獵遠征

(B) voyage 航程

(C) ferry 渡船

(D) yacht 遊艇

中譯 他畢生的雄心之一就是到非洲肯亞狩獵遠征，拍獅子和老虎。

解析 由 lions and tigers 可知為 safari 狩獵遠征。ambition 雄心、抱負。

16. They cruised all around the Mediterranean for eight weeks last summer and stopped off at a number of uninhabited islands.

(A) campaigned 參加活動

(B) cruised 巡遊

(C) commuted 通勤

(D) circulated 流通

中譯 他們去年夏天航遊地中海 8 週，並在一些無人島上短暫停留。

解析 由 Mediterranean 可知答案為 cruised 巡遊。cruise ship 載客長途航行的遊輪；uninhabited 無人居住的、杳無人跡的。

17. Even though John has returned from Bali for two weeks, he is still <u>savoring</u> the memories of his holidays.

(A) missing 想念

(B) forgetting 忘記

(C) savoring 細細品味

(D) remembering 記得

中譯 即便約翰已經從峇里島回來兩個星期了，他仍然對他的假期回憶<u>念念不忘</u>。

解析 savor 細細品味。savor 在此即為 enjoy 的意思。

18. Thailand is a pleasure for the senses. Tourists come from around the world to visit the nation's gold-adorned temples and sample its delicious <u>cuisine</u>.

(A) sky diving 跳傘

(B) cuisine 美食

(C) bungee jumping 高空彈跳

(D) horseracing 賽馬

中譯 泰國是個讓人感官感到愉悅的地方。來自世界各地的觀光客來拜訪此國家以黃金裝飾的廟宇並品嚐<u>美食</u>。

解析 重點單字為 cuisine 美食。

19. Paris' Cultural Calendar may be bursting with fairs, salons and auctions, but nothing can quite <u>compete with</u> the Biennale des Antiquaires.

(A) compete with 比得上

(B) comment on 評論

(C) complain about 抱怨

(D) compose of 由～組成

中譯 巴黎的文化節目可能有展覽、講座和拍賣會，但沒有一個可以和巴黎古董<u>雙年展相比</u>。

解析 bursting with 充滿；auction 拍賣；compete with 比得上。

01 航空交通

02 飯店住宿

03 餐廳飲食

04 旅遊觀光

05 介紹台灣

06 帶團職責

20. Macau, a small city west of Hong Kong, has turned itself into a casino headquarters in the East. Its economy now depends very much on tourists and visitors whose number is more than double that of the local population.

(A) man 男人

(B) shop 商店

(C) worker 工人

(D) population 人口

中譯 澳門，位於香港西邊的小城市，現在已成為東方的賭場總部。其經濟仰賴比當地人口多上兩倍的觀光客。

解析 headquarters 總部、總公司。由 tourists and visitors 可推論是比人數，故選 population。

21. Strictly speaking, Venice is now more of a tourism city than a maritime business city.

(A) waterfront 濱水地區

(B) Italian 義大利的

(C) tourism 觀光業

(D) modern 現代的

中譯 嚴格來說，威尼斯比較像觀光城市，而不是海洋商業城市。

解析 strictly speaking 嚴格地說；tourism 觀光業。

22. I like Rome very much because it has many historic sites and it is friendly to visitors.

(A) stories 故事

(B) glory 光榮

(C) sites 遺址

(D) giants 巨人

中譯 我非常喜歡羅馬，因為它有很多歷史遺跡，當地人對遊客也很友善。

解析 historic sites 歷史遺址；site 地點、場所、網站、遺址。

01 航空交通

02 飯店住宿

03 餐廳飲食

04 旅遊觀光

05 介紹台灣

06 帶團職責

23. With its palaces, sculptured parks, concert halls, and museums, Vienna is a <u>steeped</u> city in cultures.

(A) chronic 長期的　　　　　　　　(B) elite 精英

(C) provincial 省份的　　　　　　　(D) steeped 充滿的

中譯 維也納有皇宮、用雕刻裝飾的公園、音樂廳和博物館，是一座充滿文化的城市。

解析 be steeped in 充滿著、沉浸於，如 The castle is steeped in history. 這座城堡充滿了歷史。

24. The oldest of all the main Hawaiian islands, Kauai is <u>known</u> for its secluded beaches, scenic waterfalls, and jungle hikes.

(A) due 由於　　　　　　　　　　(B) known 知名的

(C) neutral 中立的　　　　　　　　(D) ripe 成熟的

中譯 身為夏威夷群島最古老的島嶼，考艾島以隱密性的海灘、美景瀑布與叢林健走聞名。

解析 known for / famous for / well known for 都為某事物「知名」之意。secluded 隱蔽的、僻靜的。

25. Hong Kong is one of the world's most thrilling Chinese New Year travel destinations. The <u>highlight</u> is the spectacular fireworks display on the second day of the New Year.

(A) highlight 亮點　　　　　　　　(B) limelight 引人注目的中心

(C) insight 洞察力　　　　　　　　(D) twilight 黎明

中譯 香港是世界上最令人興奮的中國新年旅遊景點之一。最精彩的部分是大年初二壯觀的煙火表演。

解析 thrilling 令人興奮的；spectacular 壯觀的、壯麗的。

26. This monument <u>honors</u> the men and women who died during the war.

(A) presides 主持

(B) honors 榮耀

(C) monitors 監控

(D) memorizes 熟記

中譯 此紀念碑是為了榮耀在戰爭期間陣亡的男男女女。

解析 honor 此處為動詞，不論為名詞、動詞，都是榮耀之意。monument 為紀念碑，memorial hall 為紀念堂，如 Chiang Kai-shek Memorial Hall 中正紀念堂。

27. The <u>results</u> of the New Seven Wonders of the World campaign were announced on July 7th, 2007, and the Great Wall of China is one of the winners.

(A) sources 來源

(B) results 結果

(C) revolts 反叛

(D) shelters 遮蔽物

中譯 新世界七大奇景的結果於 2007 年 7 月 7 日公布，中國的萬里長城為優勝者之一。

解析 Wonders of the world 為世界奇景，announce 為宣布。此題為宣布結果，故選 result。考生可能誤選為 source 來源，但以最後一句的 winners 即可推論是結果出爐。

28. <u>Spectacular</u> fireworks shows lit up the sky of cities around the world as people celebrated the start of 2012.

(A) Invisible 看不見的

(B) Spectacular 壯觀的

(C) Dull 遲鈍的

(D) Endangered 瀕臨絕種的

中譯 當人們慶祝 2012 年的開始，壯觀的煙火照亮了世界上許多城市的天空。

解析 spectacular 壯觀的，考題中也常見 breath-taking 令人屏息的、amazing 令人驚豔的這兩個形容詞來描述風景。

01 航空交通

02 飯店住宿

03 餐廳飲食

04 旅遊觀光

05 介紹台灣

06 帶團職責

29. The landscape of this natural park is best seen on bike or foot, and there are <u>numerous</u> trails in the area. All paths offer breath-taking sceneries.

(A) sole 單獨的

(B) simultaneous 同時發生的

(C) numerous 許多的

(D) indifferent 冷淡的

中譯 騎單車或是步行最能看出這個自然公園的景色。園內也有許多步道，路徑上都能看到令人屏息的風景。

解析 numerous 許多的，其實就是常見的 many。breath-taking 令人屏息的，考題中也常見用 amazing 令人驚豔的、spectacular 壯觀的這兩個形容詞來描述風景。landscape 風景、景色；path 小徑、小路。

30. The view of <u>cascading</u> waterfalls in the rainforest is spectacular.

(A) ascending 上升

(B) cascading 成瀑布落下

(C) flourishing 繁榮的

(D) overflowing 溢出的

中譯 雨林中階梯狀的瀑布景色是很壯觀的。

解析 cascade 為動詞，表疊層成瀑布落下；spectacular 壯觀的。考題中也常見 breath-taking 令人屏息的、amazing 令人驚豔的這兩個形容詞來描述風景。

31. Costa Brava is a popular tourist destination in northeastern Spain, thanks to its <u>moderate</u> climate, beautiful beaches, and charming towns.

(A) dreadful 可怕的

(B) contemporary 現代的

(C) moderate 溫和的

(D) bitter 苦的

中譯 西班牙東北部的布拉瓦海岸是很受歡迎的觀光景點，多虧了它溫和的氣候、美麗的海灘和迷人的小鎮。

解析 由 popular tourist destination 可知其氣候是 moderate 溫和的。

32. A good place to end a tour of Rome is the Trevi Fountain. Legend has it that if you toss a single coin into the Trevi, you are <u>guaranteed</u> a return to Rome.

(A) preserved 保存　　　　　　　(B) obtained 獲得

(C) dedicated 專注　　　　　　　(D) guaranteed 保證的

中譯 特雷維噴泉是結束羅馬之旅的好地方。傳說只要投一枚硬幣到噴泉內，就保證可以再訪羅馬。

解析 toss 拋、投；guarantee 保證，常見用法還有 refund guarantees 保證退款。

33. Palm Beach is a coastline <u>resort</u> where thousands of tourists from all over the world spend their summer vacation.

(A) airport 機場　　　　　　　　(B) resort 名勝

(C) pavement 人行道　　　　　　(D) passage 通過

中譯 棕櫚灘是海岸度假勝地，來自世界各地的上千名遊客都到此來度過暑假時光。

解析 必考單字：resort 名勝。常見的 retreat 則是僻靜之地。

01 航空交通
02 飯店住宿
03 餐廳飲食
04 旅遊觀光
05 介紹台灣
06 帶團職責

# 5 介紹台灣

## 一、歷屆考題精選

( ) 1. Bopiliao, _____ in Wanhua District, Taipei, and serving as the setting for the film, Monga, is a popular tourist spot. 101 英導

    (A) selected     (B) featured     (C) located     (D) directed

( ) 2. Chichi is a town in Central Taiwan that is _____ by rail. 101 英導

    (A) accessible     (B) approached     (C) available     (D) advanced

( ) 3. One of Hualien's long-standing traditions is stone carving, which is not surprising considering the city's main _____ is marble. 100 英導

    (A) mission     (B) jewelry     (C) leisure     (D) export

( ) 4. Taroko National Park _____ high mountains and steep canyons. Many of its peaks tower above 3,000 meters in elevation. 101 英導

    (A) lacks     (B) features     (C) excludes     (D) disregards

( ) 5. Many tourists are fascinated by the natural _____ of Taroko Gorge. 98 英領

    (A) sparkles     (B) spectacles     (C) spectators     (D) sprinklers

( ) 6. Many people consider Yangmingshan National Park a pleasant _____ from the bustle of the city. 100 英領

    (A) retreat     (B) removal     (C) departure     (D) adventure

( ) 7. Besides participating in local cultural activities, people who desire to explore the ecology of Kenting can _____ plenty of wildlife and plants. 99 英導

    (A) observe     (B) pick up     (C) object     (D) plan

( ) 8. Taiwan is well known for its mountain _____ spots and urban landmarks such as the National Palace Museum and the Taipei 101 skyscraper. 101 英導

    (A) scenic     (B) neutral     (C) vacant     (D) feasible

( ) 9. When visiting Alishan, one of the most popular tourist destinations in Taiwan, it's worth spending a few days to learn about the indigenous people living in mountain villages and _____ the marvelous scenery. `102 英導`

(A) prick on      (B) take in      (C) put off      (D) pick up

( ) 10. Cloud Gate, an internationally _____ dance group from Taiwan, demonstrated that the quality of modern dance inAsia could be comparable to that of modern dance in Europe and North America. `101 英導`

(A) refunded      (B) reflected      (C) retained      (D) renowned

( ) 11. Taiwan has more than 400 museums. The most famous of these is the National Palace Museum, which holds the world's largest _____ of Chinese art treasures. `98 英導`

(A) supply      (B) catalogue      (C) collection      (D) addition

( ) 12. The National Palace Museum opens daily from 9 a.m. to 5 p.m.. However, for Saturdays, the hours are _____ to 8:30 p.m.. `102 英領`

(A) closed      (B) moved      (C) lasted      (D) extended

( ) 13. In southern Taiwan, people's ties to rural folk culture are strongest. Local gods are more fervently worshipped. Tainan, for instance, has a temple heritage second to _____. `100 英導`

(A) one      (B) none      (C) any      (D) some

( ) 14. Pineapple cakes and local teas are some of the most popular _____ of Taiwan. `102 英領`

(A) sights      (B) souvenirs      (C) services      (D) surprises

( ) 15. Taiwan Mountain Tea and Red Sprout Mountain Tea are _____ subspecies of the island. They were discovered in Taiwan in the 17th century. `102 英領`

(A) inscribed      (B) indigenous      (C) incredible      (D) industrial

( ) 16. Tourists enjoy visiting night markets around the island to taste _____ local snacks. `99 英導`

(A) authentic      (B) blend      (C) inclusive      (D) invisible

01 航空交通

02 飯店住宿

03 餐廳飲食

04 旅遊觀光

05 介紹台灣

06 帶團職責

( ) 17. The _____ of our trip to Southern Taiwan was A Taste of Tainan where we had a lot of delicious food. 101 英導

(A) gourmet     (B) highlight     (C) monument     (D) recognition

( ) 18. Night markets in Taiwan have become _____ tourist destinations. They are great places to shop for bargains and eat typical Taiwanese food. 101 英導

(A) tropical     (B) popular     (C) edible     (D) responsible

( ) 19. An open-minded city, Taipei _____ Asia's first Gay Pride parade which has now become an annual autumn event. 100 英導

(A) expanded     (B) governed     (C) hosted     (D) portrayed

( ) 20. The World Games of 2009 will take place in Kaohsiung, Taiwan, from July 16th to July 26th, 2009. The games will _____ sports that are not contested in the Olympic Games. 98 英導

(A) feature     (B) exclaim     (C) bloom     (D) appeal

| | | | | |
|---|---|---|---|---|
| 1.（C） | 2.（A） | 3.（D） | 4.（B） | 5.（B） |
| 6.（A） | 7.（A） | 8.（A） | 9.（B） | 10.（D） |
| 11.（C） | 12.（D） | 13.（B） | 14.（B） | 15.（B） |
| 16.（A） | 17.（B） | 18.（B） | 19.（C） | 20.（A） |

## 二、試題中譯＋解析

1. Bopiliao, <u>located</u> in Wanhua District, Taipei, and serving as the setting for the film, Monga, is a popular tourist spot.

   (A) selected 選擇　　　　　　　(B) featured 以～為特色

   (C) located 位於　　　　　　　(D) directed 指揮

   **中譯** 剝皮寮位於台北萬華區，曾是電影《艋舺》拍片的場景，是個受歡迎的觀光景點。

   **解析** 由 in Wanhua District 即可推知為 located 位於。tourist spots / tourist attractions 為觀光景點。

2. Chichi is a town in Central Taiwan that is <u>accessible</u> by rail.

   (A) accessible 可到達的　　　　(B) approached 接近的

   (C) available 可用的　　　　　(D) advanced 先進的

   **中譯** 集集是中台灣一個可以經由鐵路到達的城鎮。

   **解析** 形容某處的交通時，經常用 accessible by car / rail 來形容是否能開車、搭火車到達。

3. One of Hualien's long-standing traditions is stone carving, which is not surprising considering the city's main <u>export</u> is marble.

   (A) mission 任務　　　　　　　(B) jewelry 珠寶

   (C) leisure 悠閑　　　　　　　(D) export 出口

   **中譯** 花蓮屹立不搖的傳統之一就是石雕，因此此城市的主要出口為大理石也就不足為奇了。

   **解析** 此題考 export 為出口，import 則為進口。

4. Taroko National Park <u>features</u> high mountains and steep canyons. Many of its peaks tower above 3,000 meters in elevation.

(A) lacks 缺少

(B) features 具特色的

(C) excludes 不包含

(D) disregards 不理會

**中譯** 太魯閣國家公園以高山和陡峭的峽谷<u>為特色</u>。許多高峰海拔都超過 3,000 公尺。

**解析** feature 為重點單字，當動詞時，feature 為「以～為特色」，如考題 The zoo features more than 1,000 animals in their natural habitats.；當名詞時，feature 為「特色」，如 Her eyes are her best feature. 她的雙眼是她最大的特色。elevation 高度、海拔、提高，此作海拔。

5. Many tourists are fascinated by the natural <u>spectacles</u> of Taroko Gorge.

(A) sparkles 火花

(B) spectacles 奇觀

(C) spectators 觀眾

(D) sprinklers 灑水機

**中譯** 許多觀光客為太魯閣的自然奇觀所著迷。

**解析** spectacles 奇觀；fascinate 迷住、強烈地吸引。fascinating（形容某事迷人的）、fastened（人被迷住了）。

6. Many people consider Yangmingshan National Park a pleasant <u>retreat</u> from the bustle of the city.

(A) retreat 隱居

(B) removal 遷居

(C) departure 出發

(D) adventure 冒險

**中譯** 許多人認為陽明山國家公園是個遠離城市喧囂的<u>僻靜之處</u>。

**解析** 由 from the bustle of the city 可知為 retreat。bustle 鬧哄哄地忙亂。

01 航空交通

02 飯店住宿

03 餐廳飲食

04 旅遊觀光

05 介紹台灣

06 帶團職責

7. Besides participating in local cultural activities, people who desire to explore the ecology of Kenting can <u>observe</u> plenty of wildlife and plants

(A) observe 觀察

(B) pick up 撿起

(C) object 反對

(D) plan 計畫

**中譯** 除了參與當地的文化活動外，想在墾丁探訪生態環境的人也可以觀察豐富的野生動物與植物。

**解析** 由 desire to explore the ecology of Kenting 想探訪墾丁的生態環境，可得知 observe plenty of wildlife and plants 觀察豐富的野生動物與植物。

8. Taiwan is well known for its mountain <u>scenic</u> spots and urban landmarks such as the National Palace Museum and the Taipei 101 skyscraper.

(A) scenic 風景的

(B) neutral 中立的

(C) vacant 空的

(D) feasible 行得通的

**中譯** 台灣以其高山風景景點以及城市的地標聞名，像是故宮博物院和台北 101 摩天大樓。

**解析** scenic spots 風景景點，tourist spots / tourist attractions 觀光景點，此兩處景點經常出現於考題中。scenery 則為風景（名詞）。well known / famous 都是有名的意思，亦為常考單字。urban 城市的；rustic 則是鄉下的。

9. When visiting Alishan, one of the most popular tourist destinations in Taiwan, it's worth spending a few days to learn about the indigenous people living in mountain villages and <u>take in</u> the marvelous scenery.

(A) prick on 刺上

(B) take in 欣賞、參觀

(C) put off 推遲

(D) pick up 撿起

**中譯** 當去最受歡迎的台灣景點——阿里山旅遊時，很值得花幾天去學習原住民的高山生活方式，和擁抱絕美風光。

**解析** take in 欣賞、參觀；indigenous 本地的；marvelous scenery 絕美風光。

10. Cloud Gate, an internationally <u>renowned</u> dance group from Taiwan, demonstrated that the quality of modern dance in Asia could be comparable to that of modern dance in Europe and North America.

(A) refunded 退還

(B) reflected 反映

(C) retained 保留

(D) renowned 有名

中譯 雲門，來自台灣的國際知名舞蹈團體，證明亞洲現代舞水準媲美歐洲以及北美的現代舞。

解析 renowned 也可以用 famous 替換，此處由 comparable to that of modern dance in Europe and North America 可知為 internationally renowned 國際上知名的。demonstrate 論證、證明。

11. Taiwan has more than 400 museums. The most famous of these is the National Palace Museum, which holds the world's largest <u>collection</u> of Chinese art treasures.

(A) supply 供應

(B) catalogue 目錄

(C) collection 收藏、收集

(D) addition 附加

中譯 台灣有超過 400 間以上的博物館。其中最有名的為故宮博物院，它擁有世界上最多的中華文物收藏品。

解析 hold 除了手握，亦可為舉辦，此處則為擁有。

12. The National Palace Museum opens daily from 9 a.m. to 5 p.m.. However, for Saturdays, the hours are <u>extended</u> to 8：30 p.m..

(A) closed 關門

(B) moved 移動

(C) lasted 持續

(D) extended 延長

中譯 故宮博物院每天從早上 9 點開放至下午 5 點。但每個禮拜六的開放時間則延長到晚上 8 點半。

解析 此處考生可能會誤選為 lasted 持續；但 extended 才能表達延長之意。daily 每天；opening hours 營業時間、開放時間。

01
航空交通

02
飯店住宿

03
餐廳飲食

04
旅遊觀光

05
介紹台灣

06
帶團職責

13. In southern Taiwan, people's ties to rural folk culture are strongest. Local gods are more fervently worshipped. Tainan, for instance, has a temple heritage second to <u>none</u>.

(A) one 一個

(B) none 沒有

(C) any 任何

(D) some 一些

**中譯** 南台灣人與民俗文化的連結是最強的。當地的神明被熱烈崇拜。例如台南。

**解析** rural 農村的、田園的；second to none 不亞於任何人、首屈一指。

14. Pineapple cakes and local teas are some of the most popular <u>souvenirs</u> of Taiwan.

(A) sights 景點

(B) souvenirs 紀念品

(C) services 服務

(D) surprises 驚喜

**中譯** 鳳梨酥和當地的茶葉是台灣最受歡迎的紀念品。

**解析** souvenirs 紀念品為常考重點單字，例句：The tour guide persuaded him into buying some expensive souvenirs. 這名導遊說服他買昂貴的紀念品。（100 英領）

15. Taiwan Mountain Tea and Red Sprout Mountain Tea are <u>indigenous</u> subspecies of the island. They were discovered in Taiwan in the 17th century.

(A) inscribed 落款

(B) indigenous 本地的

(C) incredible 難以置信的

(D) industrial 產業

**中譯** 台灣高山茶和紅芽高山茶是島上<u>土生土長</u>的品種。他們被發現於 17 世紀的台灣。

**解析** indigenous 土生土長的、本地的，例句：Kangaroos are indigenous to Australia. 袋鼠是澳洲本地的動物。

16. Tourists enjoy visiting night markets around the island to taste authentic local snacks.

(A) authentic 真正的

(B) blend 融合

(C) inclusive 包含的

(D) invisible 無形的

中譯 遊客喜歡在島上到處參訪夜市，嚐嚐真正的道地小吃。

解析 local snacks 道地小吃。由 local 可推知為 authentic 真正的。authentic 真正的，例句：This restaurant features authentic Northern Italian dishes that reflect the true flavors of Italy. 這間餐廳的特色為反映義大利口味的道地北義大利菜。（101 英導）

★其他關於夜市的考題

Night markets in Taiwan have become popular tourist destinations.

They are great places to shop for bargains and eat typical Taiwanese food.

台灣的夜市已經成為受歡迎的觀光景點，他們是殺價和吃傳統台灣料理的好地方。（101 英導）

17. The highlight of our trip to Southern Taiwan was A Taste of Tainan where we had a lot of delicious food.

(A) gourmet 美食家

(B) highlight 亮點

(C) monument 紀念碑

(D) recognition 承認

中譯 南台灣之旅的亮點就是台南小吃，我們在那裡吃了很多美食。

解析 由 we had a lot of delicious food 可推知，是此趟旅程的 highlight 亮點。

01 航空交通

02 飯店住宿

03 餐廳飲食

04 旅遊觀光

05 介紹台灣

06 帶團職責

18. Night markets in Taiwan have become popular tourist destinations. They are great places to shop for bargains and eat typical Taiwanese food.

(A) tropical 熱帶的

(B) popular 受歡迎的

(C) edible 可食用的

(D) responsible 負責任的

中譯 台灣的夜市已經成為受歡迎的觀光景點。他們是殺價和吃傳統台灣料理的好地方。

解析 觀光景點的各類用法請務必牢記：tourist destinations、tourist spots、tourist attractions。destination 目的地。

19. An open-minded city, Taipei hosted Asia's first Gay Pride parade which has now become an annual autumn event.

(A) expanded 使擴張

(B) governed 管理

(C) hosted 主辦

(D) portrayed 描寫

中譯 身為一座心胸開放的都市，台北主辦亞洲第一屆同志遊行，其也成為每年於秋天所舉辦的活動。

解析 舉辦活動有兩個常見單字：① host 主辦（帶有主辦人的意思），例句：Rio will host the 2016 Summer Olympic Games. 里約將主辦 2016 年夏季奧運。② hold 舉行、舉辦，例句 1：The Olympic Games are held every four years. 奧運每四年（被）舉辦一次。例句 2：The first Taipei Lantern Festival was held in 1990. Due to the event's huge popularity, the festival has been expanded every year. 第一屆的台北燈籠節於 1990 年舉行。而因為這場活動受到極大的歡迎，活動一年比一年盛大。（98 英導）

20. The World Games of 2009 will take place in Kaohsiung, Taiwan, from July 16th to July 26th, 2009. The games will <u>feature</u> sports that are not contested in the Olympic Games.

(A) feature 特色
(B) exclaim 呼喊
(C) bloom 開花
(D) appeal 呼籲

**中譯** 2009 年的世界運動大會將於 7 月 16 至 26 日於台灣的高雄舉辦。此運動大會是以奧運未舉辦的比賽項目為特色。

**解析** 某事件 take place / be held 發生、被舉辦，若是主辦單位為主詞，則可換成 Kaohsiung will host the World Games of 2009。

# 6 帶團職責

## 一、歷屆考題精選

( ) 1. A good tour guide has to be _____ to the people in his group. `101 英導`

    (A) considered    (B) conditioned   (C) confided     (D) committed

( ) 2. A tour guide is _____ informing tourists about the culture and the beautiful sites of a city or town. `101 英領`

    (A) afraid of                    (B) responsible for

    (C) due to                     (D) dependent on

( ) 3. As a tour guide, you will face new _____ every day. One of the hardest parts of your job may be answering questions. `98 英導`

    (A) dooms      (B) challenges   (C) margins    (D) floods

( ) 4. Mingling with tourists from different backgrounds helps tour guides _____ and learn new things in answering curious visitors' various questions. `102 英導`

    (A) blow their own horn        (B) take their breath away

    (C) fall from grace            (D) broaden their horizons

( ) 5. The tour guide is a _____ man; he is very polite and always speaks in a kind manner. `101 英導`

    (A) careless    (B) persistent   (C) courteous   (D) environmental

( ) 6. The local tour guide has a _____ personality. Everybody likes him. `101 英導`

    (A) windy       (B) stormy     (C) sunny     (D) cloudy

( ) 7. Before we left the hotel, our tour guide gave us a thirty-minute _____ on the local culture. `101 英導`

    (A) exhibition    (B) presentation   (C) construction  (D) invitation

01 航空交通

02 飯店住宿

03 餐廳飲食

04 旅遊觀光

05 介紹台灣

06 帶團職責

( ) 8. Being a tour guide is a very important job. In many cases, the tour guide is the traveler's first _____ of our country. 98 英導

(A) difference    (B) impression    (C) dictation    (D) influence

( ) 9. Mr. Jones has got the hang of being a tour guide. 100 英領

(A) Mr. Jones quit his job.

(B) Mr. Jones needs our help now.

(C) Mr. Jones met some strangers on his way home.

(D) Mr. Jones has learned the skills of being a tour guide.

( ) 10. The tour guide _____ him into buying some expensive souvenirs. 100 英領

(A) persuaded    (B) dissuaded    (C) suggested    (D) purified

( ) 11. We were asked by our tour guide on the shuttle bus to _____ seated until we reached our destination. 98 英導

(A) endure    (B) maintain    (C) remain    (D) adhere

( ) 12. We're going to be driving through farmland for the next twenty minutes or so, so just _____ and relax until we're closer to the city. 98 英導

(A) sit back    (B) pull over    (C) fall through    (D) wind up

( ) 13. If you want to become a successful tour manager, you have to work _____ and learn from the seniors. 98 英領

(A) hard    (B) hardly    (C) harshly    (D) easily

( ) 14. In order to make traveling easier, especially for those who rely on public transportation, the Tourism Bureau worked with local governments to _____ the Taiwan Tourist Shuttle Service in 2010. 102 英導

(A) terminate    (B) initiate    (C) annotate    (D) depreciate

( ) 15. _____ you need to get in touch with me, you can reach me at 224338654 at my travel agency. 98 英領

(A) Those times    (B) In case    (C) At times    (D) Sometimes

( ) 16. For tours in peak seasons, travel agents sometimes have to make reservations a year or more _____. 99 英導

(A) above all     (B) beyond all     (C) in advance     (D) afterwards

( ) 17. The travel agent says that we have to pay a deposit of $2,000 in advance in order to _____ the reservation for our hotel room. 98 英導

(A) cancel     (B) protect     (C) remove     (D) secure

( ) 18. The travel agent _____ the delay. 100 英領

(A) astonished at  (B) astonished     (C) apologized     (D) apologized for

01 航空交通

02 飯店住宿

03 餐廳飲食

04 旅遊觀光

05 介紹台灣

06 帶團職責

## 標 準 答 案

| 1. ( D ) | 2. ( B ) | 3. ( B ) | 4. ( D ) | 5. ( C ) |
|----------|----------|----------|----------|----------|
| 6. ( C ) | 7. ( B ) | 8. ( B ) | 9. ( D ) | 10. ( A ) |
| 11. ( C ) | 12. ( A ) | 13. ( A ) | 14. ( B ) | 15. ( B ) |
| 16. ( C ) | 17. ( D ) | 18. ( D ) | | |

01 航空交通

02 飯店住宿

03 餐廳飲食

04 旅遊觀光

05 介紹台灣

06 帶團職責

## 二、試題中譯＋解析

1. A good tour guide has to be <u>committed</u> to the people in his group.

   (A) considered 考慮　　　　　　(B) conditioned 適應

   (C) confided 透露　　　　　　　(D) committed 承諾

   中譯 一名好的導遊必須致力於照顧他的團員。

   解析 tour guide 的責任即為對團員負責任，故選 committed。

2. A tour guide is <u>responsible for</u> informing tourists about the culture and the beautiful sites of a city or town.

   (A) afraid of 害怕　　　　　　(B) responsible for 對～有責任

   (C) due to 由於　　　　　　　(D) dependent on 依靠

   中譯 導遊應負責介紹該城鎮的文化和美麗景點給旅客。

   解析 responsible for / take responsibility to do / be responsible for doing sth. 對～有責任。

3. As a tour guide, you will face new <u>challenges</u> every day. One of the hardest parts of your job may be answering questions.

   (A) dooms 厄運　　　　　　　(B) challenges 挑戰

   (C) margins 邊緣　　　　　　　(D) floods 水災

   中譯 身為導遊，你每天會面臨到新的挑戰。工作上最困難的部分之一也許就是回答問題。

   解析 此處的 challenge 為名詞，而 challenge 亦可為動詞，也為挑戰之意。

4. Mingling with tourists from different backgrounds helps tour guides broaden their horizons and learn new things in answering curious visitors' various questions.

   (A) blow their own horn 自吹自擂

   (B) take their breath away 使他們大吃一驚

   (C) fall from grace 失寵

   (D) broaden their horizons 開拓視野

   中譯 與不同背景的觀光客打交道能讓導遊開拓視野，也能讓導遊學習回答好奇旅客不同的新問題。

   解析 mingle 使混合、使相混；broaden their horizons 開拓視野，直譯為擴大海平面。

5. The tour guide is a courteous man; he is very polite and always speaks in a kind manner.

   (A) careless 粗心的                    (B) persistent 堅持不懈的

   (C) courteous 禮貌的                   (D) environmental 環境的

   中譯 導遊是一個有教養的男生，他非常有禮貌，談吐也得宜。

   解析 courteous / well-mannered / polite 都有「禮貌」的意思，而沒禮貌則為 discourteous / ill-mannered / impolite。manner 態度、禮貌。

6. The local tour guide has a sunny personality. Everybody likes him.

   (A) windy 大風的                       (B) stormy 暴風雨的

   (C) sunny 陽光的                       (D) cloudy 陰天的

   中譯 這位當地的導遊有著陽光開朗的性格。每個人都喜歡他。

   解析 sunny 陽光性格的；outgoing 外向；shy 害羞，都為形容個性的常考單字；humble / modest 為「謙虛」的常考單字。此處的答案選項都是描述天氣的形容詞：windy 大風的；stormy 暴風雨的；sunny 陽光的；cloudy 陰天的。

7. Before we left the hotel, our tour guide gave us a thirty-minute presentation on the local culture.

(A) exhibition 展覽

(B) presentation 介紹

(C) construction 建造

(D) invitation 邀請

**中譯** 在我們離開旅館之前，我們的導遊給我們做了 30 分鐘當地文化的介紹。

**解析** presentation 直譯上來看是呈現，但口語中多半為簡報、介紹，在台灣報名許多旅遊行程時，旅行社多半也會提供事前的說明，亦為 presentation。

8. Being a tour guide is a very important job. In many cases, the tour guide is the traveler's first impression of our country.

(A) difference 不同、差異

(B) impression 印象

(C) dictation 口述

(D) influence 影響

**中譯** 當一位導遊是一份很重要的工作。在許多情形下，導遊是遊客對我們國家的第一印象。

**解析** first impression 第一印象；traveler 亦可替換為 tourist，皆為遊客之意。

9. Mr. Jones has got the hang of being a tour guide.

(A) Mr. Jones quit his job. 瓊斯先生辭職了。

(B) Mr. Jones needs our help now. 瓊斯先生現在需要我們的幫忙。

(C) Mr. Jones met some strangers on his way home.

瓊斯先生在回家途中遇到一些陌生人。

(D) Mr. Jones has learned the skills of being a tour guide.

瓊斯先生已經學習到當一位領隊的技巧。

**中譯** 瓊斯先生已經學習到當一位領隊的技巧。

**解析** get the hang of sth. 掌握某事的訣竅。

10. The tour guide <u>persuaded</u> him into buying some expensive souvenirs.

(A) persuaded 說服　　　　　　(B) dissuaded 勸阻

(C) suggested 建議　　　　　　(D) purified 淨化

中譯 這名導遊說服他買昂貴的紀念品。

解析 persuade into Ving 說服；souvenir 紀念品。

11. We were asked by our tour guide on the shuttle bus to <u>remain</u> seated until we reached our destination.

(A) endure 忍受　　　　　　(B) maintain 維護、保持

(C) remain 維持　　　　　　(D) adhere 黏著

中譯 導遊要求我們在接駁車上維持就座，直到我們抵達目的地。

解析 此題考生易誤選為 maintain 維護，maintain 通常是維護、保持某物；故選擇 remain 維持。shuttle bus 為接駁車、交通車之意，各類的飯店或是景點則會提供 shuttle bus service 接駁車的服務。

12. We're going to be driving through farmland for the next twenty minutes or so, so just <u>sit back</u> and relax until we're closer to the city.

(A) sit back 休息　　　　　　(B) pull over 靠邊停

(C) fall through 失敗　　　　　(D) wind up 結束

中譯 接下來的 20 分鐘我們會駛經農田，所以在接近市區之前，請放鬆休息。

解析 sit back 直譯為坐好，口語上則為 relax 放鬆、rest 休息之意；在飛機上常可聽到廣播「sit back and fasten your seatbelt」，就是請坐好並繫緊安全帶之意。

13. If you want to become a successful tour manager, you have to work hard and learn from the seniors.

(A) hard 努力地

(B) hardly 幾乎不

(C) harshly 嚴厲地

(D) easily 容易地

中譯 如果你想成為一名成功的領隊，你必須很努力地工作並向資深領隊學習。

解析 常聽到的 play hard, work hard 認真玩樂、認真工作，也是同樣用法。the seniors 長者，也可作前輩、資深人士。

14. In order to make traveling easier, especially for those who rely on public transportation, the Tourism Bureau worked with local governments to initiate the Taiwan Tourist Shuttle Service in 2010.

(A) terminate 終止

(B) initiate 開始

(C) annotate 註解

(D) depreciate 貶值

中譯 為了讓旅遊更方便，特別是對那些仰賴大眾運輸的人，觀光旅遊局與當地政府一起於 2010 年開始執行台灣旅遊巴士。

解析 rely on / depend on / count on 依靠、信賴；Shuttle Service 快捷公車（直達公車）。

15. In case you need to get in touch with me, you can reach me at 224338654 at my travel agency.

(A) Those times 這些時間

(B) In case 萬一

(C) At times 有時

(D) Sometimes 有時

中譯 萬一你需要和我聯繫，你可以打 224338654 到我的旅行社和我聯絡。

解析 get in touch with 與～取得聯繫。

01 航空交通

02 飯店住宿

03 餐廳飲食

04 旅遊觀光

05 介紹台灣

06 帶團職責

16. For tours in peak seasons, travel agents sometimes have to make reservations a year or more in advance.

(A) above all 首              (B) beyond all 超乎範圍

(C) in advance 事先        (D) afterwards 之後

中譯 對於旺季的出遊,旅行社有時必須早在一年甚至更早之前就先預定好行程。

解析 由 peak seasons 得知,出發前一定得 make reservations in advance 事先預約。

17. The travel agent says that we have to pay a deposit of $2,000 in advance in order to secure the reservation for our hotel room.

(A) cancel 取消            (B) protect 保護

(C) remove 除去          (D) secure 確保

中譯 旅行社説我們必須事先支付 $2,000 訂金,來確保飯店訂房。

解析 常考單字:travel agent 旅行社;deposit 訂金;make reservation 訂位; secure reservation 確保訂位 / 房;re-confirmation 再確認。

18. The travel agent apologized for the delay.

(A) astonished at             (B) astonished

(C) apologized              (D) apologized for 道歉

中譯 旅行社因為行程延誤而道歉。

解析 apologize to 人 for 某事,意思是為某事向某人道歉,故選 ( D )。

# 7 健康

## 一、歷屆考題精選

( ) 1. Many people have <u>put on</u> some pounds during the New Year vacation. 98 英領

(A) dressed up　　(B) gained　　(C) gambled　　(D) turned into

( ) 2. Shelly has adhered _____ a low-fat diet for over two months and succeeded in losing 12 pounds. 102 英領

(A) on　　　　　　　　　　(B) at

(C) in　　　　　　　　　　(D) to

( ) 3. Diabetes is a _____ disease which is difficult to cure. Management concentrates on keeping blood sugar levels as close to normal as possible without presenting undue patient danger. 100 英導

(A) gigantic　　(B) chronic　　(C) lunatic　　(D) pandemic

( ) 4. Caused by the _____ of our "body clock", jet lag can be a big problem for most travelers in the first few days after they have arrived at their destination. 98 英導

(A) aspiration　　(B) inspiration　　(C) disruption　　(D) motivation

( ) 5. I seem to have a fever. May I have a _____ to take my temperature? 101 英導

(A) thermometer　(B) manometer　(C) calculator　(D) scale

( ) 6. _____ has become a very serious problem in the modern world. It's estimated that there are more than 1 billion overweight adults globally. 99 英領

(A) Depression　(B) Obesity　　(C) Malnutrition　(D) Starvation

( ) 7. The chemicals in these cleaning products can be _____ to our health. 102 英領

(A) hazardous　　(B) hapless　　(C) rueful　　(D) pitiful

(　　) 8.　Scientists have found a _____ for the rare contagious disease, and some patients now have the hope of recovery. 99 英導

(A) replacement　(B) penalty　　　(C) cure　　　　(D) passion

(　　) 9.　Scarlet fever is a/an _____ disease, which is transferable from one person to another. 99 英導

(A) different　　(B) contagious　(C) important　(D) special

(　　) 10.　Middle-aged smokers are far more likely than nonsmokers to _____ dementia later in life, and heavy smokers are at more than double the risk, according to a new study. 100 英導

(A) deflect　　　(B) demote　　　(C) deliberate　(D) develop

# 標 準 答 案

| | | | | |
|---|---|---|---|---|
| 1. （B） | 2. （D） | 3. （B） | 4. （C） | 5. （A） |
| 6. （B） | 7. （A） | 8. （C） | 9. （B） | 10.（D） |

1. Many people have <u>put on</u> some pounds during the New Year vacation.

(A) dressed up 打扮

(B) gained 獲得

(C) gambled 賭博

(D) turned into 使變成

中譯 新年假期期間，許多人的體重都增加了不少。

解析 gain weight / put on weight 都是增重之意。例句：Please don't order so much food! I have been putting on weight for the last two months. 拜託別點太多食物！這2個月我已經開始變胖了。 100 領隊

2. Shelly has adhered <u>to</u> a low-fat diet for over two months and succeeded in losing 12 pounds.

(A) on

(B) at

(C) in

(D) to

中譯 雪麗遵循低卡飲食2個多月，並且成功瘦下了12磅。

解析 adhered to 堅持；英文領隊考題經常出現關於減重的主題。例句1：Please don't order so much food! I have been putting on weight for 拜託別點太多食物！這2個月我已經開始變胖了。（100英領）例句2：Many people have put on some pounds during the New Year vacation. 新年假期期間，許多人的體重都增加了不少。（98英領）

3. Diabetes is a <u>chronic</u> disease which is difficult to cure. Management concentrates on keeping blood sugar levels as close to normal as possible without presenting undue patient danger.

(A) gigantic 巨大的

(B) chronic 慢性的

(C) lunatic 精神錯亂的

(D) pandemic 全國流行的

中譯 糖尿病是一種慢性且難以治癒的疾病。日常管理上須注意血糖高低是否接近正常值，不要讓病人有過度危險的狀況發生。

解析 由 difficult to cure 即可推知為 chronic 慢性的，cure 治癒。

4.  Caused by the disruption of our "body clock", jet lag can be a big problem for most travelers in the first few days after they have arrived at their destination.

    (A) aspiration 志向

    (B) inspiration 靈感

    (C) disruption 中斷

    (D) motivation 刺激

    中譯 由於生理時鐘的混亂，對於大多數的旅客來說，在抵達目的地的前幾天，時差會是一大問題。

    解析 此題易誤選為生理時鐘遭受 motivation 刺激，但 jet lag 時差則是因為時鐘的 disruption 中斷而造成。

5.  I seem to have a fever. May I have a thermometer to take my temperature?

    (A) thermometer 溫度計

    (B) manometer 壓力計

    (C) calculator 計算機

    (D) scale 比例尺

    中譯 我好像感冒了。可以給我溫度計量體溫嗎？

    解析 由 fever 跟 temperature 都可猜出答案為 thermometer 溫度計。

6.  Obesity has become a very serious problem in the modern world. It's estimated that there are more than 1 billion overweight adults globally.

    (A) Depression 沮喪

    (B) Obesity 肥胖

    (C) Malnutrition 營養失調

    (D) Starvation 飢餓

    中譯 肥胖已經成為現代世界很嚴重的問題。預估全球有超過 10 億的成人過重。

    解析 由 overweight 可推知為 obesity 肥胖。estimate 估計、估量；globally 全球地。

7.  The chemicals in these cleaning products can be hazardous to our health.

    (A) hazardous 有害的

    (B) hapless 不幸的

    (C) rueful 悔恨的

    (D) pitiful 可憐的

    中譯 清潔用品中的化學物質對我們的健康可能有害。

    解析 hazardous 有害的，例句：Smoking can be hazardous to health. 吸菸對健康有害。

8. Scientists have found a <u>cure</u> for the rare contagious disease, and some patients now have the hope of recovery.

(A) replacement 替代法

(B) penalty 處罰

(C) cure 治療

(D) passion 激情

中譯 科學家已經發現治癒罕見接觸傳染性疾病的療法，有些病人現在對於痊癒懷抱希望。

解析 由 the hope of recovery 對於痊癒懷抱希望，可猜出答案為 cure 治療。

9. Scarlet fever is a/an <u>contagious</u> disease, which is transferable from one person to another.

(A) different 不同的

(B) contagious 接觸傳染的

(C) important 重要的

(D) special 特別的

中譯 猩紅熱是一種接觸性的傳染病，是經由人與人接觸傳染。

解析 由 transferable from one person to another 人與人接觸傳染，可得知是 contagious 接觸傳染的疾病。

10. Middle-aged smokers are far more likely than nonsmokers to <u>develop</u> dementia later in life, and heavy smokers are at more than double the risk, according to a new study.

(A) deflect 偏斜

(B) demote 使降級

(C) deliberate 仔細考慮

(D) develop 發展

中譯 根據一項新的研究，中年吸菸的人比不吸菸的人在往後的日子裡更容易得到失智症，而有菸癮的人更有超過 2 倍以上的風險。

解析 develop a new symptom 出現新症狀。例句：Fresh air and exercise develop healthy bodies. 新鮮空氣和運動能使身體健康。

# 8 職場學校

## 一、歷屆考題精選

( ) 1. According to the meeting _____ , three more topics are to be discussed this afternoon. 101 英導

    (A) agenda    (B) invoice    (C) recipe    (D) catalog

( ) 2. It has been my honor and pleasure to work with him for more than 10 years. His insight and analysis are always _____ . 101 英導

    (A) distant    (B) superficial    (C) impressive    (D) premature

( ) 3. As Tim has no experience at all, I _____ he is qualified for this job. 102 英領

    (A) describe    (B) deliberate    (C) develop    (D) doubt

( ) 4. _____ unemployed for almost one year, Henry has little chance of getting a job. 101 英領

    (A) Having been    (B) Be    (C) Maybe    (D) Since having

( ) 5. All the employees have to use an electronic card to _____ in when they arrive for work. 101 英領

    (A) clock    (B) access    (C) enter    (D) apply

( ) 6. The non-smoking policy will apply to any person working for the company _____ of their status or position. 101 英領

    (A) regardless    (B) regarding    (C) in regard    (D) as regards

( ) 7. I would like to express our gratitude to you _____ behalf of my company. 101 英領

    (A) at    (B) on    (C) by    (D) with

( ) 8. My boss is very _____; he keeps asking us to complete assigned tasks within the limited time span. 98 英領

    (A) luxurious    (B) demanding    (C) obvious    (D) relaxing

(　　) 9. We all felt _____ when the manager got drunk. `100 英領`

    (A) embarrassed                 (B) embarrassing

    (C) being embarrassed         (D) been embarrassed

(　　) 10. If you want to work in tourism, you need to know how to work as part of a team. But sometimes, you also need to know how to work _____. `99 英領`

    (A) separately    (B) confidently    (C) creatively    (D) independently

(　　) 11. John has to _____ the annual report to the manager before this Friday; otherwise, he will be in trouble. `100 英領`

    (A) identify        (B) incline        (C) submit        (D) commemorate

(　　) 12. _____, the applicant was not considered for the job. `100 英領`

    (A) Due to his lack of experience

    (B) Because his lack of experience

    (C) His lack of experience

    (D) Due to his experience lack

(　　) 13. Before the applicant left, the interviewer asked him for a current _____ number so that he could be reached if he was given the job. `101 英領`

    (A) connection    (B) concert    (C) interview    (D) contact

(　　) 14. Most _____ private schools are highly competitive – that is, they have stiffer admissions requirements. `100 英領`

    (A) fastidious    (B) obscure    (C) ponderous    (D) prestigious

(　　) 15. One of the most important parts of these activities is for students to share the _____ of a group discussion with the rest of the class. `102 英領`

    (A) lowlights    (B) brightlights    (C) highlights    (D) headlights

(　　) 16. A group of young students has taken the _____ through social media to organize a rally against the austerity plans. `100 英領`

    (A) invitation    (B) initiative    (C) instruction    (D) inscription

(　) 17. Stay calm and clear-minded. I'm sure you'll have no problem _____ the exam. 102 英領

     (A) to pass      (B) passing      (C) pass      (D) passed

(　) 18. Bonnie signed up _____ dancing classes in the Extension Program. 100 英領

     (A) on          (B) in          (C) for          (D) about

## 標準答案

| | | | | |
|---|---|---|---|---|
| 1. （A） | 2. （C） | 3. （D） | 4. （A） | 5. （A） |
| 6. （A） | 7. （B） | 8. （B） | 9. （A） | 10. （D） |
| 11. （C） | 12. （A） | 13. （D） | 14. （D） | 15. （C） |
| 16. （B） | 17. （B） | 18. （C） | | |

## 二、試題中譯＋解析

1. According to the meeting agenda, three more topics are to be discussed this afternoon.

   (A) agenda 議程                    (B) invoice 發票

   (C) recipe 食譜                    (D) catalog 目錄

   **中譯** 根據會議議程，這個下午還有 3 個議題要討論。

   **解析** agenda 為議程、應辦事項，而由 meeting 可將其他選項刪除。

2. It has been my honor and pleasure to work with him for more than 10 years. His insight and analysis are always impressive.

   (A) distant 遙遠的                  (B) superficial 表面的

   (C) impressive 令人印象深刻的        (D) premature 早熟的

   **中譯** 能與他共事超過 10 年以上是我的榮幸。他的洞見和分析總是令人印象深刻。

   **解析** 由 it has been my honor and pleasure to work with him 可知其洞見和分析總是 impressive 令人印象深刻的。insight 洞察力、眼光、見識。

3. As Tim has no experience at all, I doubt he is qualified for this job.

   (A) describe 形容                   (B) deliberate 故意的

   (C) develop 發展                    (D) doubt 懷疑

   **中譯** 因為提姆沒有任何經驗，我懷疑他是否有資格能勝任這份工作。

   **解析** 由 no experience 和 qualified for this job 對比，可知答案為 doubt 懷疑。

4. <u>Having been</u> unemployed for almost one year, Henry has little chance of getting a job.

(A) Having been

(B) Be

(C) Maybe

(D) Since having

中譯 因為亨利已經幾乎 1 年沒有工作了,他找到工作的機會很小。

解析 此為簡化的副詞子句,在副詞子句的主詞與主要子句相同時,我們可將副詞子句中的連接詞及主詞去掉,並將動詞改為 Ving(動詞為主動語態,須為「現在分詞 Ving」;被動語態,須變為「過去分詞 PP」),即為簡單分詞構句。原句為 Since he has been unemployed = Having unemployed。little chance 幾乎毫無機會。

5. All the employees have to use an electronic card to <u>clock</u> in when they arrive for work.

(A) clock 打卡

(B) access 訪問

(C) enter 進入

(D) apply 申請

中譯 當抵達辦公室時,所有的員工都必須使用電子卡來打卡。

解析 clock in 打卡上班,clock out 打卡下班,clockless worker 彈性工時員工,clock+less 也就是不用打卡的意思。

6. The non-smoking policy will apply to any person working for the company <u>regardless</u> of their status or position.

(A) regardless 無論

(B) regarding 關於

(C) in regard 關於

(D) as regards 至於

中譯 禁菸政策將適用於任何在公司工作的人,不管其地位或職位。

解析 regardless 無論如何;regarding 關於某事的 3 種用法為 regarding something / with regard to something / as regards something。

07 健康

08 職場學校

09 人格個性

10 社交禮儀

11 金錢買賣

12 社會時事

7. I would like to express our gratitude to you on behalf of my company.

(A) at                         (B) on

(C) by                        (D) with（皆為介系詞）

中譯 我代表公司對你表達我們的感激。

解析 常考片語：on behalf of 代表，例句：The Union has filed a protest on behalf of the terminated workers. 公會已經代表被資遣的員工發起抗議。（102 英領）

8. My boss is very demanding; he keeps asking us to complete assigned tasks within the limited time span.

(A) luxurious 豪華的            (B) demanding 苛求的

(C) obvious 明顯的              (D) relaxing 令人放鬆的

中譯 我的老闆很嚴苛，他一直要求我們在有限的時間內完成指定任務。

解析 由 assigned tasks within the limited time span 可推知為 demanding 苛求的（現在分詞當形容詞，形容人）；assign 分配、分派。

9. We all felt embarrassed when the manager got drunk.

(A) embarrassed                (B) embarrassing

(C) being embarrassed          (D) been embarrassed

中譯 當經理喝醉時，我們都感到很不好意思。

解析 embarrassing 使人尷尬的，指事物；embarrassed 感到尷尬的，形容人。由 felt 得知是人感到尷尬，故選 embarrassed。

10. If you want to work in tourism, you need to know how to work as part of a team. But sometimes, you also need to know how to work <u>independently</u>.

(A) separately 個別地

(B) confidently 確信地

(C) creatively 創造性地

(D) independently 獨立地

中譯 如果你想要在旅遊業工作,你需要知道如何和團體工作,但有時候你也需要知道如何獨立作業。

解析 work as a team 團體工作;work independently 獨立工作。

11. John has to <u>submit</u> the annual report to the manager before this Friday; otherwise, he will be in trouble.

(A) identify 識別

(B) incline 傾斜

(C) submit 提交

(D) commemorate 慶祝

中譯 約翰必須在這週五之前提交年度報告給經理,不然他就完蛋了。

解析 submit 提交;submit a plan 提出一項計畫;otherwise 否則、不然。

12. <u>Due to his lack of experience</u>, the applicant was not considered for the job.

(A) Due to his lack of experience

(B) Because his lack of experience

(C) His lack of experience

(D) Due to his experience lack

中譯 由於他的經驗不足,這名申請者不在錄取這份工作的考慮名單內。

解析 此題以剔除法即能選出答案,先刪除 His lack of experience,名詞片語不能放於句首;再刪除 Because his lack of experience,because 後應接句子,故不符;剩下兩個 due to 開頭的選項,但由於 experience lack 明顯錯誤(lack 為形容詞,應放於名詞之前),故選 Due to his lack of experience。consider 考慮。

13. Before the applicant left, the interviewer asked him for a current <u>contact</u> number so that he could be reached if he was given the job.

(A) connection 連接　　　　(B) concert 演唱

(C) interview 面試　　　　**(D) contact 聯絡**

**中譯** 在應徵者離開之前，面試人員和他要他的<u>聯絡</u>電話，以便錄取時聯絡。

**解析** contact number 聯絡電話。其他面試相關的例句：Beatrix's friend had given her a mock interview before she actually went to meet the personnel manager of the company she was applying to. 貝翠絲的朋友在她真的要和所申請工作公司的人事主管面試之前，給她一個模擬的面試。（100 英導）

14. Most <u>prestigious</u> private schools are highly competitive – that is, they have stiffer admissions requirements.

(A) fastidious 挑剔的　　　(B) obscure 模糊的

(C) ponderous 沉悶的　　　**(D) prestigious 聲望很高的**

**中譯** 大部分有<u>名氣的</u>私立學校都很競爭，也就是說，他們有比較嚴格的入學條件。

**解析** competitive 競爭的；requirements 需求。

15. One of the most important parts of these activities is for students to share the <u>highlights</u> of a group discussion with the rest of the class.

(A) lowlights 弱光　　　　(B) brightlights

**(C) highlights 重點**　　　(D) headlights 大車燈

**中譯** 這些活動最重要的部分之一，就是讓學生和班上分享團體討論的<u>重點</u>。

**解析** highlights 重點、最精彩的部分，為最常考的單字之一，例句：The highlight of our trip to Southern Taiwan was A Taste of Tainan where we had a lot of delicious food. 南台灣之旅的亮點就是台南小吃，我們在那吃了很多美食。（101 英導）

16. A group of young students has taken the <u>initiative</u> through social media to organize a rally against the austerity plans.

(A) invitation 邀請

(B) initiative 倡議

(C) instruction 指令

(D) inscription 題詞

**中譯** 一群年輕學生透過社群媒體提出倡議以組織來對抗緊縮政策。

**解析** 此處為名詞，為主動性，若為形容詞則為初步的。

17. Stay calm and clear-minded. I'm sure you'll have no problem <u>passing</u> the exam.

(A) to pass

(B) passing 通過

(C) pass

(D) passed

**中譯** 保持冷靜和清晰的思路。我敢保證你會順利地通過考試。

**解析** have no problem + Ving 做某事沒有問題；have problems / trouble / difficulty + Ving 做某事有問題、困難。

18. Bonnie signed up <u>for</u> dancing classes in the Extension Program.

(A) on

(B) in

(C) for

(D) about

**中譯** 邦妮報名了推廣教育的舞蹈課。

**解析** sign up for 報名登記。

07 健康

08 職場學校

09 人格個性

10 社交禮儀

11 金錢買賣

12 社會時事

# 9 人格特性

## 一、歷屆考題精選

( ) 1. People love to socialize, and Facebook makes it easier. The shy become more _____ online. `101 英導`

    (A) modest     (B) outgoing     (C) pious     (D) timid

( ) 2. The local tour guide has a _____ personality. Everybody likes him. `101 英導`

    (A) windy     (B) stormy     (C) sunny     (D) cloudy

( ) 3. As children grow and mature, they will leave behind _____ pursuits, and no longer be so selfish and undisciplined as they used to be. `99 英導`

    (A) masculine     (B) childish     (C) philosophical   (D) honorable

( ) 4. _____ people are sensitive to others' wants and feelings. `99 英導`

    (A) Blunt     (B) Considerate   (C) Arrogant   (D) Dominant

( ) 5. People who have a great sense of _____ are often very popular, because they are usually intelligent, open-minded, and witty. `99 英導`

    (A) frustration     (B) humor     (C) betrayal     (D) inferiority

( ) 6. A _____ person is usually welcomed by everyone, because he never irritates people. `99 英導`

    (A) selfish     (B) naughty     (C) pessimistic   (D) humble

( ) 7. Elaine Hadley has many _____, such as horse-back riding, dancing, and playing with animals. `99 英導`

    (A) devices             (B) sensations

    (C) temperaments     (D) hobbies

( ) 8. Sarah, who often attends symphony concerts, has a great _____ for music. `99 英導`

    (A) anxiety     (B) disregard   (C) appreciation   (D) headline

(　　) 9.　The book is about a very _____ boy who always breaks things. 99 英導

(A) clumsy　　　(B) appropriate　(C) evident　　(D) fragrant

(　　) 10. Professor Nelson, who is rather strange, displays some _____ behavior from time to time. 99 英導

(A) ordinary　　　　　　　(B) eccentric

(C) comprehensive　　　　　(D) logical

# 標 準 答 案

| 1. ( B ) | 2. ( C ) | 3. ( B ) | 4. ( B ) | 5. ( B ) |
|----------|----------|----------|----------|----------|
| 6. ( D ) | 7. ( D ) | 8. ( C ) | 9. ( A ) | 10. ( B ) |

1. People love to socialize, and Facebook makes it easier. The shy become more <u>outgoing</u> online.

   (A) modest 謙虛的

   (B) outgoing 外向的

   (C) pious 虔誠的

   (D) timid 易受驚嚇的

   **中譯** 人們喜歡社交，而臉書讓此變得更容易。害羞的人在網路上得以變得更<u>外向</u>。

   **解析** humble / modest 都為「謙虛」的常考單字。outgoing 外向的、shy 害羞的、sunny 陽光性格的，都為形容個性的常考單字。

2. The local tour guide has a <u>sunny</u> personality. Everybody likes him.

   (A) windy 大風的

   (B) stormy 暴風雨的

   (C) sunny 陽光的

   (D) cloudy 陰天的

   **中譯** 這位當地的導遊有著<u>陽光</u>開朗的性格。每個人都喜歡他。

   **解析** sunny 陽光性格的、outgoing 外向、shy 害羞，都為形容個性的常考單字；humble / modest 為「謙虛」的常考單字。此處的答案選項都是描述天氣的形容詞：windy 大風的；stormy 暴風雨的；sunny 陽光的；cloudy 陰天的。

3. As children grow and mature, they will leave behind <u>childish</u> pursuits, and no longer be so selfish and undisciplined as they used to be.

   (A) masculine 男子氣概的

   (B) childish 幼稚的

   (C) philosophical 哲學家的

   (D) honorable 尊敬的

   **中譯** 當小孩長大變成熟後，他們將會把<u>幼稚</u>的行為拋下，且不再跟以前一樣自私且沒有紀律。

   **解析** mature 變成熟；leave behind 留下；pursuit 追求；undisciplined 沒有紀律的；discipline（名詞）教條；disciplined（形容詞）有紀律的；no longer 不再。

4. Considerate people are sensitive to others' wants and feelings.

(A) Blunt 遲鈍的

(B) Considerate 體貼的

(C) Arrogant 傲慢的

(D) Dominant 支配的

中譯 體貼的人對他人的需求以及感覺很敏感。

解析 considerate 體貼的；thoughtful 也為體貼的，體貼的人對人際關係通常比較 sensitive 敏感的，故選 considerate 體貼的。

5. People who have a great sense of humor are often very popular, because they are usually intelligent, open-minded, and witty.

(A) frustration 挫折

(B) humor 幽默

(C) betrayal 背叛

(D) inferiority 劣質

中譯 非常有幽默感的人通常很受歡迎，因為他們通常是聰明、大方機智的。

解析 有這樣特質的人 are often very popular 通常很受歡迎，可得知是 sense of humor 幽默感。open-minded 心胸寬的、無先入為主之見的。

6. A humble person is usually welcomed by everyone, because he never irritates people.

(A) selfish 自私的

(B) naughty 調皮的

(C) pessimistic 悲觀的

(D) humble 謙虛的

中譯 一個謙虛的人通常會受到每個人的歡迎，因為這樣的人從不激怒其他人。

解析 humble 謙虛的；down-to-earth 樸實的；irritate 使惱怒、使煩躁。

7. Elaine Hadley has many hobbies, such as horse-back riding, dancing, and playing with animals.

(A) devices 裝置

(B) sensations 感覺

(C) temperaments 氣質

(D) hobbies 嗜好

中譯 依蓮‧海德力有許多嗜好，像是騎馬、跳舞以及與動物們玩耍。

解析 hobby 嗜好（單數），hobbies（複數）；由 horse-back riding, dancing, and playing with animals 得知為各類的 hobbies。

8. Sarah, who often attends symphony concerts, has a great appreciation for music.

(A) anxiety 焦慮

(B) disregard 忽視

(C) appreciation 鑑賞

(D) headline 頭條

中譯 莎拉常常參加交響音樂會，對於音樂有極高的鑑賞力。

解析 由 often attends symphony concerts 常常參加交響音樂會可得知，對音樂有 appreciation 鑑賞力。

9. The book is about a very clumsy boy who always breaks things.

(A) clumsy 笨手笨腳的

(B) appropriate 適當的

(C) evident 明顯的

(D) fragrant 芳香的

中譯 這本書是關於一名笨手笨腳的男生，他總是打破東西。

解析 由 breaks things 打破東西可知，這男孩很 clumsy 笨手笨腳的。句子可拆成以下來看，The book is about / a very clumsy boy / who always breaks things. 這本書是關於 / 一名笨手笨腳的男生 / 他總是打破東西。

10. Professor Nelson, who is rather strange, displays some <u>eccentric</u> behavior from time to time.

(A) ordinary 普通的

(B) eccentric 反常的

(C) comprehensive 包容的

(D) logical 邏輯的

**中譯** 尼爾森教授是一個相當奇怪的人，他有時會表現出一些<u>怪異</u>的行為。

**解析** 此處的 displays 可換成 shows，為表現之意。解題可由 strange 奇怪的，來推測是 <u>eccentric</u> behavior 怪異的行為。from time to time 有時。

# 10 社交禮儀

一、歷屆考題精選　➤

( 　 ) 1.　In most western countries, it's ＿＿＿ for you to bring a bottle of wine or a box of candy as a gift when you are invited for dinner at someone's home. 98 英導

(A) temporary　　(B) invalid　　(C) customary　　(D) stubborn

( 　 ) 2.　Dress codes are basically some ＿＿＿ about what people wear in an organization or on a particular occasion. 102 英導

(A) pros and cons　　　　　　(B) ups and downs

(C) dos and don'ts　　　　　　(D) ways and means

( 　 ) 3.　If we remember our social ＿＿＿, particularly in a big crowd, we shall win people's admiration though we may not feel it. 102 英導

(A) ages　　(B) manners　　(C) news　　(D) recruits

( 　 ) 4.　When Americans shake hands, they do so firmly, not loosely. In the American culture, a weak handshake is a sign of weak ＿＿＿. 98 英導

(A) personnel　　(B) currency　　(C) character　　(D) parade

( 　 ) 5.　In many Western cultures, it is rude to ask about a person's age, weight, or salary. However, these topics may not be as ＿＿＿ in East Asia. 99 英導

(A) economical　　(B) polluted　　(C) governed　　(D) sensitive

( 　 ) 6.　Table manners differ from culture to culture. In Italy, it is considered ＿＿＿ for a woman to pour her neighbor a glass of wine. 99 英導

(A) inappropriate　(B) inconsistent　(C) incomplete　(D) infinite

( 　 ) 7.　Do not be afraid to eat with your hands here. When in Rome, do ＿＿＿ the Romans do. 100 英領

(A) for　　(B) as　　(C) of　　(D) since

( ) 8. It is said that there are only a few lucky days _____ for getting married in 2010. 99 英領

    (A) elated      (B) available      (C) elected      (D) resentful

( ) 9. Mary is _____ divorce because her husband is having an affair with his secretary. 99 英領

    (A) controlling to          (B) filing for

    (C) calling for             (D) accustomed to

( ) 10. The newlyweds are on their _____ tour. 100 英領

    (A) blossom      (B) bosom      (C) begotten      (D) bridal

( ) 11. While many couples opt for a church wedding and wedding party, a Japanese groom and a Taiwanese bride _____ in a traditional Confucian wedding in Taipe. 101 英領

    (A) tied the knot          (B) knocked off

    (C) wore on              (D) stepped down

## 標 準 答 案

| | | | | |
|---|---|---|---|---|
| 1. (C) | 2. (C) | 3. (B) | 4. (C) | 5. (D) |
| 6. (A) | 7. (B) | 8. (B) | 9. (B) | 10. (D) |
| 11. (A) | | | | |

## 二、試題中譯＋解析

1. In most western countries, it's <u>customary</u> for you to bring a bottle of wine or a box of candy as a gift when you are invited for dinner at someone's home.

   (A) temporary 臨時的　　　　　(B) invalid 有病的；無效的

   (C) customary 約定俗成的　　　(D) stubborn 固執的

   中譯 在大多數的西方國家中，當你被邀請去其他人家作客時，帶一瓶紅酒或是一盒糖果當作伴手禮是種基本禮儀。

   解析 custom 為風俗；customary 為約定俗成；customs 為海關。此 3 個單字常出現於考題中。而符合約定俗成也就是符合基本禮儀。

2. Dress codes are basically some <u>dos and don'ts</u> about what people wear in an organization or on a particular occasion.

   (A) pros and cons 優缺點　　　(B) ups and downs 高低起伏

   (C) dos and don'ts 注意事項　 (D) ways and means 方法

   中譯 穿衣法則基本上就是一些人們在哪個機構或是特殊場合穿著的行為準則。

   解析 dos and don'ts 可做與不可做的（注意事項）。dress code 穿衣法則；occasion 場合。

3. If we remember our social <u>manners</u>, particularly in a big crowd, we shall win people's admiration though we may not feel it.

   (A) ages 年紀　　　　　　　　(B) manners 禮貌

   (C) news 新聞　　　　　　　　(D) recruits 新成員

   中譯 如果我們遵守我們的社交禮儀，特別是在群眾社交中，即便我們沒有感覺到，我們應該也會更容易贏得人們的尊敬。

   解析 social manners 社交禮儀。

4. When Americans shake hands, they do so firmly, not loosely. In the American culture, a weak handshake is a sign of weak <u>character</u>.

(A) personnel 人員

(B) currency 貨幣

(C) character 性格

(D) parade 遊行

中譯 當美國人握手時,會握得較為強而有力,而非隨便握過。在美國人的文化中,蜻蜓點水的握手方式是軟弱特質的象徵。

解析 此題可能會將 personnel 人員誤看成 personality 人格;character 指的是內在的特質,如價值觀,而 personality 則指外在的性格,像是內向、外向、活潑等。為一般大眾所接受的是,孩子於早期所得的經驗大部分決定其內在 character 價值觀,隨後所得的經驗才決定其外在 personality 人格。

5. In many Western cultures, it is rude to ask about a person's age, weight, or salary. However, these topics may not be as <u>sensitive</u> in East Asia.

(A) economical 經濟的

(B) polluted 汙染的

(C) governed 管理的

(D) sensitive 敏感的

中譯 在許多西方文化中,問他人的年齡、體重或是薪水是很無禮的。然而這些話題在東亞可能就不是如此敏感。

解析 sensitive 敏感的,可以是對人觀察很細微的敏感,或是需要很慎重處理的重要議題的敏感之意。

6. Table manners differ from culture to culture. In Italy, it is considered <u>inappropriate</u> for a woman to pour her neighbor a glass of wine.

(A) inappropriate 不適宜

(B) inconsistent 不一致

(C) incomplete 不完整

(D) infinite 無限的

中譯 每個國家文化的餐桌禮儀都不同。在義大利,女士幫鄰座倒酒就被視為不恰當的行為。

解析 table manners 餐桌禮儀;appropriate 合宜,inappropriate 不合宜;polite 禮貌,impolite 不禮貌。Watch your table manners. 注意你的餐桌禮儀。

7. Do not be afraid to eat with your hands here. When in Rome, do <u>as</u> the Romans do.

(A) for

(B) as

(C) of

(D) since

**中譯** 在這裡不要害怕用手吃飯,要入境隨俗。

**解析** When in Rome, do as the Romans do. 入境隨俗。

8. It is said that there are only a few lucky days <u>available</u> for getting married in 2010.

(A) elated 興高采烈的

(B) available 可獲得的

(C) elected 當選的

(D) resentful 忿恨的

**中譯** 據說 2010 年只有幾天好日子<u>可以</u>結婚。

**解析** available 可獲得的;stock available 貨源充足;unavailable 不可獲得的; Goods unavailable 無貨可供。

9. Mary is <u>filing for</u> divorce because her husband is having an affair with his secretary.

(A) controlling to 操控

(B) filing for 申請

(C) calling for 需要

(D) accustomed to 習慣於

**中譯** 瑪莉<u>提出</u>離婚訴訟是因為她的丈夫與其祕書有染。

**解析** file 除了當名詞「檔案」外,當動詞有「提出」的意思。例句:The hotel services are far from satisfactory. I need to <u>file</u> a complaint with the manager. 飯店的服務讓人無法滿意。我需要向經理客訴。(98 英領) divorce 離婚;have an affair with 與~有染。

10. The newlyweds are on their bridal tour.

(A) blossom 開花 　　　　　　　(B) bosom 胸部

(C) begotten 獨生子 　　　　　　(D) bridal 婚禮的

中譯 新婚夫婦正在蜜月旅行。

解析 newlyweds 新婚夫婦；bridal tour / honeymoon 蜜月旅行。

11. While many couples opt for a church wedding and wedding party, a Japanese groom and a Taiwanese bride tied the knot in a traditional Confucian wedding in Taipei.

(A) tied the knot 結婚 　　　　　(B) knocked off 敲昏

(C) wore on 時間推移 　　　　　(D) stepped down 降低

中譯 當許多情侶選擇在教堂舉辦婚禮以及婚宴時，一對日本新郎以及台灣新娘選擇在台北進行傳統的儒家婚禮互訂終身。

解析 tie the knot 為結婚的慣用說法，若不熟此片語，仍可由關鍵字 wedding 將其他選項剔除。groom 新郎；bride 新娘。

07 健康

08 職場學校

09 人格個性

10 社交禮儀

11 金錢買賣

12 社會時事

# 11 金錢買賣

## 一、歷屆考題精選

( ) 1. You can get cash from another country at the _____ at the airport. `100 英導`

   (A) information desk　　　　(B) currency exchange

   (C) customs office　　　　　(D) check-in counter

( ) 2. We don't recommend exchanging your money at the hotel because you won't get a _____ rate. `98 英領`

   (A) humble　　(B) partial　　(C) dull　　(D) fair

( ) 3. May I have two hundred U.S. dollars in small _____. `98 英領`

   (A) accounts　　(B) balance　　(C) numbers　　(D) denominations

( ) 4. Client: I would like to change 500 US dollars into NT dollars.
     Bank clerk: Certainly, sir. Please complete this form and make sure _____.
     `100 英領`

   (A) you jot down the capital appreciation

   (B) you put the full name in capitals

   (C) you visited the capitals of other countries

   (D) you vote against capital punishment

( ) 5. I would like to _____ $500 from my savings account. `102 英領`

   (A) give in　　(B) put out　　(C) withdraw　　(D) reject

( ) 6. This traveler's check is not good because it should require two _____ by the user. `102 英領`

   (A) insurances　　(B) accounts　　(C) signatures　　(D) examinations

( ) 7. I would like to _____ my American Express card, please. `102 英領`

   (A) choose this to　　　　(B) charge this to

   (C) chain this to　　　　　(D) change this to

( ) 8. I'm afraid your credit card has already _____. Would you like to pay in cash instead? 99 英領

(A) cancelled     (B) booked     (C) expired     (D) exposed

( ) 9. A _____ is simply another name for a small specialty shop. 102 英導

(A) boutique     (B) body shop     (C) bonus     (D) beauty parlor

( ) 10. Sara bought a beautiful dress in a _____ in a fashionable district in Milan.
101 英導

(A) boutique                 (B) brochure

(C) bouquet                  (D) balcony

( ) 11. Parents should teach their children to _____ their money at an early age. Otherwise, when they grow up, they will not know how to manage their money.
98 英導

(A) inspire     (B) budget     (C) instill     (D) assert

( ) 12. If you want to find the cheapest airplane ticket, _____ can usually be found through the Internet. 99 英導

(A) bargains     (B) destinations     (C) reservations     (D) itinerary

( ) 13. All drinks served on the airplane are complimentary. 98 英領

(A) for extra cost            (B) of self service

(C) free of charge           (D) first come, first served

( ) 14. You will pay a _____ of fifty dollars for your ferry ride. 98 英領

(A) fan     (B) fate     (C) fair     (D) fare

( ) 15. If you have any problems or questions about our new products, you are welcome to use our _____-free service line. 99 導遊

(A) tax     (B) toll     (C) money     (D) fee

( ) 16. If the tapes do not meet your satisfaction, you can return them within thirty days for a full _____. 98 英領

(A) fund     (B) refund     (C) funding     (D) fundraising

( ) 17. Am I _____ to compensation if my ferry is canceled? 102英領

(A) asked      (B) entitled      (C) qualified      (D) requested

( ) 18. If you have the receipts for the goods you have purchased, you can claim a tax _____ at the airport upon departure. 98英領

(A) relief      (B) rebate      (C) involve      (D) reply

( ) 19. Because of its inexpensive yet high-quality medical services, medical tourism is _____ in Taiwan. 98英導

(A) declining      (B) blowing      (C) booming      (D) collapsing

( ) 20. Thanks to India's economic _____ and the booming growth of its airline industry, more Indians are flying today than ever before. 101英導

(A) prosperity      (B) souvenir      (C) decline      (D) evidence

( ) 21. Tourism has helped _____ the economy for many countries, and brought in considerable revenues. 99英領

(A) boast      (B) boost      (C) receive      (D) recall

( ) 22. In time of economic _____, many small companies will downsize their operation. 98英領

(A) appreciation      (B) progression      (C) recession      (D) reduction

( ) 23. International _____ allows countries to buy what they need from other countries. 99英導

(A) trade      (B) field      (C) port      (D) trip

( ) 24. Since the economy is improving, many people are hoping for a _____ in salary in the coming year. 99英導

(A) raise      (B) rise      (C) surplus      (D) bonus

( ) 25. We have seen a marked increase in the number of visitors to the theme park, but cannot understand why the total income indicates _____. 98英領

(A) a demand      (B) a decline      (C) a distinction      (D) a disruption

(　　) 26. Our company has been on a very tight _____ since 2008. ▋99 英領▋

        (A) deficit　　　(B) management　(C) budget　　　(D) debt

(　　) 27. You will be _____ for littering in public places. ▋98 英領▋

        (A) fined　　　(B) found　　　(C) founded　　　(D) funded

# 標 準 答 案

| | | | | |
|---|---|---|---|---|
| 1.（B） | 2.（D） | 3.（D） | 4.（B） | 5.（C） |
| 6.（C） | 7.（B） | 8.（C） | 9.（A） | 10.（A） |
| 11.（B） | 12.（A） | 13.（C） | 14.（D） | 15.（B） |
| 16.（B） | 17.（B） | 18.（B） | 19.（C） | 20.（A） |
| 21.（B） | 22.（C） | 23.（A） | 24.（A） | 25.（B） |
| 26.（C） | 27.（A） | | | |

1. You can get cash from another country at the currency exchange at the airport.

(A) information desk 服務台

(B) currency exchange 匯兌

(C) customs office 關稅局

(D) check-in counter 登機手續櫃台

中譯 你可以在機場的換匯櫃台兌換其他國家的現金。

解析 常考重點為 currency exchange 匯兌、換匯。

2. We don't recommend exchanging your money at the hotel because you won't get a fair rate.

(A) humble 謙虛

(B) partial 部分

(C) dull 遲鈍

(D) fair 公平

中譯 我們不建議在飯店兌換你的錢，因為你不會拿到公平的匯率。

解析 exchange money 換匯；exchange rate 匯率。recommend + Ving 推薦做某事。

3. May I have two hundred U.S. dollars in small denominations?

(A) accounts 帳目

(B) balance 尾款

(C) numbers 號碼

(D) denominations 面額

中譯 我可以兌換 200 美元的小額鈔票嗎？

解析 denominations 面額，例句：In what denominations? 要什麼面額的？

07 健康

08 職場學校

09 人格個性

10 社交禮儀

11 金錢買賣

12 社會時事

4. Client: I would like to change 500 US dollars into NT dollars.
   Bank clerk: Certainly, sir. Please complete this form and make sure <u>you put the full name in capitals</u>.

   (A) you jot down the capital appreciation 記錄資產增值

   (B) you put the full name in capitals 用大寫寫全名

   (C) you visited the capitals of other countries 參觀其他國家首都

   (D) you vote against capital punishment 投票反對死刑

   中譯 客戶：我想要將 500 美元換成新台幣。
   　　　銀行行員：沒問題，先生。請填寫此表格並且確保<u>用大寫寫全名</u>。

   解析 in capitals 用大寫。

5. I would like to <u>withdraw</u> $500 from my savings account.

   (A) give in 屈服　　　　　　　　(B) put out 熄滅

   (C) withdraw 提領　　　　　　　(D) reject 拒收

   中譯 我想從我的儲蓄帳戶內提領 500 美元。

   解析 withdraw 提領；deposit 存入；savings account 儲蓄存款戶頭。

6. This traveler's check is not good because it should require two <u>signatures</u> by the user.

   (A) insurances 保險　　　　　　(B) accounts 帳戶

   (C) signatures 簽名　　　　　　(D) examinations 考試

   中譯 旅行支票不好用是因為它需要 2 份持有者的簽名。

   解析 sign 簽名（動詞）；signatures 簽名（名詞）。

7. I would like to charge this to my American Express card, please.

(A) choose this to 選擇　　　　(B) charge this to 付費

(C) chain this to 鍊　　　　　　(D) change this to 交換

中譯 我希望可以用我的美國運通卡付費，麻煩了。

解析 charge 名詞為費用，動詞為收費、掛帳，此題為動詞。名詞例句：All drinks served on the airplane are free of charge. 所有在飛機上所供應的飲料都是免費的。動詞例句：The hospitals charge the patients for every aspirin. 醫院的每一片阿斯匹靈都要病人付錢。

8. I'm afraid your credit card has already expired. Would you like to pay in cash instead.

(A) cancelled 取消　　　　　　(B) booked 預定

(C) expired 屆期　　　　　　　(D) exposed 揭穿

中譯 恐怕你的信用卡已經過期了。你希望改以付現代替嗎？

解析 expired 屆期、過期的。

9. A boutique is simply another name for a small specialty shop.

(A) boutique 專賣流行衣服的小商店　(B) body shop 車身修理廠

(C) bonus 獎金　　　　　　　　　　(D) beauty parlor 美容院

中譯 boutique 就是專賣流行衣服的小商店的另一種稱呼。

解析 boutique 專賣流行衣服的小商店、精品店。

07 健康

08 職場學校

09 人格個性

10 社交禮儀

11 金錢買賣

12 社會時事

10. Sara bought a beautiful dress in a <u>boutique</u> in a fashionable district in Milan.

(A) boutique 流行女裝店　　　　(B) brochure 小冊子

(C) bouquet 花束　　　　　　　(D) balcony 陽台

中譯 莎拉在米蘭流行時尚區的一間<u>流行女裝店</u>買了一件漂亮的洋裝。

解析 由 Sara bought a beautiful dress 即 可 推 知 為 boutique 流 行 女 裝 店。district 區、地區。

11. Parents should teach their children to <u>budget</u> their money at an early age. Otherwise, when they grow up, they will not know how to manage their money.

(A) inspire 鼓舞　　　　　　　(B) budget 編列預算

(C) instill 注入　　　　　　　　(D) assert 聲稱

中譯 父母應該在孩子還小時就教導他們如何<u>控制花費</u>。否則，當小孩長大時，他們將不知如何理財。

解析 budget 在此為動詞；budget 亦可作為名詞。我們俗稱的「廉價航空公司」即為 budget airline 或是 low-cost airline。

12. If you want to find the cheapest airplane ticket, <u>bargains</u> can usually be found through the Internet.

(A) bargains 特價商品、便宜貨　　(B) destinations 目的地

(C) reservations 預定　　　　　　(D) itinerary 旅程

中譯 如果你想要找最便宜的機票，通常可以在網路上找到<u>特惠商品</u>。

解析 A bargain is a bargain. 說話要算話。bargain-hunting 四處尋找採購便宜貨。

13. All drinks served on the airplane are complimentary.

(A) for extra cost 額外費用

(B) of self service 自助服務

(C) free of charge 免費

(D) first come, first served 先到者優先服務

中譯 所有在飛機上所供應的飲料都是免費的。

解析 complimentary 免費，例句：A complimentary breakfast of coffee and rolls is served in the lobby between 7 and 10 am. 免費的早餐有咖啡和捲餅於早上 7 點到 10 點在大廳供應。（102 英領）

charge 名詞為費用，動詞為收費、掛帳。Breakfast is provided at no extra charge. 供應早餐，不另收費（此處為名詞）。I would like to charge this to my American Express card, please. 我希望可以用我的美國運通卡付費，麻煩了（此處為動詞）。（102 英領）

14. You will pay a fare of fifty dollars for your ferry ride.

(A) fan 電風扇                    (B) fate 命運

(C) fair 博覽會                   (D) fare 費用

中譯 你要付 50 元的費用來搭乘渡輪。

解析 fees 和 fare 的差別：

fee 服務費：pay the lawyer's fees 付律師費；a bill for school fees 學費帳單。

fare（大眾運輸）票價：What is the bus fare to London? 到倫敦的公共汽車費是多少？ travel at half / full / reduced fare 半價 / 全價 / 減價；Most taxi drivers in Kinmen prefer to ask for a flat fare rather than use the meter. 大部分金門的計程車司機喜歡使用單一費率，而非使用計程表。（100 英導）

15. If you have any problems or questions about our new products, you are welcome to use our <u>toll</u>-free service line.

(A) tax 稅

(B) toll 通行費

(C) money 錢

(D) fee 費用

中譯 如果你對於我們的新產品有任何的問題或是疑問，歡迎撥打我們的免付費服務專線。

解析 toll-free service line 免付費服務專線，也有 free call / free phone 的用法。

16. If the tapes do not meet your satisfaction, you can return them within thirty days for a full <u>refund</u>.

(A) fund 資金

(B) refund 退款

(C) funding 提供資金

(D) fundraising 募款

中譯 如果這些膠帶不能讓你滿意，你可以在 30 天內退還並獲得全額退款。

解析 refund 退款為常考單字，例句：We can refund the price difference. 我們可以退還差價。meet satisfaction 達到滿意的程度。

17. Am I <u>entitled</u> to compensation if my ferry is canceled?

(A) asked 要求

(B) entitled 有權享有

(C) qualified 有資格

(D) requested 要求

中譯 如果我的遊輪行程被取消了，我有權力要求補償嗎？

解析 entitled to 有～資格的；compensation 補償、彌補。補償的相關考題例句：Prohibited items in carry-on bags will be confiscated at the checkpoints, and no compensation will be given for them. 隨身行李中的違禁品將會於檢查站被沒收，且沒有任何的補償。（101 英領）

18. If you have the receipts for the goods you have purchased, you can claim a tax
    <u>rebate</u> at the airport upon departure.

    (A) relief 減輕

    (B) rebate 折扣

    (C) involve 包含

    (D) reply 回答

    中譯 如果你有購物收據，離境時可於機場要求退稅。

    解析 rebate 折扣；goods 商品；purchase 購買；departure 出發、起程。

19. Because of its inexpensive yet high-quality medical services, medical tourism
    is <u>booming</u> in Taiwan.

    (A) declining 衰退

    (B) blowing 吹氣

    (C) booming 蓬勃發展

    (D) collapsing 倒塌

    中譯 因為醫療服務價格不貴品質又高，台灣的醫療觀光正蓬勃發展中。

    解析 booming 為景氣好的；而另一常見的 blooming 開花，常用於興榮、興盛
    之意，如 a blooming business 興隆的事業。

20. Thanks to India's economic <u>prosperity</u> and the booming growth of its airline
    industry, more Indians are flying today than ever before.

    (A) prosperity 繁榮

    (B) souvenir 紀念品

    (C) decline 衰退

    (D) evidence 證據

    中譯 歸功於印度的經濟繁榮，以及該國航空業的成長，如今有更多印度人搭飛機。

    解析 由 the booming growth 蓬勃的成長，可推知 prosperity 繁榮。I wish you
    all prosperity. 則是「我祝你萬事如意」的意思。booming 景氣好的；
    growth 成長。

07 健康

08 職場學校

09 人格個性

10 社交禮儀

11 金錢買賣

12 社會時事

21. Tourism has helped <u>boost</u> the economy for many countries, and brought in considerable revenues.

(A) boast 自誇

(B) boost 提振

(C) receive 收到

(D) recall 想起

中譯 旅遊業在許多國家已經幫忙振興經濟，且帶來許多可觀的收入。

解析 boost the economy 振興經濟；economic recession 經濟蕭條；revenue 稅收。

22. In time of economic <u>recession</u>, many small companies will downsize their operation.

(A) appreciation 賞識

(B) progression 發展

(C) recession 不景氣

(D) reduction 減少

中譯 在經濟不景氣時期，很多小公司都會縮減他們的經營模式。

解析 由 downsize 裁減（員工）人數可推知為 recession 不景氣。economic recession 經濟蕭條為慣用說法，而非 economic reduction 經濟減少，無此說法。

23. International <u>trade</u> allows countries to buy what they need from other countries.

(A) trade 貿易

(B) field 領域

(C) port 港口

(D) trip 旅程

中譯 國際貿易讓各個國家可以向其他國家購買所需的東西。

解析 trade 可當名詞以及動詞，都為貿易、做生意之意。由 buy what they need from other countries 可得知為 International trade 國際貿易。

24. Since the economy is improving, many people are hoping for a <u>raise</u> in salary in the coming year.

(A) raise 提高

(B) rise 升高

(C) surplus 過剩

(D) bonus 獎金

**中譯** 既然經濟已經好轉，許多人希望明年能加薪。

**解析** raise 此處當名詞，為加薪，例句：Since our economy has been improving recently, I hope that my boss will give me a big raise this year. 因為我們的經濟情況最近一直持續好轉，我希望我的老闆今年可以幫我大加薪。（99 英導）

salary 薪資、薪水。raise（raised, raised）是及物動詞，必須接受詞。例句 1：Please raise your hand if you know the answer. 如果你知道答案，請舉手。例句 2：The company will raise salaries by 5%. 公司將加薪 5%。例句 3：Many concerns were raised about South Africa hosting the World Cup in 2010, but in the end South Africa pulled it off and did an excellent job. 對於南非舉辦 2010 年世界盃的疑慮逐漸升高，但最後南非消除了這些疑慮且表現出色。（101 英導）

25. We have seen a marked increase in the number of visitors to the theme park, but cannot understand why the total income indicates <u>a decline</u>.

(A) a demand 需求

(B) a decline 下降

(C) a distinction 區別

(D) a disruption 中斷

**中譯** 我們看到主題樂園的遊客數已有顯著的增加，但不懂為何總收入卻下滑。

**解析** decline / decrease 都是下降、減少的意思。

26. Our company has been on a very tight budget since 2008.

(A) deficit 虧損        (B) management 管理

(C) budget 預算        (D) debt 債務

**中譯** 自從 2008 年開始，我們公司的預算就很緊縮。

**解析** budget 預算，為名詞，亦可當成動詞，為編列預算。例句：Parents should teach their children to budget their money at an early age. Otherwise, when they grow up, they will not know how to manage their money. 父母應該在孩子還小時就教導他們如何控制花費，否則當小孩長大時，將不知如何理財。（99 英導）

budget 在此為動詞。我們俗稱的廉價航空公司即為 budget airline 或是 low-cost airline。

27. You will be fined for littering in public places.

(A) fined 處以罰金        (B) found 創立

(C) founded 有基礎的        (D) funded 提供資金

**中譯** 在公共場所亂丟垃圾會被罰錢。

**解析** fine 處以罰金；litter 亂扔廢棄物。國外路邊常見的標示為：Do not litter / No littering 都是不要隨意丟棄垃圾的意思。

## 一、歷屆考題精選

(     ) 1. A bill to legalize gay marriage in Washington State has won final legislative _____ and taken effect starting 2012. `102 英導`

(A) approval     (B) rejection     (C) veto     (D) admission

(     ) 2. Despite facing an imminent labor shortage as its population ages, Japan has done _____ to open itself up to immigration. `100 英導`

(A) small     (B) little     (C) none     (D) less

(     ) 3. According to a new study, the continuing _____ of immigrants to American shores is encouraging business activity and producing more jobs with the supply of abundant labors. `102 英導`

(A) threat     (B) arrival     (C) removal     (D) selection

(     ) 4. The financial _____ that started in the U.S. and swept the globe was further proof that - for better and for worse - we can't escape one another. `102 英導`

(A) data     (B) tadpole     (C) advent     (D) crisis

(     ) 5. Taiwan's premier said 2010 was a boom year for tourism in Taiwan and he _____ the success to the improvements in cross-strait relations. `100 英導`

(A) administered     (B) advertised     (C) acclaimed     (D) attributed

(     ) 6. Most countries take a _____ every ten years or so in order to count the people and to know where they are living. `100 英導`

(A) census     (B) censure     (C) censor     (D) censorship

(     ) 7. People who earn little or no income can receive public assistance, often called _____. `100 英導`

(A) hospitality     (B) budget     (C) pension     (D) welfare

(　　) 8.　Public _____ to voting is a problem in many democratic countries with low turnouts in elections. 98 英領

(A) interpretation (B) intervention　(C) contribution　(D) indifference

(　　) 9.　Simply put, no society can truly _____ if it smothers the dreams and productivity of half its population, women. 102 英導

(A) deteriorate　　(B) flourish　　(C) ravage　　　(D) smuggle

(　　) 10.　The cellphone is very _____ because it connects us with the world at large and even provides us with the necessary information on crucial moments. 102 英導

(A) expensive　　(B) rare　　　(C) fashionable　(D) handy

(　　) 11.　The notion that fashionable shopping takes place only in cities is _____, thanks to the Internet. 101 英導

(A) outdated　　(B) approximated (C) rehearsed　　(D) motivated

(　　) 12.　The Industrial Revolution, which began in the nineteenth century, caused widespread _____ as machines replaced workers. 100 英導

(A) postponement　　　　　　(B) curtailment

(C) unemployment　　　　　　(D) abandonment

(　　) 13.　_____ areas are more densely populated than rural areas. That is, they have more people per square mile. 100 英導

(A) Advanced　　(B) Bureaucratic　(C) Metropolitan　(D) Spacious

(　　) 14.　Demographers study population growth or decline and things like _____, which means the movement of populations into cities. 100 英導

(A) classification　　　　　　(B) normalization

(C) industrialization　　　　　(D) urbanization

(　　) 15.　As introductory English now begins in elementary, rather than secondary school, and classes have begun to focus more on the spoken language, travelers to Taiwan can _____ without having to attempt any Mandarin or Taiwanese. 100 英導

(A) take in　　　(B) stop off　　(C) get by　　　(D) pass along

(　　) 16. The public education in Taiwan has been _____ from primary school through junior high school since 1968. `100 英導`

(A) compulsory　(B) disciplinary　(C) regulatory　(D) ordinary

(　　) 17. Living in a highly _____ society, some Taiwanese children are forced by their parents to learn many skills at a very young age. `99 英領`

(A) compatible　(B) prospective　(C) threatened　(D) competitive

## 標 準 答 案

| | | | | |
|---|---|---|---|---|
| 1. (A) | 2. (B) | 3. (B) | 4. (D) | 5. (D) |
| 6. (A) | 7. (D) | 8. (D) | 9. (B) | 10. (D) |
| 11. (A) | 12. (C) | 13. (C) | 14. (D) | 15. (C) |
| 16. (A) | 17. (D) | | | |

1. A bill to legalize gay marriage in Washington State has won final legislative <u>approval</u> and taken effect starting 2012.

   (A) approval 贊同

   (B) rejection 拒絕

   (C) veto 否決

   (D) admission 承認

   中譯 華盛頓州同性婚姻合法的法案已經通過了最後立法同意，並於 2012 年生效。

   解析 bill 在此為法案。由 taken effect 可推知答案為 approval。

2. Despite facing an imminent labor shortage as its population ages, Japan has done <u>little</u> to open itself up to immigration.

   (A) small 小的

   (B) little 很少

   (C) none 沒有

   (D) less 較少

   中譯 即便隨著人口高齡化，勞工短缺的問題近在眼前，日本在開放移民方面還是做得很少。

   解析 little 表示少到幾乎沒有。imminent 逼近的、即將發生的。

3. According to a new study, the continuing <u>arrival</u> of immigrants to American shores is encouraging business activity and producing more jobs with the supply of abundant labors.

   (A) threat 威脅

   (B) arrival 到來

   (C) removal 移除

   (D) selection 選擇

   中譯 根據新的研究，美國沿岸持續到來的移民者會讓商業發展更佳，也會有更多的工作機會。

   解析 arrival 到來。

4. The financial crisis that started in the U.S. and swept the globe was further proof that - for better and for worse - we can't escape one another.

(A) data 數據　　　　　　　　(B) tadpole 蝌蚪

(C) advent 來臨　　　　　　　(D) crisis 危機

中譯 金融危機始於美國且影響了全球，這也證明了，我們誰都逃不過。

解析 financial crisis 金融危機。

5. Taiwan's premier said 2010 was a boom year for tourism in Taiwan and he attributed the success to the improvements in cross-strait relations.

(A) administered 管理　　　　(B) advertised 做廣告

(C) acclaimed 喝采　　　　　(D) attributed 歸因

中譯 台灣的行政院長説 2010 年是台灣旅遊業大幅成長的一年，他將此成功歸因於兩岸關係的改善。

解析 attribute sth. to 認為某事物是～的屬性、把某事物歸功於～；cross-strait relations 兩岸關係。

6. Most countries take a census every ten years or so in order to count the people and to know where they are living.

(A) census 人口普查　　　　(B) censure 責難

(C) censor 審查　　　　　　(D) censorship 審查制度

中譯 大部分的國家每 10 年做一次人口普查，以計算人口以及了解其居住地。

解析 常考跟人口相關的單字為 census 人口普查，也常出現 metropolitan / urban areas 都會區和 rural areas 鄉村（郊區）的比較。

7.  People who earn little or no income can receive public assistance, often called underline{welfare}.

(A) hospitality 好客

(B) budget 預算

(C) pension 退休金

(D) welfare 福利

中譯 賺很少或沒賺錢的人可以受到大眾救助，通常稱為福利。

解析 失業補助金即為 welfare 福利的一種，income 收入、所得。

8.  Public underline{indifference} to voting is a problem in many democratic countries with low turnouts in elections.

(A) interpretation 解釋

(B) intervention 調停

(C) contribution 貢獻

(D) indifference 不重視

中譯 大眾對於投票的漠不關心是許多低投票率民主國家的問題。

解析 indifference漠不關心；difference不同之處，例句：Her daughter's indifference to her makes her very sad. She wishes her daughter would show more concern for her. 她女兒對她的漠不關心讓她相當難過。她希望女兒能夠更關心她。（98 英導）democratic 民主的。

9.  Simply put, no society can truly underline{flourish} if it smothers the dreams and productivity of half its population, women.

(A) deteriorate 惡化

(B) flourish 蓬勃發展

(C) ravage 毀滅

(D) smuggle 走私

中譯 簡單來說，沒有一個社會可以真正地蓬勃發展，如果它阻擋了一半的人口——女性的夢想以及生產力。

解析 flourish 蓬勃發展。

07 健康

08 職場學校

09 人格個性

10 社交禮儀

11 金錢買賣

12 社會時事

10. The cellphone is very <u>handy</u> because it connects us with the world at large and even provides us with the necessary information on crucial moments.

(A) expensive 昂貴的

(B) rare 罕有的

(C) fashionable 流行的

(D) handy 方便的、便利的

中譯 手機非常的方便，因為它讓我們充分跟世界溝通，甚至在重要時刻提供我們所需的資訊。

解析 handy 方便、便利的；at large 充分地，另做「未被捕的」。

11. The notion that fashionable shopping takes place only in cities is <u>outdated</u>, thanks to the Internet.

(A) outdated 過時的

(B) approximated 近似的

(C) rehearsed 排練

(D) motivated 有動機的

中譯 歸功於網路，去大城市購物才時髦這樣的觀念已經過時了。

解析 take place 發生；outdated 過時，相反詞則為 modern 現代的。請注意 notion 為觀念、看法的意思，而不是 nation 國家的意思。

12. The Industrial Revolution, which began in the nineteenth century, caused widespread <u>unemployment</u> as machines replaced workers.

(A) postponement 延期

(B) curtailment 縮減

(C) unemployment 失業

(D) abandonment 放棄

中譯 工業革命始於 19 世紀，由於機器取代勞工，導致普遍的失業。

解析 考 unemployment 失業，延伸單字：employee 員工；employer 雇主。replace 取代。

13. Metropolitan areas are more densely populated than rural areas. That is, they have more people per square mile.

(A) Advanced 高級的          (B) Bureaucratic 官僚的

(C) Metropolitan 大都市的       (D) Spacious 廣大的

中譯 大都市區的人口密度比鄉村來得高。也就是每平方英里有比較多的人。

解析 metropolitan 大都市的，也常考 urban 都會的，rural 則是鄉村的。

14. Demographers study population growth or decline and things like urbanization, which means the movement of populations into cities.

(A) classification 分類         (B) normalization 正常化

(C) industrialization 工業化     (D) urbanization 都市化

中譯 人口統計學家研究人口的成長或是削減，以及像是都市化表示人口往城市移動。

解析 由 populations into cities 即可猜出答案 urbanization 都市化，字根 urban 為都市。demographers 人口統計學家；decline 下降、減少。

15. As introductory English now begins in elementary, rather than secondary school, and classes have begun to focus more on the spoken language, travelers to Taiwan can get by without having to attempt any Mandarin or Taiwanese.

(A) take in 接受          (B) stop off 中途停留

(C) get by 勉強過得去       (D) pass along 路過

中譯 現在英語入門始於小學而非國中，且課程也已變得著重在口語，到台灣的旅客可以勉強用英文溝通，而不用講中文或是台語。

解析 由 without having to attempt any Mandarin or Taiwanese 可知為 get by 勉強過得去；attempt 企圖、嘗試。

16. The public education in Taiwan has been <u>compulsory</u> from primary school through junior high school since 1968.

(A) compulsory 義務的

(B) disciplinary 訓誡的

(C) regulatory 控制的

(D) ordinary 普通的

中譯 台灣的大眾教育自 1968 年以來，從小學到國中都是<u>義務</u>教育。

解析 compulsory 義務的。

17. Living in a highly <u>competitive</u> society, some Taiwanese children are forced by their parents to learn many skills at a very young age.

(A) compatible 能共處的

(B) prospective 預期的

(C) threatened 受到威脅的

(D) competitive 競爭性的

中譯 生活在高度<u>競爭的</u>社會，有些台灣小孩從小就被逼著學很多技能。

解析 由 learn many skills 可知社會是很 competitive 競爭性的。

07 健康

08 職場學校

09 人格個性

10 社交禮儀

11 金錢買賣

12 社會時事

# memo

附錄 如何準備
英語導遊口試？

# 如何準備英語導遊口試？

　　一般考生聽到英文口試，第一個反應通常都會先冒冷汗、倒退三步，但若從近年的口試錄取率都超過8成來說，其實不需太過擔心。如果英文筆試可以及格，口試只要稍加準備，及格絕對非難事！

## 口 試 資 格

　　外語導遊人員以筆試成績滿60分為錄取標準，也就是說筆試的各科平均成績要先滿60分才會有口試的資格，而口試成績則以兩位口試委員評分總和之平均成績計算。筆試成績占總成績75%，口試成績占25%，合併計算後為考試總成績。

## 口 試 題 數 與 時 間

　　每年口試題目與應考時間略有不同，不過大約都是3-5題，時間約10分鐘左右。

## 評 分 標 準

　　外語個別口試之評分項目及配分如下：
　　外語表達能力60分，語音與語調20分，才識、見解、氣度20分。

## 考 題 方 向

　　每年主管機關所公布的考題範圍稍有差異，但準備方向都是一樣的，如102年口試問題範圍為「自我介紹」、「本國文化與國情」、「風景、節慶與美食」。英語導遊口試的出題範圍，其實可以簡單歸納成一句話，就是「用英文介紹自己、介紹台灣」。但該如何介紹台灣？網路上有非常多的資源，簡單介紹如下。

## 推薦網站

　　這裡先列了最相關的7個網站,但其實和台灣旅遊相關的英文網站,除了台灣官方的觀光網站(如觀光局、國家公園),也有外國人經常造訪的旅遊網站(在首頁上打上Taiwan就能搜尋出所有台灣相關的資料)、以及國內英文新聞網站,建議每一個網站都可以點進去瀏覽。除此之外,有沒有最簡單、最不費力的英文導遊口試的準備方法?那就是每天逛一個相關網站,把自己當成是外國遊客,用英文看看哪裡好玩,還可以順便規劃一下自己週休二日的旅遊景點,在不知不覺中,就能累積關於台灣的知識以及英文能力,真是一舉數得!

❋ **交通部觀光局(英文版)**

http://eng.taiwan.net.tw/
除了旅遊資訊之外,一定要看Discover Taiwan這個分類的資訊,裡頭包含General Information / Climate / History / People 等台灣的基本介紹,對於國情概況這類的題目,非常有幫助!

❋ **台北旅遊網**

http://www.taipeitravel.net/en/
很用心製作的網站,特別推薦考生點Tourist Guide分類當中的Tourist Audio Guide(遊客導覽講解),這些導覽知名景點的英文解說,對於想要加強口說的考生而言,千萬不能錯過。

## ❈ 新北市觀光旅遊網

http://tour.ntpc.gov.tw/tom/lang_en/index.aspx

資訊雖然沒有台北旅遊網豐富，但比較特別的是分類中多了「Tour theme」（主題旅遊），可分成Old Street Tour（老街旅遊）、Rail Tour（鐵道旅遊）等。

★補充：除了台北旅遊之外，其他縣市的相關英文旅遊資源該怎麼找？最快的方法為到該縣市的文化局官網，只要點選English就能找到許多當地文化、旅遊等的英文資料。

## ❈ 台灣國家公園

http://np.cpami.gov.tw/english/index.php

這是最能詳細了解台灣自然風光的英文旅遊網站，若覺得自然資源等的英文太難，至少也要了解台灣北中南有哪些國家公園！特別推薦Photo Gallery裡國家公園的簡單解說以及圖説。

❋ 中國英文郵報

http://www.chinapost.com.tw/
travel/

特別推薦Travel Topics，裡面分成
Northern Taiwan / Central Taiwan / Southern Taiwan / East-
ern Taiwan / Taiwan Offshore
Islands，可以依照自己的所在地點
選，用英文了解自己的家鄉。

❋ Lonely Planet 寂寞星球旅遊書出版社

http://www.lonelyplanet.com
Lonely Planet為全球最大的旅
遊書出版社，官網也有相當豐
富的內容，只要在搜尋欄上打
上Taiwan，即能看到許多國外
作者撰寫介紹台灣的文章，相
當生動有趣。

❋ 台灣光華雜誌

http://www.sinorama.com.tw/en/
index.php

以英文報導台灣的本土萬象，正因為
有各個面向的台灣報導，所以對於
增進口試題目的廣度非常有幫助。此
外，網站內的字彙通（Vocab note-
book）還有英文發音，對要練習發音
的考生而言，絕對不能錯過。

更多網站說明與連結，請上https://www.facebook.com/tourguideEnglish

**國家圖書館出版品預行編目資料**

英語領隊導遊考試總整理 全新修訂版：400題必考
題型＋250個必考單字＋230題歷屆考題與解析 /
陳若慈著
-- 修訂初版 -- 臺北市：瑞蘭國際, 2019.10
272面；19 x 26公分（專業證照系列；14）
ISBN：978-957-9138-45-1（平裝）
1.英語 2.讀本

805.18                                                108016662

專業證照系列 **14**

# 英語領隊導遊考試總整理 全新修訂版
## 400題必考題型＋250個必考單字＋230題歷屆考題與解析

作者｜陳若慈
責任編輯｜葉仲芸
校對｜陳若慈、葉仲芸、王愿琦

英語錄音｜Terri Pebsworth
錄音室｜純粹錄音後製有限公司
封面設計｜劉麗雪、陳如琪
版型設計｜林士偉
內文排版｜林士偉、陳如琪

瑞蘭國際出版
董事長｜張暖彗·社長兼總編輯｜王愿琦
**編輯部**
副總編輯｜葉仲芸·副主編｜潘治婷·副主編｜鄧元婷
設計部主任｜陳如琪
**業務部**
副理｜楊米琪·組長｜林湲洵·組長｜張毓庭

出版社｜瑞蘭國際有限公司·地址｜台北市大安區安和路一段104號7樓之一
電話｜(02)2700-4625·傳真｜(02)2700-4622·訂購專線｜(02)2700-4625
劃撥帳號｜19914152 瑞蘭國際有限公司
瑞蘭國際網路書城｜www.genki-japan.com.tw

法律顧問｜海灣國際法律事務所　呂錦峯律師

總經銷｜聯合發行股份有限公司·電話｜(02)2917-8022、2917-8042
傳真｜(02)2915-6275、2915-7212·印刷｜科億印刷股份有限公司
出版日期｜2019年10月初版1刷·定價｜450元·ISBN｜978-957-9138-45-1
　　　　2021年08月初版2刷

PRINTED WITH
SOY INK　本書採用環保大豆油墨印製